CW00406951

Also by John de Lange:

Chickenshit Farm
The Consultants

Irbuvia Press

DYING IS AN EXPENSIVE BUSINESS

JOHN DE LANGE

For Loretta

WHAT'S IN THE BOOK?

FIRST HALF

WHO'S IN THE BOOK?

Janice: Receptionist at The Poplars
Mrs Sedge: Proprietor of The Poplars, an Old People's Home
Mrs Edna Gellatly, a Guest at The Poplars*
Cynthia Forsyte, Mrs Gellatly's daughter
Charles Forsyte, her husband
Henry Warren, son of Joe Warren
Sam Clodd, The Home's gardener/odd-job man
Juanita Standish, the Home's matron
Dr Mingus, the Home's doctor
Joe Warren, a Guest at the Poplars
Lizzie, a carer
Violet, a carer
Anne, a carer
Mr Gladwyn, an undertaker
Avril Prime, a housewife and mother
Edward Prime, her husband
Martha Prime, his mother
Myron Lillywhite, a New York advertising executive
Sally Lillywhite, his wife
Edith Clarence, Sally's aunt
Augustus Wimpole, a solicitor
Eric Stubble, a Detective Inspector
Wilhelmina Bonnie, a Guest at The Poplars*
Gerald Borland, a school teacher
Lucy Borland, his wife
Millie Borland, Gerald's mother
Mr Tubbs, a Guest at The Poplars*
Mrs de Havilland, a Guest at The Poplars*
Miss Caraway, a Guest at The Poplars*
Roger Dade, a sea captain
Joshua Benin, one of his crew
Dr Caine, an abortionist*

Pollyanna Goldberg, a pregnant American teenager
Mrs Kinloch, a Guest at The Poplars*
Alastair Kinloch, her son
Cameron Kinloch, her son
Tadeusz, a computer hacker

*deceased

CHAPTER ONE
Mrs Gellatly passes on.

Janice picked up the typed card headed NOTIFYING RELATIVES OF A DEATH for the third time, wondering why it fell to her to make these calls. She reached out her hand to pick up the telephone and drew it back again.

The phone rang, making her jump. With her heart in her boots she picked it up. It was sure to be Mr Forsyte. It wasn't. It was just someone wanting Peter, the Catering Manager as he styled himself. A cook and not a very good one was Janice's opinion, since she had to eat lunch every day in the residents' dining room. Mrs Sedge made quite a fuss about the staff eating with the residents. "I like our guests to think of The Poplars as our home, as much as theirs." she enthused at every possible opportunity.

It wasn't Janice's home. She went back to her mum every night. It wasn't anyone's home, except Mrs Sedge's. No-one lived at The Poplars except Mrs Sedge and Matron and Sam, and of course, the thirty-seven Guests, which is what Mrs Sedge called them. Guests was not a word Janice would have used. Guests don't pay several hundred pounds a week to stay with you. Guests don't get their food cut up and spooned into their mouths, don't get helped into and out of bed every day. Guests can take themselves to the toilet and bath themselves. Guests can put their own clothes on.

The Waiters, Sam called the Guests. "They be waiting for to go on their last journey, my love," was how he put it. Sam was the handyman/gardener and general dogsbody. He lived in the cellar where he looked after the boiler. Sam got on with his work and didn't talk much; for some reason he seemed to have taken a shine to Janice, and occasionally stopped for a chat when he happened to pass her desk.

Mrs Sedge lived all by herself in her flat on the top floor, from which she would descend graciously from time to time to spend what she called Quality Time With My Guests. Matron, who actually did all the work, had a bedroom/office on the first floor. The rest of the staff came in from the village, like Janice who stiffened a sinew and dialled the Forsytes' number, still wishing she didn't have to. It rang and rang. Surely they had not gone to work already at, she checked the clock on the wall facing her, at twenty past eight. She was just making up her mind to phone Mr Forsyte's office number when he picked up the phone.

"Mr Forsyte?" Janice wondered why she asked him that. Who else might it be?

"Yes. Sorry, I was in the shower."

"It's Janice at The Poplars here. I'm afraid I've got bad news."

"My mother-in-law?"

"I'm afraid so. Mrs Gellatly passed away this morning. I'm so sorry. Could you come over?"

"Of course. We'll be there as soon as we can. You've called the doctor, I take it?"

"He expects to be in about ten o'clock."

"Thank you. Good bye."

Janice heaved a sigh of relief and read again the typed card which set out the way Mrs Sedge thought relatives should be advised of their loved ones' demises. She had not used a word of it.

Mr Forsyte had not sounded upset. His tone had been sort of businesslike; he didn't really sound sorry, or even ask how it was at the end. But then Janice had noticed that when her gran died her mum didn't seem to take it in for a day or so. It was only after the funeral that it hit her that gran was never coming back that she got upset. But Mrs Gellatly wasn't Mr Forsyte's mother, was she? She was just his Mother-in-law. Maybe Mr Forsyte hadn't been best friends with her. It was Mrs Forsyte who was more likely to be sad.

It wasn't as though death was an infrequent visitor at The Poplars. "Last stop before the terminus" Sam called it. You didn't get to be a Guest at The Poplars unless you were on the way out of this life. You had to fail one of the five tests to get on the waiting list for the home and there always was a waiting list. These were the five simple tests:

Can you get up in the morning and dress yourself without help?

Can you bath yourself?

Can you feed yourself?

Can you go to toilet on your own?

Can you be left alone without falling over or setting the place on fire?

If you answered "no" to any one of these questions, then you passed the test and became a candidate for The Poplars and the many other similar old people's homes, rest homes and retirement homes dotted up and down the country.

Some were good, some indifferent, some downright awful. The good were full of residents moving about, reading, watching television, talking to each other. The indifferent ones could be identified by the old ladies (for some reason not many old gentlemen lived long enough to need care) sitting round the room staring into space or muttering to themselves. The bad ones had empty lounges and residents who emerged from their rooms for meals and promptly shuffled back to them afterwards.

A visitor could make a quicker quality assessment by sniffing to see if a smell of stale urine was hanging over the place. The Poplars did not smell. Mrs Sedge made sure of it. No-one who was the slightest bit incontinent was admitted and any Guest who did dare to lose control once admitted was watched like a hawk until they were quietly eased out. Any accident was cleaned up immediately and generous libations of scented sprays and air fresheners applied. The Poplars made an effort to be classified as Good.

The home's lavishly illustrated brochure was full of carefully taken pictures of freshly decorated bedrooms, warm comfortable lounges, an inviting dining room presided over by chef in impeccable whites and sunny gardens rich with flowers. "A home from home with all the facilities of a first-class hotel where gracious living is the watchword" proclaimed the introduction, and indeed the minor stately home which had come down in the world and was now The Poplars promised all this. The spacious communal rooms were always kept in apple-pie order. True, what had been commodious bedrooms had been partitioned to cram as many customers in as possible, but they were still quite adequate. Mrs Sedge made sure every picture included at least one smiling happy guest, and for the most part the camera did not lie. The Guests did smile. Occasionally.

Janice put the NOTIFYING A DEATH card back into its box and looked through the appointments diary. A Mr Warren was due at ten o'clock to look over the home which was exactly when Doctor Mingus was due to come and see to Mrs Forsyte's mother. That meant Matron would have to deal with the doctor and the bereaved Forsytes while Mrs Sedge would be taking Mr Warren round the home. Mrs Sedge liked to show possible customers round the retirement home as she considered herself best able to answer any awkward questions.

And here was Mrs Sedge herself flowing regally down the stairs, a heavily built dream in lilac chiffon. Janice thought she was walking around as if she owned the place, and then reminded herself that she really did. She called out "Good morning Janice, what a beautiful morning. I hear we lost poor Mrs Gellatly last night." Janice confirmed that this was the case and that she had called the doctor and notified the family.

Mrs Sedge nodded. "So we have a vacancy. I believe we have a Prospective coming this morning?"

Janice went through the motions of checking the diary on her desk "A Mr Warren; looking for a place for his father, at ten o'clock."

"Father? That's unusual. Well it will be nice to have an extra man about the place. You'll let me know when he arrives, won't you Janice?"

"Of course, Mrs Sedge, and I'll ask Matron to see to the doctor and look after Mr and Mrs Forsyte, since they're coming at the same time."

"Well done, Janice. I'm glad to see you're picking up our routines so quickly. One thing though, It's not Mrs Sedge, it's Maureen. We're all friends here. We all muck in together, don't we?"

"Yes, Maureen," replied Janice dutifully, reflecting as she watched Mrs Sedge sailing into the dining room that when it came to money she bet Mrs Sedge was getting much more muck than she was. The Poplars was by no means one of the best paying employers in the district, but jobs were hard to come by, and working there was better in every respect than being at school. She wasn't well paid, but she had lots more money than any of her friends who had decided to stay on and take their A levels.

It wasn't as if she intended staying at The Poplars for the rest of her life.

Dr Mingus got there earlier than expected and had already gone by the time Mr and Mrs Forsyte got to The Poplars. They happened to arrive at precisely the same time as Mr Warren who was promptly snatched away by Mrs Sedge who was lurking by the door ready to show him over the home.

The bereaved Forsytes were taken in hand by Matron, who took them off to the dining room for the customary cup of tea sugared with sympathy, followed by a discussion of What Happens Next. She handed the doctor's Death Certificate to Mr Forsyte and explained that he would need to take it to the Registrar who would issue a Green Form, which the undertaker would need to have before proceeding with The Arrangements.

"Do you have a preference for any particular undertaker?" asked Matron. Not getting any reaction from the Forsytes she went on "We always use Gladwyns. We find they are quietly efficient and very reasonable. Would you like us to deal with them, or would you prefer to talk to them yourselves?"

"I believe my mother arranged everything with them and even paid them in advance when she came to live here. She was a very careful woman, liked to have everything organised" said Mrs Forsyte.

"In that case I'll let them know," said Matron. "One of you will have to go to the Registrar in Dununder with the Death Certificate I've just given you. He'll give you the Green Form to give to the undertaker. After that it's all quite straightforward, Gladwyns will take care of everything. The Registrar's office is in the Shambles; you know where that is?"

Mr Forsyte affirmed he did.

Matron turned to his wife. "Do you know if your mother wanted to be buried or cremated?"

"Buried." Mr Forsyte answered on his wife's behalf.

"Of course," Matron remarked, "a lot of people opt for cremation these days. Personally I think it's more decorous and you can do what you like with the ashes. People often like to scatter them in some spot the loved one was happy, like their garden. I've left instructions for my own body to be cremated when I go,"

Mr Forsyte said "Which we hope will not be for many years.".

"I also hope not." Matron smiled thinly. "Anyway, the choice is up to you. Think it over and let me know."

"My husband just told you mother wants to be buried." said Mrs Forsyte.

"Oh, cremation's a lot cheaper, and you save by not having a stone."

"A stone?" Mrs Forsyte looked puzzled.

"A tombstone." explained Matron, "They do come quite expensive. "You could plant a rose tree in the crematorium instead. That's very popular, but it's something that can wait until later."

Mr Forsyte was asking himself how much commission Matron got from the crematorium. His wife had come to the conclusion Matron must be a little deaf the way she went on and on about cremation. She yelled "So we need to go to the Registrar right away, is that right?"

Why did the woman need to shout like that? Matron told herself bereavement affected people in odd ways. "The Registrar's office is open until four o'clock, so there's no hurry."

"Best get it out of the way so we can get things moving." said Mr Forsyte, standing up. Mrs Forsyte followed his example. "Thank you so much for all your help, Matron."

"Anything we can do, don't hesitate to ask." "I'll phone Mr Gladwyn to ask him to come and collect your mother."

Mr Forsyte thanked her.

"You've been so helpful." yelled Mrs Forsyte to Matron as she held the door open for them.

As she watched them drive down the gravel drive Matron reflected on two things: Mrs Forsyte had not asked to see her mother's body and she had not asked what the old lady died of. Neither she nor her husband had even glanced at the death certificate

"And this is our Activities Room," Mrs Sedge told Mr Warren." We do like to keep our Guests as active as possible, both mentally and physically."

Mr Warren was not impressed. "I can't see my father using it. He's not what you'd call sociable. Doesn't like being ordered about, and now he can't do things for himself he gets very frustrated."

"Mrs Sedge tried to reassure him. "We're used to dealing with frustration here. Old people get easily upset when they find they can't do things they've done all their lives, you know."

"Well you shouldn't complain. You'd be out of business if we all died in the bloom of middle age with all our faculties intact." pointed out Mr Warren.

"I like to think we don't see it like that. We try to encourage optimum quality of life at The Poplars." purred Mrs Sedge.

"Quality of life!" snorted Mr Warren. "He'd be better off dead. You should have seen him ten years ago. I came home once and caught him cutting down a tree. He was fantastic for a man of his age, and now he's stuck in that wheelchair."

"Our Guests often arrive like zombies and after a couple of months of the PLC we give them they start showing an interest, even talking." simpered Mrs Sedge.

Mr Warren snorted . "PLC? What's that? I thought it meant Public Limited Company."

"Poplars Loving Care. Wonderful medicine. We've got one lady, her family reckoned she was at death's door, and she's still with us after six years."

"My father won't last six years."

Mrs Sedge asked herself whether that was a statement, a question or an expression of hope. She said: "Well, that's pretty much all there is to see in the house. Perhaps you'd like a walk round the garden? It's so nice for the guests to sit out in the sun, when there is any sun, of course."

"When can you take him?" asked Mr Warren abruptly.

"Well, we do have a waiting list."

"How much do you charge?"

Mrs Sedge told him.

"Add a hundred a week to that. And a year's payment in advance. That make a difference?"

"We did lose one of our guests last night. Maybe I could stretch a point," said Mrs Sedge, as if to herself.

Warren was not a man to mess about. "Right. I'll get the old fellow packed and here in time for tea. That suit you?"

"We'd have to assess him, see if he fits in. Most people come for a week or two to see if they like it." said Mrs Sedge.

"He'll like it. Don't you worry?"

Mrs Sedge demurred, "we can't be sure of that, can we?"

"Who do I write the cheque to?"

Mrs Sedge put any scruples she might have had back in her handbag. "I look forward to meeting your father. I'm sure he'll be very happy here."

"I'm sure he will." said Warren, tearing off his cheque and handing it to her

Mr Gladwyn the undertaker and his assistant slid the body bag containing Mrs Forsyte's mother's body into his Private Ambulance, closed the doors, and then found Matron to give her a receipt for it.

"I'll get the relatives to phone you when they come back from the Registrar so they can sort out the Arrangements with you." she assured him.

He thanked her and took himself off. She went out to Janice in reception and asked her if she knew where Sam was, only to see him ambling towards her.

"You busy just now, Sam?" she asked.

"Fair busy. I got to finish trimming me hedge and there's the lawn needs mowing. It's getting a bit on the long side with all this rain we've been having,"

"They can wait an hour or so," said Matron. "Mr Gladwyn has just taken Mrs Gellatly away, so we need to get her room cleared."

Janice couldn't work out who Mrs Gellatly was for a moment, and then remembered she had been Mrs Forsyte's mother.

"There's a bookcase and a sewing box and a funny old chair she brought in." Matron was telling Sam. "They've got to be put into the storeroom until the relatives tell us what to do with them. Violet is stripping the bed and packing up her clothes and bits and her bobs already. The new guest is coming in at teatime today so we've got to put our skates on. It's a Mr Warren."

"I'll need help," Sam protested.

Matron looked around as if expecting another Sam to materialise by magic. Instead her eyes lit upon Janice. "Can you give Sam a hand for a few minutes?" she asked.

"Who'll be on the switchboard?"

"Switch it through Mrs Sedge's flat."

When they got to the late Mrs Gellatly's room the sheets were already off the bed and Violet, a heavily built lady from Jamaica in her forties who was never seen without a smile was carefully wrapping the old lady's ornaments and keepsakes in newspaper and putting them into one of the tea chests kept ready for the purpose. Matron went immediately to the wardrobe and started packing Mrs Gellatly's clothes into the suitcases they had arrived in only a few months before.

Sam took hold of the chair, heaved it into the corridor, hoisted it onto his head upside down and walked to the lift.

"You get the books off the bookcase" Matron ordered Janice. "Pile them on the floor. The relatives are almost certain to donate them to our library."

Janice looked at the titles as she took them off the shelves. Most of them seemed to be about geology. She could not imagine what use they would be to the other guests. Then she happened to notice one whose author was M.J.Gellatly. It was called "Structure of the Empty Quarter". She wondered what the Empty Quarter could be and idly opened the book to see if she could find out. She was surprised to see a picture of a much younger Mrs Gellatly staring out at her.

"Interested?" came Matron's voice from over her shoulder. She stood up and showed her the picture. "That must be her. You'd never have thought she wrote books."

Violet spoke up: "Oh yes. She told me all about it. She was a geologist, used to go all over the world looking for oil."

"She must have been quite a girl." said Janice.

"It's so easy to forget they were all young once." Matron stopped folding dresses for a moment. She sighed. "I suppose we'll all end up like that one day."

Sam came back, collected the little sewing box and a coffee table and disappeared again.

"We'll need something to put those books in." Matron said.

Janice suggested the books could be put back in the bookcase when it was in the basement.

"Good idea. We still need something to carry them in so Sam can put them back on the shelves."

"I could do that. I wouldn't mind staying a little longer before I go home to do it," said Janice, who wanted to have a closer look at the books. She wanted to know more about Mrs Gellatly.

"I'm not sure Sam will welcome you down there in his kingdom. Still, no harm in asking."

Sam arrived again with some black plastic bags to put the books in. "There you are; Sam thinks of everything," Matron remarked.

They stuffed the books into the black bags and then Sam asked Janice to help him with the bookcase. "Grab hold of one end, love, and I'll take the other, we'll have it downstairs in no time."

Even with the two of them carrying it the bookcase was surprisingly heavy. Janice wondered what would happen when the lift got to the basement. Would Sam let her into his kingdom, as Matron called it?

In the event he almost made her welcome. The lift took them down to a large cellar which had a neatly made bed against one wall, a kitchen table and chair, an old armchair, and a wardrobe. In one corner stood an ancient fridge and a small cupboard with a portable gas ring and a basin with some dishes in it. Janice wondered why Matron thought he would make a fuss about her seeing where he lived.

"Let's put it down for a moment, love" said Sam. She lowered her end of the bookcase thankfully. Her arms were beginning to feel the strain.

"Got to find somewhere to put it," said Sam, disappearing through a door in the far corner of the cellar. Janice heard the sound of things being moved about and then he emerged, saying "Come on – I've made a space for it."

They hauled the bookcase into the other room and Janice found herself in an even larger cellar, packed from floor to ceiling with all sorts of packing cases, suitcases and other bits of luggage, and an immense assortment of bits of furniture, piled one on top of another.

"Impressive, ain't it," said Sam. "Proper Aladdin's cave. Don't know what's going to happen when it's full up. I'd feed some of this stuff into the boiler, only it's an oil burner, so I can't, can I?"

Janice was fascinated. She had never seen anything like this in her young life. "Do you live down here?" she asked tactlessly.

"That's right, love. This is my home now." Sam sounded as though he was going to say more but he switched out the light and said "Come on, look sharp, they'll be waiting for us upstairs."

When they got there they found Matron vacuuming the carpet while Violet made the bed with a set of brand new sheets.

"Thank you Janice, I think we can cope now." said Matron. "Sam can carry the rest of the things downstairs. You go back to your own job."

"I might as well carry a few books, as I'm going down," suggested Janice.

"Good thinking, girl," said Sam, handing her a black bag which did not seem to have very many books in, filled a bag for himself and led her out to the lift.

"I can see you're interested in them books," he said as it went down. "Any time you want to come down to my celler and read them in peace and quiet out of the way of you know who, you're welcome."

Janice thanked him and went back to her post in reception. She thought she might take Sam up on his offer. But then again, she might not. Not when Sam was there, any road, you never knew, did you?

When Janice returned to her desk she found Mr and Mrs Forsyte had come back from the registrar and were waiting for her.

Mr Forsyte asked "What do we have to do now?"

"I'll go and find Mrs Sedge. She'll tell you everything," Janice told them". "Would you like a cup of tea?"

"That would be very nice, said Mrs Forsyte, collapsing into one of the chintz armchairs that were designed to make the reception area look homely and inviting.

Mr Forsyte took his wife's hand. "She's at peace at last. That's the great thing."

Mrs Forsyte began to sob quietly.

She was still crying when Janice came back with the tea. "Nice cup of tea," she said brightly as she put the tray down on a conveniently placed coffee table.

"Try a cup," said Mr Forsyte letting go his wife's hand. "It'll make you feel better."

"Milk and sugar?" asked Janice.

"Thank you, just a little sugar," said Mrs Forsyte, trying to compose herself.

"No sugar for me," said her husband.

"Ah, I see Janice is looking after you," Mrs Sedge's voice boomed as she came down the staircase. I'm afraid various practicalities have to be dealt with. I wish we didn't have to at a time like this, but officialdom never lets up, does it?"

"I see you have the Green Form," she said, almost snatching it out of Mr Forsyte's hand. "I'll take care of that; Mr Gladwyn will need it to allow him to proceed. Now, did Mother ever say anything about her funeral?"

The Forsytes looked puzzled.

"Some people make arrangements in advance, like reserving a plot next to their spouses, or if they were regular worshippers they want to be in the churchyard. I notice your mother was C of E."

"I don't think she went to church much, if at all."

"Where is her husband buried?" asked Mrs Sedge.

"In Amman, they were both geologists. He was in the desert looking for oil-bearing strata when he had a heart attack. They helicoptered him to hospital in Amman, but it was too late."

Mrs Forsyte added. "Mother was in Saudi Arabia at the time. They did their best to get her to him but he was dead by the time she arrived. She decided to bury him there. There didn't seem any point in bringing him home." Her eyes filled with tears again. She searched in her bag for a tissue and wiped her eyes. She smiled bravely.

"A drop more tea?" asked Mrs Sedge brightly. Mr Forsyte nodded. There were a few moments' silence while cups were refilled and Mrs Forsyte dried her eyes.

"We've put Mother's things in store for the moment." said Mrs Sedge, when she felt it was safe to get back to the business in hand. "There's no hurry to take them away, and of course we won't be pressing you for any money we're owed, not at a time like this. You'll need to talk to Mr Gladwyn about the Arrangements. I imagine, since your mother was not religious, you'll opt for cremation."

"Oh, no." said Mrs Forsyte, "Mother would not like that at all. She was a geologist, you see. She told me several times that when she died she wanted to be reunited with the earth's crust. I'm pretty sure there's something about it in her will."

"Ah, her will." said Mrs Sedge with the air of someone who has been presented with another can of worms to go with the one she was already trying to sort out. "Her will. She had a solicitor, of course. You'll need to contact him as soon as possible."

"Mr Wimpole," said Mr Forsyte. "I've phoned him already."

"He's very highly thought of," added his wife dutifully.

"You are obviously ahead of me," said Mrs Sedge. "All I can say is that if there is anything else we can do to help, anything at all, here we are."

"You've been most kind." said Mrs Forsyte." I don't know what we'd have done without The Poplars."

"I'd like to show our appreciation to the staff." said Mr Forsyte.

"Very nice of you," said Mrs Sedge. "Would you like to do something for the people who were directly involved with Mother, or would you prefer me to share it out among everyone on the staff?"

"If you would look after it for me, I'd be very grateful. I know Lizzie, Violet and Anne actually looked after her but there are lots of other people, like cooks and cleaners, who helped Mother without ever perhaps even meeting her. Oh, and I'd like to give Sam something. He and Mother were great friends."

"Very thoughtful," purred Mrs Sedge."

"I'll drop by to thank Sam, Lizzie Violet and Anne personally and I'll let you have a letter in the next few days with a cheque for the rest of the staff."

"That would be very nice of you. A thank you letter on the notice board is always good for staff morale. It's not an easy job, and it is nice for them to feel their efforts are appreciated."

"The least we could do." breathed Mrs Forsyte.

"Oh, and when you've fixed a date," said Mrs Sedge, "please do let us know about the funeral. I'm sure some of our staff would like to attend to say their last goodbyes." she put her cup and saucer on the table by her side and stood up as a sign to the Forsytes that it was time to go. They took the hint. "I'm sure you must be very busy," said Mrs Forsyte, "thank you so much for sparing us so much of your time."

"Don't mention it. If there is anything at all we can do to help, do please let us know." said Mrs Sedge again as she showed them to the door.

"There's something about that woman that gives me the creeps", Mr Forsyte remarked to his wife as they drove away.

Mrs Sedge had brought her conversation with the Forsytes to an abrupt halt when she spied Mr Warren's estate car coming through the gates.

"How nice to see you!" she oozed, stretching out her hand to welcome Mr Warren's father.

The old man peered at her hand with a look that might have been disdain, or curiosity, or just plain puzzlement. His own hand stayed firmly under the red plaid blanket where it was warm and snug. He looked Mrs Sedge up and down and then spoke.

"Don't think much of your taste, son!" he exclaimed.

His son raised his eyes heavenwards, and then spread his hands as if to say "You see what I mean?" and said "This is going to be your new home, Dad. They'll look after you here."

The old man snorted contemptuously. "Too old for you, I'd say. Can't see what you see in her. What's she like in bed?"

Mrs Sedge shrugged. "It's all right; we're used to this sort of thing. Come and see the room we have reserved for your father." She led the way to the lift.

As the lift door closed the old man started to laugh to himself, and went on cackling as they went along the corridor to what had been Mrs Gellatly's room only a few hours before.

His son pushed him over to the window so that he could look out over the garden and the fields beyond.

"Nice?" he asked.

"Fucking awful," said his father and then burst into a tuneless rendering of Lili Marlene.

"His mind's gone," said his son.

"How old did you say he was?" asked Mrs Sedge,

"Ninety-six."

"I'm sure he'll be very happy here. Lizzie, she'll be the carer looking after your father during the day, will be along in a moment. Violet will be seeing to him at night. You'll meet Annie, his other carer, next week, it's her week off just now. You will be visiting regularly, I imagine."

Mr Warren's son showed no trace of embarrassment as he told her "Actually no. I have to go abroad on business a great deal."

"Your wife, perhaps?"

"I'm afraid not. Leonora and dad never got on, and well, we're separated."

"I see," said Mrs Sedge. "Ah, here's Lizzie. "Lizzie, this is Mr Warren, our new Guest. I'm sure you'd like to make his acquaintance while I take his son downstairs to go through the formalities." She sniffed ostentatiously.

"Yes, Mrs Sedge" Lizzie, who was short, round and ruddy, sniffed the air and said: "Seems like he needs seeing to already."

"Thank you Lizzie," said Mrs Sedge with an air of finality, opening the door for Mr Warren, who went through it without a backward glance at his poor old father.

"And how is our new Guest settling in?" Mrs Sedge asked Matron that evening.

"Mr Warren is happy enough," Matron replied, wondering yet again where Mrs Sedge got her clothes from. She had some sort of bright red ostrich feather scarf draped round her shoulders.

Considering the old gentleman seemed to have no idea where he was, or rather thought he was in a different place every ten minutes, from the siege of Mafeking to the Alhambra Music Hall to the corner grocers, Matron wondered why Mrs Sedge bothered to ask.

The only nurse on the staff was always called Matron. It gave the place tone. There was an implication that The Poplars was run on good old-fashioned lines, delivering good old-fashioned care, which was true enough. There was a computer in Matron's office, but not very much else in the way of labour-saving devices; people came cheap in that part of the country. Visitors and inspectors to The Poplars often commented favourably on the high ratio of staff to residents.

Matron was called Matron for another reason. If her name were known the home would have emptied like a shot, and the local authority would have closed it down. Which Matron would have thought damned unfair. She had never actually been charged with anything, and now she was rebuilding her life and trying to be a respectable citizen doing a worthwhile job in the community.

Only Mrs Sedge knew who she was, and Mrs Sedge wouldn't say anything, because no-one else would work for the peanuts Matron was happy to accept.

"Has Dr Mingus seen Mr Warren yet?"

"He should have popped in this evening, but he had some urgent cases, so he's promised to come tomorrow to check him out."

"Excellent, excellent," trilled Mrs Sedge. "Keep up the good work Matron!"

"Your Ladyship!" said Matron said under her breath, curtseying to Mrs of Sedge's retreating back.

Dr Mingus was a good old-fashioned doctor. The worn Gladstone bag together with the navy pinstriped suit, blue and white striped shirt topped by a pristine stiff white collar and discreet dark red tie told the world that here was a confident, competent professional. He was exactly right for the part of a doctor whose practice was mainly made up of residents of old peoples' homes. The Doctor's wonderful bonhomie and reassuring bedside manner concealed the fact that while medical science had moved on by leaps and bounds since he qualified, his knowledge of it had stayed exactly where it was. Dr Mingus had managed to be an antique in his own lifetime.

He strode into Mr Warren's room where he found Lizzie feeding him his breakfast.

"This is Doctor Mingus, come to see you" she said brightly as she wiped a bit of scrambled egg off the old man's lip. "Have a little drink to wash your eggie down and then I'll leave you to the Doctor." She picked up the feeding cup and applied the spout to Mr Warren's mouth. He sucked his tea greedily."

"Ate nearly all our breakfast up," Lizzie told the doctor. "No problem there."

"What's the matter, old fellow?" Doctor Mingus asked as he applied his stethoscope to Mr Warren's chest.

"Crap!" shouted Mr Warren making the doctor jump back.

"Constipation?" he asked, rubbing his ears and sorting out his stethoscope which had got tangled with his tie.

Mr Warren peered at him. Who was this idiot? He said loudly " Syrup of figs. Clears the system out once a month. You try it. Sort you out in no time."

Dr Mingus sighed. His first punter of the day and he was dying for a drink already. He explained slowly and patiently "I'm all right, old man, I'm the doctor here. Are you tight or loose?"

"Wish I could get tight." came the reply. "This place is getting me down already."

"Ah. So you have a problem with your movements."

"I wouldn't be in this fucking wheelchair if I could move, would I?"

Lizzie stopped the conversation going nowhere by saying "I don't think anything's physically wrong with Mr Warren, apart from his legs. He's a new resident. You usually give new arrivals the once-over, don't you, doctor?"

"Of course, silly of me." Dr Mingus started to take Mr Warren's blood pressure, then got out his stethoscope again and had another go it to the old man's chest. He took it away, seemingly satisfied, and suddenly asked "Who's the Prime Minister?"

"You mean to say you don't know?" said Mr Warren. "Tell him, Lizzie."

"The doctor wants to know if you know. That's why he asked."

"Of course I know. It's Mr Baldwin. Bloke with a pipe. Wilson, that's it Harold Wilson."

The doctor told himself his patient living in the past. Deficient short term memory, very common in old people, but Mr Warren was not finished with him. He burst out. "Got it! Not Harold Wilson. Macmillan, Harold Macmillan. That's the boy! Knew it was a Harold!"

"Thank you," said the doctor, snapping his bag shut. "I think that's enough. Mr Warren seems fairly healthy for a man of his age, physically that is. How old did you say he is?"

"I didn't," said Lizzie, "but he's ninety-six, and as far as constipation is concerned, I don't think that's his problem, as you may be able to smell."

"Syrup of figs!" exclaimed the old man. "Can't beat it!"

Dr Mingus made for the door.

His next visit was to Mrs Sedge. She was waiting for him in reception, coffee on the table.

"Well, what do you think of our new arrival?" she asked, after pouring him a cup.

Dr Mingus drank the coffee gratefully. "Seems healthy enough for a man of his age. You should try and make him stop smoking – he's got a touch of emphysema, and his heart's a little irregular. Perhaps he should have a pacemaker. He should see a consultant about that. Do you happen to know if he has private health insurance?"

"No I don't. He only came in yesterday afternoon. His son had something urgent to go to and was in a hurry to get away. Next time he comes in I'll check with him." Then she remembered. Since he had paid in advance for a whole year's care. Mr Warren junior was not likely to be back for quite a while. "I'm not sure when that might be."

"Dumped the old boy and ran?" said Dr Mingus, holding out his cup.

"You put it so elegantly, Doctor," Mrs Sedge, smiled as she refilled it.

"My guess is that Mr Warren will be living at The Poplars for some years, unless there's an accident."

"Accident?" Mrs Sedge fiddled with her pen. "Whatever do you mean, Alfred?"

"Medical term, my dear; a blocked artery, a clot, you never know in medicine, at his age anything could happen," explained the doctor wondering how soon he could get away and grab the flask he kept in the glove box.

"Not in our Home. We don't allow accidents at The Poplars."

"I'm sure you don't. The great thing is to get the paperwork right. Then you're covered." He got up to go, desperate to get back to his car.

Mrs Sedge understood perfectly. "I'll get the details about his health insurance, if any, from Mr Warren and let you know."

"And I'll need to know who his glove box, sorry, his GP, is, or should I say was."

"Was," Mrs Sedge told him wondering what glove boxes had to do with it.

As soon as he had gone Mrs Sedge picked up the card Mr Warren had given her the night before. It was slightly old fashioned, black embossed print on a quality ivory card. She turned it over. There was the imprint of the letters on the reverse, indicating that the card was die stamped, which indicated an expensive stationer. Most people didn't bother any more, not when it meant a new die every time the telephone number changed. She turned the card right side up and read it. Henry Warren, Greengage Manor, Darleigh, Undershire, UN14 3AD. Beneath the phone and fax numbers was his e-mail: hawarren@warrens.co.uk. which told her that Mr Warren was wealthy enough to live in a manor house and had his own business. There was no indication what that business did.

She picked up the phone and dialled the number on the card. A woman's voice, young from the sound of it, answered. "You have reached Mr Henry Warren's residence in his absence. Please leave a short message after the tone. Thank you."

Mrs Sedge put the phone down. She had no wish to leave a message with an answering machine; she wanted to talk to Mr Warren. She realised she had been a little foolish. It had all been such a rush the day before. Getting such a large cheque had made her neglect the usual admission procedures. The quicker she sorted them out, the better. A chill ran up her spine. The old man might easily be diabetic or be allergic to something. Trust that old fool Mingus not to check, or if he did, not to mention it. Better put Mr Warren on a diabetic diet, just to be on the safe side. Who was the next of kin? Mustn't jump to the conclusion it was this Mr Henry Warren. It could be some other member of the family.

Mrs Sedge cursed herself for letting Mr Warren blind her with his cheque.

She tried Mr Warren's son's number again that evening. This time a real live woman answered.

"Can I speak to Mr Warren?"

"May I ask who is calling?" said the woman in a businesslike voice.

Sounds like a secretary, thought Mrs Sedge. Could be a mistress. Can't be his wife, he said they were separated.

"It's Mrs Sedge from The Poplars. It's about his father."

"I'll put you through."

Maybe Mr Warren ran his business from home. Mrs Sedge wondered again what that business might be. He came on the line. "Hallo Mrs Sedge, how is my father settling in?"

"Very well, but there are some forms and things I need you to fill in and sign. When will you next be visiting?"

"I hadn't given the matter much thought. My business takes me all over the world, so I'm afraid I won't be able to drop in very often. Could you perhaps send the forms on? I'll make sure they get dealt with and sent back to you as soon as possible. You've got my address?"

This confirmed Mrs Sedge's suspicion. The old man had been dumped. His son had been only too glad to be shot of him. She said "No problem. They'll be in the post tomorrow. If you could get them back to us as quickly as you can, please, otherwise we'll have the local authorities on our backs, and you know what they can be like."

Mr Warren laughed. "Don't I just! Drive you mad if the paperwork's not perfect. Don't worry I'll see to it, just as long as I have them before the weekend. I'm off to Canada and the States for a fortnight then.

Mrs Sedge replied. "I'll make sure you get them. There's just one thing more. We need to have the name and address of your father's doctor."

"Anything wrong?"

"No, nothing. Our doctor has to get his medical records, that's all. You don't happen to know if your father suffers from diabetes or needs any other special diet. Is he on any medication?"

"Not as far as I know. His doctor's a Dr Swallow, Enid Swallow. Hold on a moment while I find out her address."

Mrs Sedge heard the woman saying "It's in the file downstairs, I'll get it" before Mr Warren came back on the line. "Won't keep you a moment. How is my father?"

My father, not Dad, or the old fellow, or any other endearment. Just "my father." Mrs Sedge's ear was finely tuned to little nuances like these.

"Well enough. He seems quite strong for a man of his years. Don't worry, we'll look after him and keep him going. He might make a century if we try hard?"

"A hundred years! You think that's likely?"

"Certainly. We have a lady who is 102 and another even older. Mabel had her hundred and fifth birthday last week. I'm afraid she didn't know what was going on; her mind's completely gone, but we do like to celebrate these occasions; it's good for the other Guests."

"A hundred and five!" Mr Warren's son sounded more shocked than congratulatory." Hang on a moment." Mrs Scdge caught the woman saying "here's the file," then Warren came back and said "Look, perhaps it would be best if I called in at your place on Friday to sign those papers and give you Dr Swallow's details on the way to the airport."

"I'm here all the time," Mrs Sedge told him.

"Friday morning, then. Eight o'clock too early?"

"No. That will do fine."

"Good. Look forward to it." Mrs Sedge was going to say "see you then," but he had put the phone down.

Mr Warren's son never turned up Friday morning as he had promised.

Mrs Sedge tried phoning him again.. The secretary answered.

"I'm afraid you can't speak to Mr Warren. He left for Canada this morning. Can I be of assistance?"

Mrs Sedge explained.

"I'm afraid," said the woman, "that Mr Warren does not confide in me as far as personal matters are concerned. I could pass a message to him the next time he contacts me."

Mrs Sedge decided to pull out the stops. She lied: "Look, his father is not well and we must have certain details as a matter of urgency in case he passes away. Can you please give me his number in Canada so I can telephone him?"

The answer was what she expected. "I'm not in a position to divulge that information. I repeat, I shall convey your concern as soon as I hear from him."

Mrs Sedge recognised a stone wall when she walked into one and saw no point in banging her head up against it. She merely said "It is a matter of the greatest urgency. Please do all you can to help.

"Of course I shall," replied the lofty voice.

"Sodding la-di-dah bitch!" said Mrs Sedge as she put the phone down.

Mrs Forsyte's mother was laid to rest a week later in the municipal cemetery, nicely sited on the far side of Hatchet Hill, where it could not be seen from the city centre. It was a fine day and there was a seemly turnout, composed of family and friends, geologists and ladies of the Women's Institute which Mrs Gellatly had joined when she settled into retirement. Mrs Sedge, on holiday in Majorca, was represented by Matron, accompanied by Anne and Violet. Lizzie could not get away because she was on duty. Sam was there too, dressed in his only suit. Sam liked a good funeral and went to as many as he could. He regarded it as one of the perks that went with his job.

There was a large wreath from The Poplars. There always was. Mrs Sedge was of the opinion that a striking wreath was first-class publicity, cheaper than an advertisement in the local paper. During the service Mr Forsyte read Yeats' "When you are old and grey and full of sleep" which he said was his late mother-in-law's favourite. His wife broke down at the graveside and had to be helped back to the car. Afterwards everyone went back to the Forsyte residence, a mass-produced detached house in North Dununder, except Sam who stayed behind for a chat with the gravediggers.

After everybody had eaten the finger buffet, drunk the sparkling wine and taken themselves off, the Forsytes cleared the remains of the feast away and washed the dishes. When all was neat and tidy again they settled themselves in their respective armchairs.

"Well!" said Mrs Forsyte.

Her husband got up and went over to an antique globe which opened to disclose an array of bottles and glasses. He said "Let's have a drink first."

"Why not? A few moments more suspense might kill me, but I'll take a chance. Dry sherry for me."

"You've had rather a lot already."

"So have you." I'll have it in one of your whisky glasses."

"Fill it?"

"I'm still thirsty."

Her husband filled the tumbler and then poured a generous whisky for himself.

"Cheers."

"Cheers."

"Come on Charlie, open the damn thing."

He went over to the bureau that stood in the corner of the room, drew out a buff envelope. He said "I wonder why Wimpole had to send this by post, especially since it says "not to be opened until after my funeral." He could have given it to us this afternoon. Saved himself the cost of a stamp."

She mused "Some sort of legal thing, I imagine."

He pulled out his pocket knife, slit the envelope, drew out the paper inside and peered at it. He started reading. "Last Will and Testament of..."

"No need to read every bloody word," said his wife, just get to the bit when it says how much."

There was silence while he read through to legal preamble then "Here we are..... I bequeath.... I don't believe it... the fucking bitch!"

She got up and came over to see what the matter was. Looking over his shoulder she read "to my dear daughter Cynthia Emma Forsyte the sum of ....five thousand pounds! Is that all?"

"Read on." said her husband, "Take it! Read it all. It's a bloody insult." He sat down heavily, gulped down the rest of his whisky and sloshed some more into his glass.

She went on reading, "to my dear son-in-law Charles Henry Forsyte the sum of five thousand pounds and to the Geological Society of Great Britain the residue of my estate, after all expenses ....She's left the lot to the Cats' Home!"

"Not the Cats' Home, the Geological...."

"Shut up, Charlie! She must be worth a million after what Dad left her. After all we've done for her!"

"There must be some way of fighting it. I'll go and see Wimpole in the morning, see what the law says."

"Ten thousand. That's just about what it cost us for putting the granny flat in the loft!"

"I know, I know," said her husband wearily.

"After all we did for her!" Mrs Forsyte repeated numbly.

Charlie Forsyte got up from his chair and started to pace the room. "Item: we got her a place at The Poplars. Item: we went down to Brighton and brought her up here, just to be near us. Item: we cleared her flat and sold it for her. Item: we arranged the sale of all that ghastly furniture. Item: we had the loft extended to make a granny flat in case she didn't like it at The Poplars. Item: we went to see her every other Sunday, Item..."

"Bloody cow!" Mrs Forsyte interrupted him. She slumped into an armchair and grabbed her drink. "You realise what this means, Charlie? The bank is going to stop the overdraft, we only got it because you told them we were going to inherit." She wiped her nose and sniffed before going on "and the credit cards, we're never going to pay them off now, and then there's the car – they're sure to take that back."

"We're behind with the mortgage too," her husband took the opportunity of reminding her.

"Oh God," she wailed. "What are we going to do?"

Her husband poured himself another whisky. She held out her glass and he filled it up. "We're going to fight this ridiculous will, that's what we're going to do. I'll keep the bank hanging on; the ten grand she did leave us will shut them up for a bit. The other creditors will just have to sue. They'll get judgement easily enough but then they've got to get hold of their money. They'll be lucky because it isn't there!"

"They'll put the bailiffs in. Take the furniture!"

Mr Forsyte sank into a chair. His speech was slurred. "They can't take the bed. I know that. They gotter leave you your bed, your clothes and the tools of your trade. That's what the law says darling, the rest isn't ours. The bed stays!"

"The bed stays! The bloody bed stays!" She started to laugh, at first a titter, than a cackle which grew until she could not control it. She slid off the chair onto the floor where she rolled about helplessly. Eventually she regained control over herself, got up, grabbed her glass and stretched it out towards him.

He filled her glass again, then his own, and raised it aloft. "To our creditors, may they rot in hell!"

She drained her glass and echoed. "Rot in hell!" then she leaned back, closed her eyes and went to sleep.

"Shit!" he said. He stood up and looked down at her. Her mouth was open and she was starting to snore. "She never knows when to stop!"

"Nor do I, come to think of it," he said to himself as he switched out the light and made his unsteady way upstairs.

CHAPTER TWO
Mrs Prime's Dinner Party

Avril Prime took a large plastic container out of her fridge, snapped the lid and tasted the contents. She told herself her vichyssoise was as good as any in France. She put the soup back in the fridge, went over to the Aga, donned the Freddy Frog oven gloves her mother had given her last Christmas and drew a large roast joint out of the oven. She opened the drawer which should have contained her meat thermometer. It was not in its place. She swore silently. Then she remembered she had already got it out and put it on the kitchen table. She pushed it gently into the beef and waited a few seconds while the pointer rose to show the temperature inside the meat.

"Another half hour will do it," she said out loud although there was no-one to hear. "Now, how are the roast potatoes?" The potatoes were browning nicely. The treacle tart, made that morning, stood golden and perfect on one of the units. Everything was ready except herself. She had just enough time to shower and change before Mrs Hunkle from the village came to take over while she played the perfect hostess.

She ran up the stairs to the bedroom, threw her clothes on a chair and stepped into the shower in the en-suite bathroom. Ten minutes later, fresh and perfumed, she slipped into the black dress she had selected for the evening and studied herself in the mirror. Too severe. She toyed with the idea of her navy two-piece, got the jacket up and held it up in front of her and shook her head. It would have to be the black dress.

A scarf. That was it. Something colourful to lighten the mood. Hermes. No. Too formal. The grey watered silk Eddie had brought back from Milan? She put it round her neck and studied it. Classy but too plain. She leafed through her scarf drawer with an increasing feeling of desperation.

She heard a car draw up. Oh God! Eddie was here already. She'd have to go down and greet his boss half dressed. She padded to the window and peered out through the net curtain, hoping she could not be seen and realising at the same time that she could, since the light was on.

It was only Mrs Hunkle in her old Renault. "I'll be down in a moment!" she yelled down the stairs as her helper shut the front door. "Please give Mother her tea while I finish dressing."

"Right you are," Mrs Hunkle's confident voice came up the stairs. Avril thought: All right for you. Your husband's promotion doesn't depend on this evening. She went back to the scarves and discovered a tie-die one made by her daughter at school which set off the dress to perfection.

She sat down and applied her makeup, slipped into her shoes and checked the result. Just right. The capable, sophisticated, attractive, very slightly sexy, business wife, just a touch flirtatious, but coolly unavailable. She turned round and looked over her shoulder. Bum getting a bit on the heavy side. She really must get to the gym more often. Not so easy with Mother to look after. She told herself all she had to do tonight was look good, help the conversation along and produce the food, which last was pretty well dealt with.

She went downstairs to the self-contained granny flat, the garage in an earlier incarnation, where Eddie's mother lived. Mrs Hunkle was spooning semolina pudding into the old lady's mouth.

"I'll make her hot chocolate," Avril said. Darting into the kitchen she poured boiling water onto instant chocolate, leaving a generous space in the mug which she filled to the top with vodka.

"Sleep well, mummy," she said to herself as she went back to the flat with the old lady's nightcap.

While Mrs Hunkle finished off the cooking Avril went to the dining room and set the table. She polished each piece of cutlery and glass as she put it in place, then folded the serviettes carefully. She lit the two delicately scented candles and then stood back to survey the effect. Finally she uncorked the bottles of claret Eddie had bought specially for the occasion to give them time to breathe, which is what Eddie said claret needed.

She checked her watch. They could arrive any moment. She looked round the room again to make sure everything was in place, tiptoed to the granny flat to make sure her mother-in-law was fast asleep and then went back to the kitchen where Mrs Hunkle assured her all was ready.

A moment later the bell rang. Eddie was here with his boss. Avril nearly went out to greet them wearing her Betty Boop apron. She remembered to take it off just in time.

"That was the most delicious vichyssoise, you must give me the recipe" said Lorna Masters.

"Absolutely fabulous." confirmed her husband.

Eddie shot Avril a significant look that said "going well". She saw Mrs Hunkle hovering in the doorway, and nodded to her. She came in, collected the soup tureen and gathered up the dishes.

I'll just go and see to the joint" said Avril.

"A roast joint!" cried Mr Masters. "Fantastic! Haven't had a proper home-made roast for years.

His wife shot him a look and remarked "Since the children left home there didn't seem to be much point."

"Eddie enjoys the carving bit," said Avril. Taking his cue her husband seized the steel and, a touch theatrically, started to sharpen the carving knife, while she slipped into the kitchen where Mrs Hunkle was emptying Yorkshire puddings into a dish. "Everything ready?" she asked. Mrs Hunkle's terse "yes" told her she should not have asked.

"I'll take the roast," Avril told her, "and you follow with those and then bring in the vegetables."

Back in the dining room Eddie was filling his boss's glass. His wife covered hers. "I'm driving tonight." she explained.

Mike Masters ogled the joint, and when Mrs Hunkle followed with her dish of Yorkshire puddings he almost started to slaver. "Yorkshire pudding! Now I know I'm in paradise." he exclaimed. Eddie filled his half empty glass again and then, brandishing his newly sharpened carving knife like a sword, attacked the roast.

He gave a couple of slices to Lorna Masters and then piled slice after slice on her husband's plate, added two Yorkshire puddings and motioned to Mrs Hunkle to place the plate in front of him. "Help yourself to roast potatoes and veg." he said unnecessarily, since Masters was already spooning them onto his plate.

"Gravy?" asked Avril, waving a gravy boat under his nose.

"Ah Bisto!" exclaimed Masters, sniffing the aroma.

Fortunately no-one noticed the expression on Avril's face.

About half an hour and two more platefuls of beef later Mike Masters sighed and put down his knife and fork. He emptied his glass and then said "Eddie, I've got something to tell you."

"Tell me?" asked Eddie innocently, his heart beating wildly.

"This is all strictly confidential. Not to go beyond these four walls for the time being."

"Of course." said Avril.

Eddie didn't have to be told. Talk about the company opening its own office in New York had been circulating for weeks. In a moment he was going to be asked to head it up.

Masters went on: "As you know our American sales have been going up steadily over the last few years. So much so that we are going to open our own operation there instead of relying on Kodiak Agencies. Joe Kodiak's agreed to bring his New York office under the umbrella of the company instead of running his own operation, so we get a ready-made set up there. He'll join our board, of course.

Eddie's heart sank. If he wasn't going to get the New York office and the seat on the board that went with it what did Masters have in mind? What was the man doing sitting at his table eating his roast beef and drinking his claret?

Masters went on to put him straight. "Everything west of the Mississippi, including Michigan, will be run from LA, so we need someone to set up an office there. Naturally Joe's offered to do that, but I want one of our own people to be involved in what will in effect be a major expansion into the US market, with serious back-up, marketing, advertising, PR, the works. How would you feel about taking that on, Eddie?"

Eddie had given quite a lot of thought about how he was going to respond. Now the moment had come he was tempted to clasp his hands above his head and yell "Yeah! Result!" but he had not yet had enough to drink.

Masters replied for him. "You'll need time to think it over, of course and talk to Avril about it. We'd compensate you generously for the inconvenience of relocation, of course, and you've got the children's education to think about. I don't expect an answer right aw…....."

Masters stopped in mid-speech and was staring at the open door with his mouth hanging open. From where he was sitting Eddie could not see what he was staring at. "What is it? What's wrong? Are you all right?" he asked. Masters was pointing at the open door transfixed, his eyes wide. Avril, sitting next to him, had hers tight closed and an expression of horror on her face.

Through the door came Eddie's mother, babbling incomprehensibly. There were no teeth in her mouth, or clothes on her body. For a moment there was silence. Then she spoke, this time loud and clear.

"Where's me nightie? I can't find my nightie! Some bastard's gone and nicked me bloody nightie!"

Eddie's boss's mouth slowly closed.

Over breakfast the following morning, Avril declared "We've got to do something," at least five times.

"Too right," agreed her husband. Mike Masters had been very understanding really, and disaster had been averted by Mrs Hunkle's miraculous appearance bearing the treacle tart. "Did you put enough vodka in her bedtime drink?"

"Couldn't have put more. There should have been enough there to keep her asleep for a week."

"Did she drink it all? Doesn't matter. The time really has come for her to go into a home. In any case, if we're going to live in America we can't take her with us."

Avril remarked "They say The Poplars is very good."

"Be a darling and give them a ring" said Eddie getting up from the breakfast table "I've got to be off to work."

"I'm going to call them the moment you've gone" said his wife, getting up kiss him goodbye.

The day was sunny and warm. Sam was taking old Mr Warren for a walk in the garden. Mr Warren was chattering happily to himself, Sam was taking the chance to have a cigarette, since smoking was not allowed within the walls of The Poplars.

Mr Warren stopped his discussion of the Boer War in the middle of the Relief of Mafeking and sniffed. He sniffed again.

"You smoking?" he asked.

Sam instinctively hid his fag in his hand so that the smoke went up his sleeve.

"Me? Smoking? Nah!" he said, the guilt plain in his voice.

"Yes you are," insisted the old man, twisting round in his wheelchair. Come round here where I can see you."

Sam shuffled round, holding his fag behind his back.

"You've got smoke coming out of your arse," said Mr Warren. "Come on, show! Bring it out. Can't hide anything from Joe Warren."

Sam guiltily brought the gasper into view.

"I knew it!" exclaimed Mr Warren."

Sam muttered something that sounded like an apology and went to throw the fag away.

"Don't do that!" shouted Mr Warren. "Ciggies cost money!"

Sam bridled "So what you want me to do?"

"Let me have a puff. Go on!" came the reply.

Sam looked into the old man's eyes. "You won't tell?" he said.

"Cross my heart and hope to die, the old man assured him. Sam wondered if that was quite the right thing for the old bloke to be saying, but without a word he passed over his fag. Mr Warren drew deeply. When his lungs were full he handed it back to Sam. He breathed out slowly, savouring every scrap of nicotine.

"Boy, that was good," he said. Look...."

"What?" Sam thought he knew what was going to come next.

Joe Warren paused for a moment, considering how best to put what he was going to say. Then he came out with it. "You couldn't let me have one."

Sam looked suitably shocked.

The old man went on before he could say anything. "I can pay. I've got plenty of cash. Took it out of my miserable son's jacket when he was out. Look!" He reached into his pocket and pulled out a five pound note.

Sam looked at it disdainfully. "Too much. I mean, five quid for one fag."

"No, my boy," said Mr Warren. "You don't get it. That's for five ciggies. Pound a fag. Not bad eh?"

Sam reached into his pocket and was about to hand him a smooth white coffin nail when he had a touch of the seconds.

It wasn't his conscience. He muttered "Best if we goes behind them bushes 'fore we lights up."

"It was the Turks, you know. They started it." remarked Mr Warren.

"Started what?"

"Turkish delight!" exclaimed the old man and burst into a paroxysm of coughing laughter. "They invented ciggies, the Turks!" he wheezed when he had recovered.

Sam wheeled him behind the bushes, handed him his fag and lit it for him.

"Mum's the word, right?" said Mr Warren between puffs.

"More than me job's worth, so you keep your mouth shut." countered Sam.

Then he added. "I got ways of making sure you keep that mouth shut. Got me?"

Got you." said Mr Warren as he puffed happily away. "Got you, got you, got you, got you!"

CHAPTER THREE
The Lillywhites Fly the Atlantic

Six miles above the Atlantic, somewhere in the vicinity of Rockall, Myron and Sally Lillywhite were discussing their airline dinner.

"Boeuf Bourgignon," Myron read the label on the packet the stewardess had handed him. He managed to remove the red-hot aluminium cover without burning his fingers or getting the contents in his lap and poked apprehensively at the contents.

Sally deftly removed the foil and dug right in. "Delicious," she remarked after the first forkful. She ate a little more and then pushed it away.

Myron took a mouthful and savoured it before swallowing.

"AlliedAir, the Gourmet's choice of Airline." he remarked sarcastically.

Sally was incredulous. "You mean you wrote the ad without tasting the food?"

"Of course I ate the food," Myron expostulated. "In Business Class. That was the market we were aiming at. I never dreamed they served this pap to the paupers." He put the stew to one side and nibbled dubiously on the cheese and biscuits.

"Why did that lawyer send us Economy tickets?" Sally finished her beef and turned her attention to the Lemon Mousse.

"Lawyers are like that. Mean as hell as long as they're spending their own money. I did my best to get an upgrade, but let's face it, the only real argument is cash, and we're maxed on our credit cards."

"Bloody BBQ!" Sally muttered, not for the first time.

"It happens in the advertising game," Myron said stoically, also not for the first time. "You get hired, you get fired. You're as good as your last campaign, and let's face it, I haven't had a really whacko one since I sold AlliedAir on the strength of their gourmet food."

Sally giggled. "Like, well, you're having to eat your words."

.Myron looked at her and asked himself if he should take offence at her little joke. He could have done with a bit of sympathy from his wife when he had come home with the news that Ben

Brock, the BB of BBQ had told him there was no future for him at the agency. Myron had refrained from telling her Ben had also forcefully opined there was no future for Myron in any other agency.

"Don't worry, I'll get another job." he reassured her. He wished he could reassure himself. Numerous calls to contacts had yielded zilch. He had been working on his resumé when the mysterious letter with the British stamp had arrived, addressed to Sally.

Inside was a sheet of heavy notepaper headed Augustus Wimpole, Solicitor, printed in old fashioned copperplate. In stilted unfamiliar language he begged to inform Sally that her aunt, Mrs Edith Mary Clarence, was in hospital in England and it would be to their mutual advantage if Sally could see her way clear to visiting England to discuss her aunt's affairs. All reasonable expenses would be paid. .

Sally had been only vaguely aware that she had an aunt in England. She had telephoned this Augustus Wimpole, who had been unforthcoming. "It is a delicate matter which I would not care to discuss over the telephone, dear lady," he had intoned.

Sally immediately took umbrage at Wimpole's unctuous manner. "So we've got to drop everything fly across the Atlantic to have a chat with you." As the words left her mouth she realised they did not have much to drop, now that Myron was no longer with BBQ.

"Entirely your affair," Wimpole had said, "but I feel it would be in your best interest to come and see me. Your best financial interest," he had added in a portentous tone."

Sally got the message that serious money was involved and relented. Wimpole for his part began to understand that he was talking to Americans and should cut the act he put on to impress new clients and the conversation began to take a more friendly tone. When Sally realised that Myron could come too, indeed that Wimpole seemed quite happy to pay for them to spend a fortnight's holiday in Britain, all expenses paid, everything got settled very quickly.

In no time at all, dates were agreed and the next day airline and railway tickets, together with a detailed itinerary, had arrived by courier. This Wimpole was seemingly not as antiquated as he sounded.

And soon they would be landing in London. Neither of them had been out of the States before. Sally was looking forward to the experience but Myron was sure something would go wrong; they would get lost, mugged, catch some foul disease and almost certainly be ripped off. He got out the itinerary and ran through it again for what seemed the tenth time. "10.00 land London Heathrow. Take Heathrow Express train to Paddington Station. 14.00, that's two o'clock, take train from Paddington to Birmingham."

Sally said "Birmingham as in Alabama. Limey copycats." She was wondering how much longer the flight was going to take. She was getting cramp, she was sure of it.

Myron said "No honey, theirs is the original."

"Joke, sweetie."

He carried on reading out the itinerary. "Arrive Birmingham New Street Station 16.05. Take 16.35 from New Street to Dununder Castle Station. He wondered how you could have a train station in a castle. Wimpole was going to meet them off the train and take them to the County Hotel where he had made reservations.

Myron put the itinerary back in his pocket and pulled the letter which had started them on their journey from his document case and began to read it aloud. "Dear Mrs Lillywhite, "Re.: Edith Mary Clarence."

Sally peered over his shoulder at the letter. "My aunt I never met. Hardly knew she existed. Wouldn't know her if she stood in front of me. I feel sort of responsible for her,"

"Why?"

"I know it's absurd, but I do." She went back to staring out of the window. It was a clear day, not a cloud to be seen. Far down below the white feather of the wake of a ship going about its business relieved the monotony of the sea.

Myron put the letter back in his case. "What puzzles me is why we have to go and see this Mr Wimpole. Why can't he talk to us on the telephone, send us faxes, e-mails?"

"We are getting a free holiday in England, honey. Don't look a gift horse in the mouth. Besides, there's a lot of money involved. Wimpole pretty well said as much last time we spoke." Sally was sure she was getting cramp. She should have taken an aisle seat so she could stretch her legs more.

The pilot's voice announced the plane was approaching the Irish coast. Sally peered out of the window again and was rewarded by the sight of a line of white breakers, a jagged coastline and some hills far below. Everything looked very green, even from this height. She felt the cramp going away.

"I wonder what's the matter with your aunt?" Myron asked suddenly. Sally looked away from the window. "Good question, Ed. Every time I asked Wimpole he avoided the question."

"Maybe she's in a funny farm."

"Whatever Mr Mysterious Wimpole wants, I hope it won't take long. I want to see Stratford and Big Ben and London Bridge and all that, not some lawyer's office out in deadsville."

"I'm sure we'll get to see the country" said her husband as he handed the remains of the airline meal to the stewardess and got up to join the queue for the john at the back of the plane. He was feeling queasy already, and he had a fortnight of English food ahead of him. Everyone knew that was digestive death. He should be back in New York waiting for the phone to ring. He should have let Sally go on her own.

But he was her husband. How could he do a thing like that? What did she know about money? This Brit lawyer would for sure run rings round her.

"I'm afraid there is really nothing I can do about your Mother-in-law's will," Augustus Wimpole told Charlie Forsyte. "You are at liberty to contest it, of course, but you'd be wasting your time and your money. Your mother was entitled to do what she liked with her own money."

"But we did so much for her at the end. She said she'd see us right. Over and over again."

"What did she die of?"

"Heart failure, it said on the death certificate, but she had Alzheimer's. She didn't know who she was at the end."

"You can get a doctor's certificate to that effect?"

"I'm sure Dr Mingus, he's the doctor at The Poplars, will give us one." said Charlie, wondering how much that would cost. He was pretty certain Dr Mingus would help if the price was right. The man had virtually hinted as much.

"And testify in court if it comes to it," went on the lawyer, "submit himself to cross-examination?"

Charlie was not quite so sure. How would Mingus stand up to being battered about by hostile counsel? He asked Wimpole "Who is likely to fight us if we contest the will?"

Wimpole wondered, yet again, at the cupidity and stupidity of the clients who came through his door. He spelt out the obvious: "The Geological Society. They'll fight you tooth and nail. Organisations like that rely on legacies for a large part of their income. They are sure to have solicitors who specialise in contested wills."

"But it's a whole lot of old stones and fossils against a living breathing family who need the money. Surely the court will see that? It's an open and shut case."

Mr Wimpole sighed. How many times had he heard that phrase and had to explain that open and shut cases more often than not end with one's client shut out. For a moment he wondered if he should take this fool's money and fight his hopeless fight. No point. The Forsytes didn't have any money, which is why they were fighting the will. They hadn't even paid his last bill.

"You'd be wasting your time," he repeated. "Go away and think about it. Talk to your wife."

"Thanks, I'll do that," said Charlie Forsyte getting up to leave. His unspoken thoughts, as he headed for the door ran along the lines of *Perhaps I'll talk to another solicitor, one who does what his clients ask him to do.*

Mr Wimpole was rude enough to utter the mantra "If you could do something about our account?" to the back of Charlie's head as he went out, but he knew in his heart that that was another forlorn hope.

"I'm afraid we have a waiting list," said Mrs Sedge when Avril Prime phoned.

Avril didn't mince her words. "Not to put too fine a point on it, you mean we have to wait for someone to die."

"I was trying not to use that word," said Mrs Sedge. "So distressing. Everyone at The Poplars knows it's going to come to our Guests eventually, but we try not to dwell on it. We are in the business of life, Mrs Prime, prolonging life and making it as enjoyable as possible   for our Guests."

"It's a rather difficult situation," Avril repeated. "Up to now we've been looking after my mother-in-law at home; we were able to convert the garage into a flat for her where she could be independent but there if she needed us, but now everything's changed. You see, my husband's just been offered a big job in California by his firm. He's going out in a couple of weeks and I'm going to follow as soon as I can make arrangements for his mother to be looked after."

"She can't go with you?"

"No way, there's a lot of entertaining involved." and Avril went on to describe the sudden appearance of her mother-in-law, stark naked and querulous, just at the moment that Eddie had been offered the job.

Mrs Sedge smiled. "I can see that could be a problem. You've tried other homes in the vicinity, I suppose."

"Yes, but they all say the same. No vacancies. A friend recommended you, said you   might be more flexible than the others."

"Have you tried Limes Court? They have the reputation of never turning anyone away."

"Have you been there?" asked Avril.

"The smell? You get used to it after a while. Hardly notice it."

"I wouldn't want to put her in a place like that. She is my husband's mother after all."

"I thought you were desperate."

Avril shuddered at the thought of Limes Court. "Not that desperate."

Mrs Sedge had another suggestion. "Have you thought of taking her to California and finding a home for her there?"

"Aren't they rather expensive?"

"You should make enquiries. Try the American Embassy. They will know about immigration rules. Perhaps your husband's firm would contribute to the cost?"

Avril considered this for a moment. "I hadn't thought about that possibility. I'll ask my husband to find out what the position is.

Going to America would be traumatic for the old lady, though. I wonder if she'd even survive the journey."

There was something about the way Avril expressed this last thought that made Mrs Sedge say "I"d like to meet your mother-in law, in any case. You never know in this business. One moment you're full up and the next you've got more vacancies than you'd like. When would be convenient?"

Avril suggested the next day.

"Tomorrow? Perhaps the old lady would like to come and have lunch with us? Meet some of our other residents?"

"That would be lovely," agreed Avril.

Sam had the afternoon off. He went into Dununder to buy himself some cigarettes and some toothpaste, had a pint or two and then took himself off to the municipal cemetery where he sat himself down on his usual seat by the chapel wall, lit up and puffed contentedly away.

It was a fine day. Little woolly clouds chased each other across an azure sky; birds swooped and wheeled among the tombstones. Sam gazed contentedly across the tranquil scene while he calculated the amount he had saved up for his own funeral.

When his cigarette was finished he got up and strolled among the tombstones looking at the epitaphs. There were some he knew well, like Anna Jane Coombs who had arranged to have the legend "I told you I didn't feel well" carved below her name and age, and Jack Harrison who "never failed to amuse and amaze" his family.

As he stood looking at the grave of Elizabeth Goode who, according to her relicts, "never put a foot wrong" Sam tried to imagine what sort of people they must have been. Elizabeth Goode was possibly a dancer, or possibly a footballer. No, she couldn't have been a footballer. Women didn't play football in those days. He pictured Anna Jane Coombs complaining about her innards and Jack Harrison driving his wife and kids to distraction with his silly jokes.

He wandered round the cemetery comparing the headstones. There was no doubt about it, marble was rotten value. Some of the graves, only twenty years old, were already showing signs of weathering. Granite was what Sam wanted when he went. Granite lasted. Of course it was pricey, but when it came to headstones expense was never something to be spared.

He came across a new grave, the earth still freshly turned. and realised he had been by its side only a few days before. It was the grave of that old girl who had died last week, Mrs Gellatly. Nice old lady. Knew her stones too. Bet she's insisted on granite for her headstone, Sam told himself, recalling pleasant chats with the old lady about the relative merits of different rocks when it came to statuary, especially funerary statuary.

Sam didn't know it, but she had indeed insisted on granite. There was a codicil to her will stipulating the wording on her tombstone and the quarry where the stone, already cut and paid for, was to be found.

But her children never got down that far when they read her will.

"Can I offer you some tea, Mrs Lillywhite?" asked Augustus Wimpole, once Myron and Sally were safely settled on the far side of his desk. "I usually have a cup myself about now," he added by way of making his clients feel at home.

"You got any coffee?" asked Myron, "I tried your English tea yesterday."

"Of course and for you, Madam?"

"Madam." Sally liked that. She could not imagine an American lawyer being so gentlemanly.

"Now," started Wimpole, when he had ordered the coffee. "I have brought you here, as you know, to decide what to do about your aunt. I gather from our telephone conversations that you have never met the lady.

"That's right," agreed Sally. "I hardly knew she existed."

Wimpole allowed himself a dry cough before going on "I am the sole executor of her will, since at the time she made it she had no idea where you were and there were no other relatives. She has no power to change that will, as sadly, she can no longer be said to be of sound mind. Now, I hold an Enduring Power of Attorney....."

"What's that?" put in Myron. "You're an attorney, aren't you, so you've got whatever powers attorneys have in this country. I don't get it."

Wimpole took an immediate dislike to Myron. He put on his most formal solicitor's face while he prepared to launch into an explanation of the rights and duties conferred by a Power of Attorney.

Myron decided he had an equal dislike of Wimpole. He leaned back and said "I'm sure you know your business."

Wimpole knew a snide remark when he heard one. He was wondering if "With respect" is as insulting in the States as it is in England, when his secretary came in with the coffee. Wimpole fussed around with milk and sugar, while telling himself there was no point in having a row with people who could turn out to be a pair of very profitable clients.

While they drank their coffee Wimpole resumed his lecture. "Perhaps a Power of Attorney is called something different in the United States. It is a document giving someone else, a relative, say, power to act on behalf of someone who is not able to look after their own affairs, which is now the situation in the case of your aunt. When I realised your aunt was no longer able to act for herself I applied to have the Power registered, which led to my consulting her will which showed Mrs Lillywhite as the sole beneficiary.

"You mean Sally gets the lot?" asked Myron.

"Absolutely," replied Wimpole and went rapidly on laying down the law. "Mrs Clarence gave me Power of Attorney some time ago as a precautionary measure. Perhaps you would like to see it?"

Sally shook her head. "I'm sure everything's in order, Mr Wimpole."

Wimpole bowed slightly, "Normally I would simply go ahead and administer your aunt's affairs to the best of my ability, but as you are the sole beneficiary under your aunt's will, I thought you would want to be involved., indeed, since you are her next of kin although I have no duty in law I do feel a moral obligation to consult you as to what is the best thing to do with her, having due regard…..."

"So put the old bat in a home, and be done with it," Myron broke in, glancing at the clock.

"If I tell you your aunt's estate is worth at least six million pounds, will that stop you interrupting me?" said Wimpole abruptly.

"Six million pounds – that's about ten million bucks!" Myron exclaimed.

"Correct," Wimpole shot him a synthetic smile. "Your aunt is in excellent health, physically that is. It is only her mind that is affected. At the moment she is in St. Hagwina's in Wolverhampton.

Myron's suspicions rose to the surface. He knew there was a rip-off coming, there had to be where a lawyer and ten million bucks were put together, and this was it. "Saint Hagwina's? Some fancy seniors' facility I suppose. And what's that costing, eh?"

"Not one penny. St. Hagwina's is a National Health hospital specialising in geriatric medicine to which your aunt was transferred from Dudley Royal Infirmary where I gather she was taken after her fall."

"Her fall?" Sally started to see her aunt as a human being, not a legal cipher.

"Apparently she was thrown by her horse."

"Her horse?" Sally felt her credulity beginning to snap. "What was she doing on a horse, an old woman like that?"

Wimpole put on his reassuring voice. "She rode to hounds regularly, I understand. Broke her leg. They set it and saw to the bruises and abrasions in Dudley, but as far as I can make out, the shock seems to have affected her brain."

"So stick her in the nuthouse," insisted Myron

Sally's look silenced him. "That's my aunt you're talking about, Mister."

Wimpole acted swiftly to stop war breaking out between husband and wife. "I am sure we all want what is best for your aunt. I was about to go and see her myself when I managed to trace you." Wimpole leaned back in his chair and steepled his hands, a mannerism to which he had become addicted.

The two Lillywhites glared at each other, both with a single thought: *Ten million bucks.*

Wimpole's voice broke into their dreams. "I imagine you will be wanting to visit your aunt. Wolverhampton is some fifty miles from here. I could arrange transport, or maybe you would like to hire a car so you could see something of the country."

Myron said "Forget it. You don't get me driving on the wrong side of the road."

"In that case I will arrange to have a driver and car outside your hotel tomorrow morning."

Myron, ever suspicious, said. "And how much is that going to cost us?"

"I think, as your aunt's attorney, I could reasonably charge it to her account."

"You mean we won't have to pay?" said Myron

Wimpole coughed in a lawyerly sort of way. "As attorney I have to defray certain expenses. This would be one of them."

"I see," said Sally, which she didn't, but she didn't want to be left out of the conversation. They were talking about her aunt, weren't they?

Wimpole went on: "I must warn you that Wolverhampton is not one of our most beautiful cities. Not without its attractions, you understand, but not to compare with say, Stratford or York. Furthermore, I do not imagine that St. Hagwina's is one of our most modern hospitals."

"I guess we're in your hands, Mr Wimpole," said Sally.

I guess you are, thought Wimpole. Out loud he said modestly "I do my best. Will nine o'clock tomorrow do for the car to pick you up from your hotel? I shall be at your disposal to discuss your aunt's future when you have seen her. Shall we pencil in ten o'clock the day after tomorrow to meet again? We can decide that what course of action to take."

"That O.K., honey?" asked Myron

"Suits me," agreed Sally.

Wimpole ushered his new clients out of his office. When they were gone he resumed his place at his desk, his fingers together, not in prayer but in thought. Then he picked up the phone, dialled The Poplars, and asked to speak to Mrs Sedge.

Avril Prime arrived at The Poplars the following morning with her mother-in-law, who was having one of her better days. She was neatly dressed and looked like any other nice old lady. It was only when she was introduced to Mrs Sedge that any oddity appeared. She curtsied and called her "Your Grace"

The three of them made a tour of the home. As each attraction, like the lounge, the dining room, the activities room, the hairdressing and chiropody salon was displayed, old Mrs Prime remarked "Absolutely lovely, Your Grace. Eventually she was deposited in the dining room where she was introduced to some of the other residents. Avril was wondering if she would ennoble them as well, but nothing happened. Her mother-in-law discussed the weather and the food with the ladies on her table in the most ordinary way.

Mrs Sedge led Avril into her office.

"Your mother seems quite well," she opened.

"Mother-in-law," corrected Avril. "She has good days and bad days," and she went on to describe the old lady's recent escapades, not forgetting to include the incident at the dinner party.

"And you are going to live in America, I think you told me on the phone. Something to do with your husband's job?"

Avril enthused "It's the chance of a lifetime. He's going to be in charge of marketing right across the States," she told herself a little exaggeration would do no harm. "The company's going to find us a house in Los Angeles and a car of course. It's a big step up for Eddie, and we have to go with him, me and the boys, that is. I think there is going to be a lot of entertaining involved."

Mrs Sedge was understanding itself. "It must be very exciting for you."

"But there's no way Eddie"s mother can come too."

"I can see that. I don't suppose her appearing in her night-dress....."

Avril corrected her. "No. There wasn't any night-dress. She didn't have a stitch on."

Mrs Sedge sympathised. "Hardly the best atmosphere for doing business, old ladies bursting in in the altogether, is it?"

They both laughed. When their merriment died down Avril went on to explain that her husband was going at the end of the month and that she wanted to follow as soon as she could make arrangements for his mother to be looked after. "I hope we can get her in here before the end of term, which would be the ideal time for the boys to go. They need to start in their American schools in the autumn."

"All very exciting for you," repeated Mrs Sedge.

"About money....." said Avril.

Mrs Sedge trotted out her standard lecture when that word was mentioned. She intoned: We are not the cheapest home, but we like to think we are one of the best. We don't see our residents as patients but as our Guests. We like to give them everything they expect to have in the own homes, plus the facilities of a good hotel. Our watchword is ...."

Avril interrupted her. "I was going to say money would be no problem. My husband's firm will be paying – they have some sort of insurance which covers this situation."

This was music to Mrs Sedge's ears. "Oh good. It"s so much nicer when there are no money worries."

Avril reassured her. "I gather they want Eddie not to have to worry about his mother. The quicker we find somewhere the better. Of course I shall be looking at other homes, but I came to you first because you have such a fine reputation."

"We'll just have to see what we can do to help." purred Mrs Sedge. Give me a day or two to see what I can come up with. Now, let's go and see how your mother-in-law is getting on."

She was getting on very well. She was with old Mr Downing discussing the possibility of having sex together. Avril was all for letting them get on and have some fun but Mrs Sedge reckoned the Poplars didn't need the reputation of being a geriatric knocking shop and hauled the old gentleman away.

Charlie Forsyte followed his own advice and took his problem to another solicitor. Someone had told him Fry and Patel in North Street were understanding and accommodating, so he phoned them and made an appointment to meet Mr Jules Fry. His first reaction when he met Mr Fry was to ask himself if he had made a good choice. Mr Fry was very young, so young he looked as if he was still at school and he sounded more like a bookie than a solicitor.

Since he was already sitting in Mr Fry's comfortable chair in his minimalist office, its walls a dazzling white and its designer furniture in some very light wood, so different from Mr Wimpole's gloomy den, he reckoned he might as well go ahead and explain his problem.

Mr Fry listened attentively. When Charlie had finished he said "got the will, 'ave you?

Charlie handed it over and waited while the solicitor read it through. He took his time. Eventually he put the will down and said "Only one chance. Of sound mind." He went on to explain: "Your mum-in-law was in The Poplars, wasn't she? Lots of them there have got Alzheimer's. Was she all there when she signed this will?"

Charlie nodded and then lied "Now you mention it, she wasn't quite right in the head, which is why she had to go into a home."

"You will need evidence of that. From her doctor and members of the staff, people who knew her at the time. Can you supply it?"

"Possibly." Charlie thought of Dr Mingus. If ever a doctor looked bent, he did, and he was sure some of the staff would be happy to stand up in court and lie their heads off, if they were paid enough. .

"Who was her doctor?"

Charlie gave the solicitor Dr Mingus's number.

"I'll get on the horn to him and then get back to you," said Mr Fry rising from his seat and holding out his hand..

Charlie went straight home and phoned Dr Mingus, who said he would be quite happy to do a report on Mrs Gellatly's health while she had been in the Poplars. "Yes, if you say she was confused then she must have been," he assured Charlie.

Charlie raised the matter of payment. "I don't suppose doing a report for a solicitor is covered by the NHS?"

"Quite correct," the doctor confirmed. "I shall be sending in my bill in the usual way."

"Don't worry, I'll see you right."

"I'm sure you will," said Dr Mingus, working out just how high he could make that bill.

Henry Warren, back from Canada sooner than expected, came to see Mrs Sedge about his father.

"He's settled in rather well," she remarked. "Sam, our odd-job man, seems to have taken to him, perhaps too well; the two of them go out in the garden for a smoke every day."

"That'll shorten his life all right." remarked Henry.

Mrs Sedge pretended she had not heard him. "We don't object too much if they smoke, although we don't encourage it. After all, most of our Guests are nearing the end of their lives, so our policy is if they live a couple of months less but are happy, we allow them to smoke, so long as they don't burn the place down. We aim to make people comfortable in their declining years, not nag them to death." Henry wondered if he was meant to laugh at this. "Of course we don't allow smoking in the house at all. The ones who go outside for a cigarette think we can't see the smoke rising from behind bushes and trees, they don't realise the smell lingers on their clothes when they come indoors."

"I wasn't objecting" protested Henry. "On the contrary, in some ways I reckon Dad would be happier to get it over. He's not the man he was; he used to be so active. It must be terrible for him, sitting in that wheelchair day after day. I don't think I could take it myself."

"Nor me," said Mrs Sedge.

"If he were to go soon it would be better for everybody really." mused Henry Warren.

Neither of them spoke for a while. Then Henry said. "If I gave you some money to buy him some cigarettes...?"

Mrs Sedge understood him exactly. She spelt it out. "That would be hastening his death."

There was another silence and then Henry Warren simply said "Could be."

"I see," said Mrs Sedge quietly. "How much money did you have in mind? Cigarettes are very expensive these days."

Henry Warren looked out of the window for a while. He watched his father being wheeled round the garden by Sam. Then he turned to Mrs Sedge and said "Could I have a day or two to think it over."

"Take as much time as you like," purred Mrs Sedge.

CHAPTER FOUR
The Borlands are Desperate

Gerald Borland tapped the figures into his pocket calculator yet again, carefully checking them with the ones he had written on the paper by his side on the dining room table. There was no getting away from it, the total at the bottom of the page was correct. He yawned and resisted the temptation to let his eyes close, rest his head on the dining room table, and get some sleep.

He stared out of the window at the block of flats that had just been built in the next street, almost at the bottom of their garden. If only some kind developer would come along and pay handsomely for their house so as he could tear it down it would solve all their problems.

No use. Even if one came along like a fairy godmother they wouldn't sign a cheque there and then. They needed the cash now. Perhaps he could get a better job. In his dreams. The job market was not exactly begging for fifty-year-old English teachers. If Lucy didn't have to spend every minute of the day looking after her mother she could go back to work and they'd be able to get the overdraft down, but she was stuck to the house because she had to look after the old woman.

He could hear his wife's footsteps on the loose floorboards on the stairs. Up and down, up and down. The stair carpet was getting worn out with her going up and down to see to her mother. Poor Lucy was getting worn out as well as the carpet. Now her mother had become incontinent the washing machine was on every single day, sometimes twice. It was only a matter of time before that broke down. They couldn't afford a new one.

Everyone and everything was falling to bits thanks to the old woman. He tried to remember the last time they had had a proper night's sleep. Last night they had only had to get up twice. Once to change the sheets and clean her up and once because she called out that her hot water bottle was leaking. It wasn't, but it might have been. The hot water bottle, like everything else, was wearing out. Lucy and he certainly were. He wondered how long he would be able to keep his job – he was half asleep most of the time. If that went...... The possibility was too horrible to contemplate.

He heard Lucy's steps on the stairs again. She closed the door carefully behind her and sat down heavily, her head in her hands on the table. Gerald realised she was weeping silently. He got up and stood behind her, massaging her shoulders and neck. She liked that when she was upset. He said "There, there, darling. Have a good cry."

"She says she wants to die." Lucy wailed. "So why doesn't she?"

Gerald went on massaging her shoulders without saying anything. Lucy wasn't crying now. "If only we could afford to put mother into a home where she would be properly cared for."

"We can't afford it" said Gerald, thinking of the figures he had been looking at. How long could her mother go on? She was eighty-eight now. She might last a few months, in which case they could scrape through, or she might live to be a hundred. Unless they won the lottery there was no way they could even contemplate that possibility. He wondered what the chances were of getting a second mortgage.

If she went into a home she would get proper regular care, better than he and his wife could give her, but there were long waiting lists for all of them and anyhow they could not afford it. They could get help from the Council but that wouldn't cover the cost by a long way. They would have to find the rest and they hadn't got it.

"Phone The Poplars," he heard his wife saying. "They say that's the only decent place round here. We'll find the money somehow. I'll get a job."

Gerald looked at his wife. She didn't need a job; she needed a rest. Even if she got a job, what sort of job at her age? Dinner lady, shop assistant? How could it be enough to pay to keep Lucy's mother in a home? He temporised. "It's Sunday afternoon, there won't be anyone in the office."

"Don't be silly, care homes don't work a five day week." Lucy insisted.

Gerald did as he was told; asking himself if phoning on Sunday was the best way to get on the right side of whoever dealt with admissions, and how the hell they were going to pay the fees if there was a place vacant. Everyone said The Poplars was pricey. He was relieved to hear the proprietor was not in. The woman who answered asked if she could take a message.

"It's about my mother-in-law. She needs to be looked after. I was wondering whether you have a vacancy."

"If it's about an admission, there's no-one here today, you'd better phone in the morning." said the voice at the other end of the line.

Gerald put the phone down and turned to his wife. "There must be other homes. Everyone says The Poplars is expensive."

"And I hear the others are awful," said Lucy.

They had yet another row about money, interrupted by the ringing of the bell Gerald had installed by his mother-in-law's bed. Gerald went upstairs to see what she wanted and was relieved to find it was only a glass of water, which the old lady promptly spilled all over her bed.

"I don't care what it costs." Gerald told himself when the mess was cleared up. "She has got to go. She may be Lucy's mother, but either she goes or I do."

He didn't know it but Lucy was thinking exactly the same.

Midnight. Matron made her unsteady way up the drive that led to the front door of The Poplars. It was silly of her to have walked all that way home. She should have taken a taxi. But she couldn't afford a taxi, not on what Mrs Sedge paid her.

She couldn't have both. Not a taxi and a couple of drinks. It was either the one or the other. She glanced around nervously. It wasn't safe for a girl to walk these lanes at night. Some very odd characters worked on the local farms. She'd seen them outside the Lamb and Flag. Small dark characters wearing flat caps and scuffed dealer boots with the mud still on them. She was sure their sharp dark eyes were undressing her as she walked past.

She pictured them lurking behind hedges and bushes waiting to leap out onto an unsuspecting girl on her own, drag her into a field and have their wicked way with her. A girl ought to be able to walk up the lane. No, down the lane. Maybe it was along the lane. That was it. A girl ought to be able to walk along the lane without being molested.

But you weren't safe in a taxi either. Stories she'd heard. Taxis suddenly shooting off down forest tracks where no-one could hear anything, their drivers clambering over the seats to get at their passenger or hauling her out like a sack of potatoes, tearing her clothes off and driving off leaving her there when they had done with her, helpless and alone.

She needed a man to support and protect her. Fat chance. They were all out for one thing. She'd had enough experience of that, hadn't she? She'd never trust a man again. Not after what had happened to her.

She stumbled and one of her shoes fell off. She saw it lying there in the moonlight, picked it up and decided it would be easier to take the other one off and walk on the grass beside the gravel path. That felt better. She suddenly felt elated and did a little dance on the lawn. No-one at The Poplars would be watching at this time of night.

Except Sam who was peering out at her from behind a Berberis Bush.

Promptly at nine o'clock the Lillywhites were collected from the County Hotel and whisked off to Wolverhampton. The driver had some difficulty in finding St. Hagwina's, which turned out to be a depressing collection of large soot-stained Victorian buildings on the edge of the town.

"Workus," remarked the driver, a member of the monosyllabic party.

"What's that in English?" asked Myron, peering at the signboard indicating the various bits of St. Hagwina's. There seemed to be only two departments: Geriatric and Mental Health.

"The workhouse. Where they used to put you if you was broke," the driver explained. He realised his passengers might not understand him and translated. "Broke, skint, no money. Couldn't feed yourself. Hadn't got a roof over your head."

"Now they call it a hospital," said Myron.

The driver concurred. "That's your National Health for you."

He dropped them off by the main entrance. The interior of St. Hagwina's seemed as depressing as its exterior. They found themselves in a fairly spacious entrance hall painted a dismal green colour +which someone had tried to brighten up by painting a mural all over one wall. The subject chosen, an underwater scene with fishes, seaweed, seashells and so on, might have achieved this objective if the artist, a patient with severe depression, had not chosen deep colours which only served to add to the general gloom.

In front of the mural was a battered reception counter. Myron and Sally asked where they could find Sally's aunt. The receptionist looked at her screen and told them Mrs Clarence was on Lincoln ward. She then got up without a word and vanished through a door behind her. A few moments later her place was taken by a good-looking young black man who smiled in a friendly sort of way. Myron asked him how to get to Lincoln ward. The answer came back in a thick Black Country accent, totally incomprehensible to the two Americans. Myron tried again. The second answer was just as unfathomable as the first.

Sally had an inspiration. She asked for a piece of paper and wrote on it "Where is Lincoln ward?"

She waited while the receptionist wrote out the reply, which read. "Sorry, I did not realise you were both deaf. Just follow the yellow paint."

"Yellow paint?" she said. "And we are not deaf. Why don't you speak English?

The receptionist's reply did end with the word English, but was otherwise untranslatable. Seeing the puzzled looks on the visitors faces he came out from behind the counter, gently took Myron's arm and led him to a corridor which had walls painted approximately the same shade as pus. He touched the wall and pointed along the corridor.

Sally got the message. "He's telling us to follow the yellow and we'll get to the ward." The receptionist nodded happily and returned to his post where he put a call through to Lincoln ward, to prepare them for the arrival of two deaf Americans who might possibly be psychiatric cases themselves.

The yellow corridor led to a T junction where there was a sign indicating Durham ward to the left and Lincoln to the right. A few steps more and they found themselves in a long wide room with a high ceiling. Along both sides were beds with shrunken figures in them. Most seemed to be asleep, but a few were sitting up in bed, and a couple were dozing in chairs. Sally looked at the ward in amazement. "I don't believe it," she breathed. "It's like, like, like it was a hundred years ago."

"Can I help you?" said a belligerent voice behind them. They turned to face a square-jawed woman in nurse's uniform with an upside-down watch pinned to her chest. She had close cropped fair hair and wore no make-up and a stern expression. Myron was not fazed by her manner at all. He said "We were looking for Mrs Clarence."

"Visiting hours are from two to eight." came the brusque reply. "Didn't you see the notice?

"No we didn't," Myron began to get irritated. What right did this bitch have to order him about?

Sally knew her husband, and could see what might happen next. She moved in to prevent the explosion.

She told the nurse in her softest voice. "She's my aunt. We've just come all the way from America to see her. Is she still," she paused to wipe away an imaginary tear, "alive?"

The Ward Sister softened. "She most certainly is. Didn't you recognise her?"

"I haven't seen her in years." Sally felt it best not to mention she'd never actually met her aunt.

The Sister added "And she hasn't got her teeth in, either which makes a deal of difference to a face. Here she is. She's asleep at the moment, but you can sit with her by all means. What part of the States are you from?"

"New York" said Myron.

"New York? I've got a sister in Albany. That's in New York, isn't it?" said the sister brightly.

"We live in New York city. Albany's a long way from there."

Sally cut to the chase. "What's the matter with my aunt?"

"She's got Alzheimer's."

"What's that."

The Ward Sister wondered what sort of people these were who had never heard of the malady she and her patients lived with day after dreadful day. "Put it in simple terms, your aunt's brain's worn out."

"How long before she gets better?"

"I'm sorry."

"Whaddya mean, you're sorry?" Myron didn't get it.

"There's no cure. They're doing a lot of research, but so far they've not come up with anything."

"So she'll be here for the rest of her life."

The Sister coughed. "I'm afraid not. She was taken to Dudley Royal with a broken leg. Fell off her horse while she was out hunting is what she told them. Can you believe it? A woman at her age and in her state out hunting! Anyway, they set the leg and sent her home. Three months later she was found wandering along the road at three in the morning. Told the police she was going to be late for school. They noticed she was coughing a lot so brought her to the General Hospital where they diagnosed pneumonia. They took her in and sorted that out. Then they sent her here because they needed the bed. And now we need her bed for someone else, so we've got to find somewhere where she can be looked after.

"Can't she stay here?" asked Sally.

"No," the Sister told her. "She's quite well, apart from the Alzheimer's, which we can't cure, so she could go home if there was someone there to look after her there. This is a hospital, not a nursing home. We only take patients who we hope we can cure. Your aunt doesn't need to be in hospital; she is taking up the bed of someone who needs treatment."

"But she needs treatment – look at her." cried Sally.

"Not as such," said the nurse, realising this was going to be difficult. "All she needs is looking after until, well, not to put too fine a point on it, she passes on."

"How long is that like to be?" asked Myron, ignoring the dirty look Sally was shooting him.

"Could be years. If it was likely to be soon we would keep her here, but there's nothing physically wrong with her. She just needs looking after, not treatment." She paused, partly for breath and partly to think whether what she was going to say next would be a good idea. She decided it was and went on, "most of the people you see around you are dying. Only a few days before they pass away. We do our best to ease them out of this world as comfortably as possible."

Sally looked around the ward and shuddered. Most of the patients looked dead already. Her aunt suddenly woke up, looked at her and said "Hallo, Miss Meredith. How nice of you to come to tea.

And you've brought a friend. How lovely. I'll put the kettle on right away."

The nurse explained "Miss Meredith was one of her teachers. She often goes back to her childhood like this. I'll get you a cup of tea while you think things over."

When she was out of earshot Sally said "They think tea cures everything in this country. She looked round the ward. "I hate this place. I want her out of here right away."

Myron agreed. "We'll tell that lawyer to find her a seniors' facility. Leave it to him. He'll take his cut, but there will still be plenty enough left for us. Ten million dollars. It can't cost that to keep her in a home, surely."

"Look at her. Poor old thing." said Sally.

The old lady smiled at him sweetly. "Now the All Clear's gone I'm going to do some shopping. I'm going to go down to the butchers to get our corned beef ration for your supper. Pity we can't get any tomatoes to go with it. I haven't seen a tomato for years."

Myron had had enough. "What's she babbling about."

"Search me. I just know we've got to get her out of here soon as maybe."

"Sure, honey. Anything you say." Myron was half way to the door.

Aunt Edith said "There goes the siren again. No rest for the wicked is there? I hope there's room in the shelter for all of you."

"Not stopping for tea?" said Sister returning with a tray.

Myron's response puzzled her. As he moved towards the door he called out. "You'll hear from our lawyer."

"It takes all sorts," Sister told herself as the door closed behind the Lillywhites. "Oh well, looks like I'm going to have to have another cup of tea."

Lucy Borland phoned The Poplars first thing the next morning. "Can I speak to someone about my mother?" she asked

"Is she a Guest?" Janice asked her.

This was not quite the answer Lucy had expected. "Well, she's not exactly what you'd call a guest. She lives in our house so I suppose she is a guest, but then she's my mother. Your mother can't really be called a guest when she comes to stay, can she?" she pondered a moment and then continued "She's not exactly what you'd call a welcome guest, you see, that's the trouble. She getting to be more than me and Gerald, he's my husband, more than we can take."

Janice got the message that the old lady was not a Guest with a capital G, but the lady on the other end of the line wanted her to be. She said "You want to speak to Mrs Sedge, but she's away. I'm sorry."

"Is there nobody else I can talk to?"

Janice recalled Mrs Sedge telling her how everyone at The Poplars mucked in together. She was sure she should not be asking a Prospective to wait until Mrs Sedge came back. Someone ought to talk to this woman. She ran her finger down the list of internal telephone extensions, mentally crossing off each one until she came to Matron. She told the woman on the outside line to hold on and then dialled Matron's number.

.Matron was not sure if talking to a Prospective was her job, but told herself there could be no harm in it; not with Mrs Sedge away.

Janice put her through. Matron listened to Lucy Borland's problem for a little while and then suggested she come to look at The Poplars and have a chat that afternoon. "Will your mother be coming with you?" she asked.

"I'm not sure." Getting the old woman out of the house would be a problem but she couldn't leave her in the house alone. She'd ask Ann next door to come in for an hour, just to keep an eye on her. If Ann couldn't help she'd just have to force her mother to come with her somehow.

She felt so utterly weary.

"Well," said Matron, "just come and have a cup of tea this afternoon and you can tell me all about it."

CHAPTER FIVE
Mrs Bonnie Goes to a Better Place

Mrs Wilhelmina Bonnie sat propped up in bed looking out of the window. It was strangely quiet.

A magpie was strutting across the lawn, and she could hear the bees buzzing in and out of the snapdragons. Her ancient eyes could just about make out the shapes of butterflies as they gorged themselves on the buddleia under her window,

One of the butterflies, a cabbage white, flew in through the open window and perched on the end of her bed. As she watched, it slowly grew to become a rather serious-faced lady dressed in white flowing robes, with a pair of impressive wings.

"Time to go, don't you think, Wilhelmina?" said the angel.

"Thank God you've come." the old lady replied as she closed her eyes for the last time.

"Come quick, it's Mrs Bonnie in number fifteen!" cried Laura, one of the cleaners who came in part-time from the village.

"What's the matter," asked Matron, looking up from her crossword.

"I think she's dead."

"Why?"

"Well, she ain't breathing."

"You checked her pulse?"

"No, not exactly."

"You checked it approximately, I suppose, " Matron allowed herself a touch of sarcasm as she heaved herself out of her seat, but it was lost on Laura. "I dare say she's asleep but I'd better come and look."

When they got to room fifteen Mrs Bonnie was propped up in bed facing the window and looked as if she was enjoying the summer afternoon. Matron seized her wrist and searched fruitlessly for a pulse.

Mrs Bonnie had indeed departed this life. A nice peaceful death, Matron told herself.

"Excuse me miss," Laura interrupted her thoughts.

"Yes?"

"Is she all right?"

"As all right as she'll ever be," Matron answered.

Laura said nervously, "You see, I've got to pick up my little boy from school."

"You want to go?"

"Yes, matron."

"Very well, off you go, Laura." Matron put Mrs Bonnie's hand back on the bedspread. "You mustn't be late for school," she laughed as Laura took herself off.

When she had gone Matron stood up and looked at Mrs Bonnie. There was a faint smile on the old lady's face, as if she had seen someone she recognised just before she died. A slow smile spread across Matron's face as well. She had just worked out a plan which would be considerably to her advantage, if she could pull it off. Laura would have to go, but it wouldn't be difficult to think up a way of sacking her before Mrs Sedge got back. Mrs Bonnie would have to go too, but she was only a little lady. With those two out of the way it would be very bad luck indeed if she was found out.

She went over to the bed and picked up Mrs Bonnie. The body hardly weighed anything at all. It was not yet cold – she might have been lifting a live woman. For a moment she was not sure what to do next but then made her decision. She pulled the wardrobe door open and laid the body inside. It went in easily. Then she slipped Mrs Bonnie's outdoor coat off its hanger and draped it over her corpse.

"There you are dear, nice and warm and comfortable and out of sight," she said as she firmly closed the wardrobe door and locked it. Then she left the room and locked the door behind her. She felt in her pocket to make sure both keys, the room and the wardrobe, were safely there, and went about her business.

Myron and Sally Lillywhite were back in their room at the Castle Hotel. Myron was lying on the bed while Sally was putting her face on.

"Look," said Sally, if we stand to get ten million bucks, what's a few thousand spent on having her looked after......"

Myron interrupted her "You mean a few hundred thousand, maybe a cool million, if she lives for ten years. You heard what that nurse said; the old dame could go on for ever."

Sally paused, put her eyelash brush down. She turned and faced her husband "Let's have less of the old dame, that's my aunt you're talking about."

"Aunt you never knew existed until last week."

"Still my aunt. Not your aunt. Get me, buster?"

Myron got her. He got up off the bed and went over and put his arms around her. "Get off! You'll muss my make up!" she protested. "Just you give aunt Edie some respect. OK?"

"OK honey. Your aunt Edith gets all the respect you want from now on."

She finished with her eyelashes and started to apply her lipstick.

He sat himself on the end of the bed. "So we only get nine million bucks. Less dear old Mr Wimpole's cut. I don't know how these things work in this country, but don't think he's working for free. Lawyers are lawyers the world over. Tomorrow we check what he costs."

She finished her lips, rubbed them together and said "Look, Myron honey, Whatever we get it'll be a whole lot of bread, which I remind you we badly need, you not having a job, so it seems right to me she should have maximum comfort in her sunset years."

Myron swung himself off the bed and started to put his shoes on. "I suppose I've got to admit it is her money. Let's give it a rest for tonight. We're going to see that Wimpole in the morning, let's wait and see what he says, and maybe go check with another lawyer. He can't be the only one in this town. In the meantime I'm tired and I'm hungry."

She dabbed an extra puff of powder onto her nose, examined the effect and was satisfied. She put her make-up back in its case, got up and pulled him to his feet. "Me too, honey. Let's go find a top class eatery; we can afford it."

Myron looked dubious. "Top class eatery. You'll be lucky to get a decent meal in this country!"

Sally took his arm "Cheer up, honey. The concierge told me there's some village near here got a restaurant with a Michelin star."

"Michelins make tyres. You want we should eat rubber?" said her husband, pulling on his jacket.

"They got restaurants too," said Sally. "We'll catch a cab and eat our way through the card."

Matron finished giving Gerald and Lucy Borland their tour of the Poplars. She took them to the reception area which was empty, since Janice had gone home, and motioned them to sit down.

"Do you think The Poplars would suit your mother?" she asked.

Gerald Borland answered. "It's very nice. I suppose you have a long waiting list."

"We do indeed," said Matron. She had a shrewd idea what was coming next, and she was right. "What are your fees like" asked Gerald.

"It depends," said Matron thinking as quickly as she could.

Gerald Borland looked at his wife. He could sense her desperation. So could Matron. A tear slowly coursed down Lucy's cheek. "It's terrible." Gerald told Matron. "We haven't had a proper night's sleep for months. Our lives aren't our own. She's taken us over completely. I don't know how long Lucy can take it."

Matron needed no convincing because Lucy was now unable to contain herself and had begun to cry. She waited a few seconds and then came out with the suggestion she was going to make all along.

"I think" she said slowly, "I can see a way to solve your problem. We do have what we call an amenity room. We use it for Guests ......"

"Guests?" asked Gerald

"We see all our residents as Guests at The Poplars," Matron explained. "This room is for people who are not well and need special care, or for respite care, which is what we call it when a Guest comes to stay for a short period while their regular carers take a holiday. It's a sort of spare room. It isn't subject to the usual pricing structure, if you see what I mean."

"I see," said Gerald, beginning to understand what Matron was hinting at. Lucy was wiping away her tears.

"Your mother could come in immediately for a fortnight, and we could take it from there. At least you'd get a break. I can see you need one."

Matron wasn't one hundred percent sure that the Borlands would take the bait, but they did. Gerald said "That would be terrific."

"Perhaps you would like to see the room." said Matron.

"No need," said Gerald. Lucy sniffed.

"I think you had better. You might not like it," said Matron going to the door. They followed her down the corridor to the room where Mrs Bonnie was sleeping soundly in the wardrobe.

"They were both surprised. From what Matron had said they had expected some sort of poky back room in an attic or something, but this was large, light and airy. It looked out on to the garden.

"What do you think?" asked Matron.

"It's lovely." Lucy burst out. "Mum should be happy here, and she won't be able to complain that we've shoved her somewhere just to get rid of her."

"It's always difficult at first, coming into a home like The Poplars," said Matron, giving the standard lecture. "It just isn't like being in your own home, however much we try to make the Guests comfortable and look after them. It's understandable of course. How would you like to give up your independence?"

Getting their own independence back was exactly what the Borlands could see within their grasp, and Matron knew it.

"What do we have to do? I mean, what arrangements do we have to make?"

"Oh, none at all," said Matron, smiling. "Just bring the old lady along tomorrow."

"What about payment?"

Matron named her price, which was what she guessed the Borlands could afford and about half what Mrs Sedge charged. She said "If you could let me have cash in advance, you know how it is, don't you?"

The Borlands had no idea how it was, but if she had insisted on Maria Theresa Dollars or cowrie shells they would have found a way to get them. The couple who drove away from The Poplars were very different from the dejected pair who had arrived.

"It'll mean getting deeper into debt." said Gerald cheerfully

"What the hell," Lucy felt like singing. "The house is going up in value all the time, that'll cover it, and I'll be able to get a job."

"I wonder if we could we afford a holiday?" Gerald mused

"Not having mother around would be a holiday in itself" said her daughter.

Charlie Forsyte was back in the squeaky clean reception area of Fry and Patel. He looked at his watch. He had been sitting there for a quarter of an hour without so much as an apology or a cup of coffee. He got up and went over to the window which commanded a fine view of the railway station. A train was just arriving. He waited while it stopped, dropped its passengers and went on its way before resuming his seat. He surveyed the receptionist: too thin, he told himself, but a nice pair of tits. He was still admiring them when her phone rang. A few moments later she told him he could go through.

He was startled to see a well-built man in a navy pinstripe suit sitting on the other side of the desk staring at him intensely as he advanced towards it. It was not a nice stare. The man spent a few more seconds regarding Charlie before announcing that he was Rajiv Patel, the other half of the firm. Mr Fry, it seemed, was having a few days holiday.

Mr Patel spoke in an educated accent. "I asked you to call in because I did not want to delay proceedings."

Imitation Oxbridge, Charlie told himself. He said "Proceedings? I hadn't realised things moved so quickly."

"They don't" said Patel. "In fact they don't proceed at all. I used the word in the broadest sense." He allowed himself the ghost of a smile.

"Why?" asked Charlie, totally at sea.

Mr Patel's smile broadened. There was something vulpine about that smile "Why? because when we contacted Dr Mingus he readily confirmed your mother suffered from Alzheimer's disease."

A hundred pounds well invested there, Charlie told himself.

He also happened to mention the date of her arrival at the Poplars, which was fifteen years after the date this will was made."

Charlie felt himself blushing. Face to face he was not a good liar. "She had been deteriorating long before we got her into the Poplars." The explanation sounded lame even as he said it.

"You would have to get her doctor at that time to say she was not in a fit state to make her will, which I think you will find difficult. Not all doctors' memories are as malleable as Dr Mingus's"

"But she did have Alzheimer's. She'd been funny for years."

"So why didn't Mrs Rees notice it?" Mr Patel was not smiling any more.

"Who the hell is Mrs Rees?"

"Mrs Violet Rees. She was with your mother-in law when she died, which was more than you were." He passed an envelope across the desk. "Our account, Mr Forsyte. I don't imagine for one moment that it will be paid, but I feel obliged to present it. We don't like to act for clients who tell us blatant lies. Now get out of my office."

Charlie got up and without thinking held out his hand. Patel ignored it.

Charlie could not see what else he could do but take himself off. As he emerged into the reception area he muttered "Fucking Paki."

The receptionist looked up from her keyboard. "He isn't the second thing you mentioned, but he is the first." she said, "and he's rather good at it. You see, he's my husband. Now, if you'd be good enough to apologise for that remark, I might just see my way clear to pressing this button to let you out."

He muttered an apology.

"I didn't catch that!" said the receptionist

"I'm very sorry." he said sullenly.

"And so you should be," She pressed the button to let Charlie pull the door open. "Now go, and don't come back!"

Across the road a pub beckoned. Charlie went over and bought himself two double brandies. He sat there moodily reflecting on the unfairness of life. After all the trouble they had taken with the old woman she had managed to get her own back and shaft them from the grave.

And now he would have to go home and face his wife. Charlie did the only thing he could think of. He went over and ordered another double brandy.

Matron sat up until two o'clock in the morning. She tried to read but it was hopeless. Her mind was on the task ahead. She kept going to the window and looking out over the lawn. Each time she looked she cursed her luck. The full moon lit up the garden so clearly she could see Smudge, the home's cat, sitting on the lawn hoping a mouse might wander past.

Once again she surveyed the sky. Not a cloud in sight. It was just her luck it had to be the first clear night for weeks.

She looked at the moon again. There was no doubt it was sinking towards the horizon. She reckoned it would go down in about an hour. She made herself yet another cup of coffee, tried to read again, and gave up. An awful thought struck her. At this time of the year dawn would come quite early. Furiously she grabbed her diary to find out when the sun rose. There was all sorts of information, like imperial to metric conversion tables, clothing sizes across Europe, time zones, a rail network map, a London Underground map, but no sign of sunrise and sunset, nor even lighting up time which would have given her a clue. She put her diary back in her handbag and looked out of the window again. The shadows had gone! The lawn was quite dark.

Out of nowhere clouds had rolled up, especially for her. She made her way quickly and quietly to Mrs Bonnie's room, unlocked the wardrobe and picked up her frail body which was now quite cold and stiff. Hefting it onto her shoulder like a soldier's rifle she carried it through the French doors, across the lawn and through the shrubbery to Sam's shed and propped the old lady up against it.

She went inside and got a spade and fork, found the spot she had selected and began to dig. In spite of it being a chilly night she was soon sweating. Digging a hole big enough to take Mrs Bonnie's body was not as easy as she had expected. The ground was soft enough, but she kept coming across roots and stones. By the time dawn was lightening the eastern sky she had a hole wider and more irregular than she had envisaged, and not nearly as deep as she would have liked, but deep enough to get the body in and cover it. It would have to do.

She went over to fetch Mrs Bonnie and was horrified to see she had vanished. She was on the point of screaming when she saw her corpse had simply toppled over and was lying on the ground.

It didn't seem to take long to get Mrs Bonnie into the earth and cover her, but by the time Matron was able to lean on her spade and get her breath back day was dawning, and she could see that her efforts had left a very visible scar where the earth was freshly turned. In a panic she banged the surface of the soil with her spade until she realised she as making too much noise. She had to content herself with stamping on Mrs Bonnie's nice new grave. As sunlight began to stream through the leaves she realised she could do no more. She would just have to hope no-one came to this bit of shrubbery. It was unlikely anyone would and if they did they wouldn't jump to the conclusion that they were looking at a freshly dug grave.

Well, she hoped not.

She put the tools back in the shed and went back to have a last look at her work. As she turned to go she saw a finger sticking out of the ground. With her heart in her mouth she knelt by it, and saw it wasn't a finger at all but the end of a root. She broke it off and hurried back to her room.

Once safely back there she lay panting on the bed. As her heartbeats slowed she started to congratulate herself. She had been bloody bold and resolute. No-one had seen her, she was sure of that.

Now Mrs Bonnie was out of the way old Mrs Borland could move in. It was just a matter of getting her in without Mrs Sedge noticing, and Mrs Sedge was due back in the morning.

Mrs Sedge looked out of the window of the 8.15 from Paddington. One of the advantages of first class travel was the free breakfast that went with it. She soon tired of the scenery; there were only so many fields you could study before they got boring, after all. One field was full of cows, another of sheep, and a third with nothing at all. She reflected that too much excitement might spoil her breakfast.

She sat back and read her newspaper until the breakfast things were cleared away. The paper was as interesting as the fields. That left her nothing to think about but her business. The Poplars might be the most prestigious and sought-after retirement home in the district, but it was not making enough money. The routine meeting with her accountant she had had on her way home had given her food for thought..

Things could be worse. The Poplars wasn't actually losing money, but as her accountant had pointed out, if she closed the home down, took the money and invested it her income would be much the same, without the trouble, worry and actual hard work of running it. If things went on as they were doing there was no way she could look forward to the comfortable retirement she planned.

So what was she doing it for? It kept her amused, she supposed, and out of mischief.

She caught her reflection, smiling out of the train window, not at the fields which were still going past as fast as they could, but at the notion of being kept out of mischief. Maybe a bit of mischief was what was lacking in her life. Maybe she should go on a cruise or something like that. Find a man to be naughty with.

Her thoughts wandered back to The Poplars. There was a steady stream of applications from people desperate to get relatives in, and no room. Perhaps she should build an annexe in the grounds. The thought of getting planning permission, going to the bank to raise money, dealing with architects and builders horrified her. No way. The saying "if you are in a hole, stop digging" flashed through her mind. Forget building an annex.

That Mr Warren. He had the right idea. If people were so desperate to get shot of their aged relatives, then let them pay over the odds. She wasn't charging enough. That was why The Poplars wasn't paying its way, even though it was the dearest home in the district.

She supposed that in a way she was running a sort of hotel where the guests decided, sometimes quite suddenly, when they were going to leave. There ought to be a way of knowing when they were going to check out, like any other hotel.

There must be a way of making sure that anyone who could pay over the odds to have their elderly relatives looked after got the chance to do so. She had a waiting list. Who would get the next empty room? Easy. Not the next on the list as had been her custom, but the family who could pay the highest price. As soon as she got back she'd get on to those people with the daft old mother, the ones who were going to America, what was their name? Prime that was it, Eddie and Avril Prime, get them in and gently spell out the new policy. If their company was going to pay she could charge as much as she liked, within reason of course.

There was that call from Wimpole as well. Also something about America. He hadn't gone into detail since her mobile had been breaking up but it sounded as if there was serious money involved. Of course he'd want his cut. No problem. She would pay him a commission. The more they paid the more Wimpole would get. She knew Wimpole. If ever a man worshipped gold it was Augustus Wimpole.

There was only one fly in the ointment. Mrs Sedge came back to it again. The seemingly insoluble problem. She had punters desperate to get their old people into The Poplars, but The Poplars had no vacant beds. Substantial sums were waiting to be collected, but she was having to turn them away because all her rooms were filled. Their occupants insisted on going on living.

And then Mrs Sedge had an idea.

Which she put straight out of her mind. What was she doing even thinking of such a possibility?

She looked out of the window. More fields. What were those two horses doing, In full view of anyone who happened to look out of the train window?

The idea came back into her mind, unbidden. She tossed it out again, picked up her newspaper and applied herself to the crossword.

But the idea was still there when the train pulled into Dunblunder Castle Station.

Over breakfast Sally and Myron Lillywhite were discussing Sally's aunt's future. "This Wimpole will make the arrangements; we don't have to do a thing." Myron said as he sipped his coffee, "except sign the cheques."

Sally swallowed a lump of sausage before replying. "No, Ed. I want her to be somewhere nice. She's my aunt, and she can afford it. I don't want her out of that dump we saw her in yesterday and into something just as bad; or even worse." She mopped up some egg-yolk with a piece of fried bread.

"How can you eat that garbage?" Myron spread some marmalade thinly on his toast. "It's so stuffed with cholesterol it's a death sentence on a plate."

"Makes a change from alfafa, mung bean shoots and carrot juice. Don't worry honey, I'll soon burn it off when we get back."

"You know, this coffee's not bad. The food's not been as inedible as everyone said."

Sally forked her grilled tomato and agreed with him before popping it into her mouth. "Do you reckon we will get everything sorted out this morning when we see Wimpole?"

"Reckon so. Then we'll be able to get started on our holiday. We can always keep in touch with him by phone if anything comes up."

"We may have to sign forms or something."

"They've got a good mail system here," Myron assured her, "and besides he's got this Power of Attorney. If I understood what he said it means he can sign things on her behalf. He can do as he likes."

"So why's he schlepped us all the way here?"

"You know lawyers. Dot the Is, cross the Ts. Cover your back. Make sure there's not even slightest chance of a comeback. He's most likely scared some American lawyer's going to pop up and sue him."

Sally put her knife and fork down and wiped her lips. "That figures."

"Ten million bucks," said Myron pouring himself another cup of coffee. "He won't want any slip-ups with that amount involved.

"Any chance I could get some of that coffee before you finish the pot?" asked his wife, "and don't forget the mazooma isn't ours. It's hers until she dies."

"Sure. And when she does she'll leave it to us. Wimpole as good as said so. He's seen the will."

Sally carried on stirring her coffee as she said quietly: "Not to us, honey. To me."

"You're looking tired, Matron." remarked Mrs Sedge, fresh and sprightly after her break. "I feel guilty making you hold the fort all on your own while I've been away. You must be exhausted. You must take the day off. Don't worry, I'll cope for a few hours. Go in to town and enjoy yourself."

Matron protested that she was perfectly all right but Mrs Sedge was insistent. There was nothing for it but to get the bus into town, even though she could not imagine what she would do when she got there. In the event she spent a couple of hours on a bench on the bank of the Under watching the ducks and the passers-by, got bored with that so she gave herself a slap-up lunch of beans on toast and a cup of tea in a café before getting the bus back to The Poplars.

As she waited for the bus into Dununder Matron wondered what had happened to Mrs Sedge while she had been away. Her little holiday seemed to have done her some good.

It never occurred to her that her employer might have had an ulterior motive.

As soon as Matron was safely out of sight Mrs Sedge let herself into Matron's bedroom/office, locked the door and went to the filing cabinet where she started to go through the records of all the Guests. Every now and again she pulled a folder out and put it on the desk. Then she sat down and read through the files she had put on the desk more carefully.

When she had finished she put all the files back in their places, took the list she had made and left, not before looking round to check that Matron's office was just as it was before she went into it.

Upstairs in her flat she studied the list she had made. Four names: Mr Tubbs, Mrs de Havilland, Mrs Eglington and Miss Caraway.

Mr Tubbs had had an affair with a lady called Asbestos. A fascinating and dangerous lady. He had first met her in Rhodesia where he had managed a mine. When Rhodesia became Zimbabwe he had come to Britain and, with his intimate knowledge of asbestos had got a job in a factory that made brake-linings. This, together with a lifetime devoted to the goddess nicotine had left him just a little short of breath.

Mrs de Havilland and Mrs Eglington, twin sisters in their 95th year, were very frail, but remarkably healthy for ladies of their age except for galloping hypochondria. It was a rare week they did not call Dr Mingus in to look at imaginary swellings, neuralgias, strains or sprains.

As for Miss Caraway she was a walking medical dictionary. Diabetic, with a weak heart, badly corroded lungs, severe arthritis plus advanced Alzheimer's. It was a tribute to The Poplars that she was still keeping the undertakers waiting.

All four had one thing in common. They were alone in the world; none had any next of kin.

Matron lay on her bed and tried to read a book, but it was a losing battle. Her eyes closed, the book fell from her hand and she surrendered to sleep, a sleep troubled by a dream of elderly female corpses rising from their graves, bursting out of locked wardrobes, and dancing through the corridors of The Poplars, banging on every door howling for Matron.

"Matron, Matron!" The knocking and the cries got more insistent. She opened her eyes, but that did not stop the knocking. As she came back to consciousness she realised someone really was knocking on her door and calling out for her. She called out "Who is it?" and heard Mrs Sedge asking if she had had a good rest.

Mrs Sedge apologised. "I'm sorry to have to wake you up, but I find I've got to go into town for an important meeting I'd forgotten about, which could go on well into the evening. I hope you are feeling well enough to resume your duties, dear."

Dear….. Matron tried to recall when, if ever, Mrs Sedge had used the word except in connection with the price of something. Then she remembered the Borlands. This was her chance. They could come that afternoon and bring their old mother while Mrs Sedge was out of the way. She could stay at her meeting as long as she liked, just as long as the old lady was safely settled into Mrs Bonnie's room before she got back.

She said "Much better, thank you. A few hours' sleep makes all the difference, doesn't it?"

"You've been overdoing it, dear," said Mrs Sedge. "We will have to see what we can do to lighten your load."

"Oh, I am sure I can cope," said Matron. The less Mrs Sedge spent her time poking about the place the better.

"No! I insist. We have been working you too hard. You must have some sort of break so you can get away. Working here is so stressful. I should know, I've been doing it for years. We all need time away from the place. I'll have a look at the duty rota as soon as I get back. You need a proper break. A week at the seaside or something like that, paid for by The Poplars," said Mrs Sedge. "Now, are you ready to take over? I'm late already."

"Off you go. I'll see to everything." said Matron, buttoning up her blouse and wondering once again whether her employer had got religion.

That afternoon the Borlands arrived with old Mrs Borland. Matron took her to what had been Mrs Bonnie's room immediately to settle her in, which was surprisingly easy. The old lady seemed to think she was going on holiday. The Borlands expressed surprised when they saw Matron locking the door as they left the old lady. She quickly explained it was a precaution they always took with new residents, until they were sure they would not wander off.

She was wondering how to raise the subject of payment without seeming to be too grasping but there was no need. Mr Borland came right up with the cash without being asked.

"I'll see you get a receipt," she said without the slightest intention of giving him one.

The Borlands left soon after, rejoicing in their freedom. Matron retired to her room where she caressed the bundle of notes they had given her before getting her suitcase down from the wardrobe and stuffing it well down into one of her boots. By the time winter came and she needed to wear them she hoped she would be well away from The Poplars.

Downstairs, old Mrs Borland slumbered happily, unaware she had been relocated.

CHAPTER SIX
Mrs Sedge's Idea Takes Root

Mrs Sedge was in Augustus Wimpole's office, discussing Sally Lillywhite's mother. "My client," he began, "is possessed of considerable assets but I fear to say," he tapped the side of his head for emphasis, "totally non compos mentis. She is at the moment occupying a bed in a geriatric ward in an NHS hospital. She is what is known as a bed blocker. They wish to discharge her, in other words, get rid of her."

"And you thought of us," said Mrs Sedge. "How very sweet of you, Augustus."

"Well, The Poplars is the pre-eminent home in the district."

Mrs Sedge smiled. "We would love to have her, except for one thing."

Wimpole liked second-guessing people. "I can imagine what that is: you have no vacancies."

"Exactly. We have people coming to us almost daily, desperate to find somewhere comfortable for their elderly relatives."

"When do you think a vacancy might occur?" asked Wimpole.

"Very difficult to say," Mrs Sedge told him. We have to wait for someone to die or decide to go somewhere else."

Wimpole paused a moment before asking "Can they not be encouraged to go elsewhere?"

"There aren't very many elsewheres. The other homes in the district are in the same position as we are. I heard even Limes Court is turning people away."

"Limes Court?"

"I'd rather die than have to go there."

"Funny, I have not heard of it. Maybe my sort of client is not their sort of client," Wimpole paused while he considered the best way to put what he wanted to say. He decided to make it sound like a joke. He tittered "You'll just have to encourage some of your residents to, shall we say, move on to a far far better place."

Mrs Sedge understood precisely what he was getting at. She smiled and said archly "Naughty Augustus! How can you even think such a thing, let alone suggest it?"

Wimpole showed no reaction to her calling him Augustus. "You didn't think I meant it seriously." He gave a dry little laugh, "but it is a thought. Between you and me and these four walls, I have a few clients I wish would "move on."

"I sure you have," said Mrs Sedge. "We all have."

He passed her a sheet of paper. "Well, here are the details of my client. I must stress that money is not going to be a problem in this case." He wondered if he had perhaps gone too far and added "up to a point. Please add her to your waiting list."

"Thank you," Mrs Sedge folded the paper carefully and put it into her handbag.

Wimpole pressed on, "At the top of your list, dear Mrs Sedge. I will telephone you in a couple of days' time to see if any of your clients have seen their way clear to," he gave a little cough, "vacating your premises."

"By all means, dear Mr Wimpole, always happy to hear from you."

"I do so look forward to our little chats, dear Maureen, I always feel we have so much in common" replied Wimpole.

Their eyes met and held each other in mutual understanding for a few moments before Mrs Sedge got up to go.

She nearly tripped and fell down the stairs, she was so preoccupied with her thoughts as she left.

Mrs Sedge was not one to linger over a decision. A few mornings later she sashayed down the stairs, simply dressed in a grey silk blouse adorned with sequins and a long green velvet skirt. Janice guessed from her carefully composed face that someone had died.

"I'm afraid I've got to ask you to telephone Dr Mingus again, Janice. It's Mrs de Havilland. She passed away during the night, poor lady. She was never very well; the doctor saw her almost every time he visited. If it wasn't her stomach it was her legs, and if it wasn't her legs it was her heart – she was always complaining she could feel it beating. And then there was her shoulder; she had a lot of trouble with that shoulder."

Janice was already dialling the number "Good morning Dr Mingus. I have Mrs Sedge for you."

"No, no!" cried Mrs Sedge, "Just tell him what's happened. He'll know what to do. I have so much to see to I simply can't spare the time to talk to him now. Oh, and call Mr Wimpole as soon as he gets to the office, I think he gets in about nine o'clock, and tell him the news. He's her solicitor – there's no next of kin, I'm glad to say, no that's not what I meant to say but you know what I mean. I'm too upset to think straight. It's never easy breaking the news, is it?"

Janice resisted the temptation to remark that that was why she always seemed to get the job and dutifully passed the sad news to Dr Mingus and passed on to Mrs Sedge the doctor's reply that he would be over as soon as possible, tactfully omitting what he said about being allowed to finish his breakfast.

He arrived a few minutes past nine just as Janice was phoning Mr Wimpole. She was puzzled by Wimpole's reaction. He said "Already? That was quick!" and then hurriedly added "I mean, I hope it was quick at the end. I was told she was sinking."

Janice said "I'm sure I don't know. Mrs Sedge asked me to phone you and tell you."

"She must be terribly busy – so much to do when a client moves on. Would you be so kind as to ask her to telephone me as soon as she gets the chance?"

That's funny, Janice said to herself as she put the receiver down, "a client moves on." Queer way to say someone's died. Maybe it's the way solicitors talk."

She barely had time to make herself a cup of coffee before Dr Mingus and Mrs Sedge came back. She overheard him say "A massive heart attack. It must have been quite sudden. I don't think she suffered very much."

Mrs Sedge stopped and asked her "Did you phone Mr Wimpole?"

Janice assured her "Yes, Mrs Sedge, he asked you to ring him as soon as you can."

"Of course. I'll phone him as soon as Dr Mingus has finished."

"I won't be long, Mrs Sedge." the doctor assured her. I just have to make out my certificate for the Registrar. No reason to delay calling in the undertaker."

"Mr Wimpole can see to that, since there were no next of kin. He looks, I mean looked, after all her affairs."

Janice turned away. The thought of old Mrs de Havilland having an affair brought a smile to her face, a smile she thought it best her employer did not see.

As soon as the doctor had gone Janice asked Mrs Scdge if she should get Mr Wimpole on the phone.

"No, I'll go up the flat and talk to him on the direct line, Janice. It'll be more comfortable there, and I need to relax a little." Mrs Sedge bounded up the stairs as fast as her skirt would let her.

Ten minutes later she was down again. "Janice, can you do something for me? Call a taxi and take one of our brochures to Mr Wimpole. I'll answer the phone while you're away. This is his address. Quick as you like."

Janice went.

Sam decided the grass was getting a bit too long. . He got the big petrol mower out of his shed, and started making neat stripes up and down the lawn. Soon the smell of newly cut grass was drifting across the terrace, upsetting an old lady with hay fever who had come out to enjoy the sun.

It was not long before his wheelbarrow was full of grass cuttings. He made for the spot he had already determined on to dump them. "Must fork the ground over first," he told himself, "helps the worms to get in there and start making the compost."

He hummed a happy tune as he pushed his wheelbarrow. Sam liked cutting grass; there was an order and simplicity about the job that appealed to him. He stopped by the shed to collect a fork.

"That's funny!" he said to himself when he got to the spot he had selected. "You be going daft, you is, Sam Clodd. Forgetting you turned that ground over. Can't recall doing it yesterday, must have been the day before. Goes on like this you'll be getting a bed in Mrs Sedge's place except you ain't got that sort of money."

Since he had the fork in his hand he gave the newly turned earth a few prods with it and then dumped the contents of the wheelbarrow on top of Mrs Bonnie's grave.

"Come in, come in!" cried Augustus Wimpole as jovially as he knew how, coming round his desk to greet Myron and Sally Lillywhite. "I trust you found your aunt well?"

"You call that well?" said Myron, sitting himself down.

"Oh, not so good?" Wimpole put on his concerned look.

Sally sat down and smoothed her skirt. "Her mind's gone. She thought I was some schoolteacher."

"But bodily reasonably sound?" enquired Wimpole."

Sally wondered what this had to do with anything. "I didn't ask. We didn't have that sort of conversation."

"Well, I have good news, very good news. Someone has died during the night."

Myron looked at Sally, Sally looked at Myron. The word ghoul occurred to both of them. The thought crossed Myron's mind that he might be in the presence of a vampire. They had them in Europe, didn't they?

Wimpole tried to redeem his faux pas. "Sorry, not good for the deceased of course, but excellent for you. As result of the death a vacancy has occurred at the finest retirement home in the district, and they are holding the place for your aunt. I asked them send over their brochure right away and I am sure you will wish to peruse it." He handed over the booklet which Janice had delivered ten minutes earlier.

Sally took it and leafed through it slowly. "Looks nice enough," she said." Any chance we can go and have a look at this place?"

"Of course you can. In fact you really must. You can never tell from an advertisement, can you?" Myron gave Wimpole a dirty look. Coming from a lawyer that was rich. Did this limey lawyer know he was in the advertising business, or would be if he could get a job?

If Wimpole noticed Myron's expression he didn't show it. "If you are free now I will see if we can go over there right away." He picked up the phone.

Half an hour later Wimpole's car's wheels crunched on the gravel drive that led up to The Poplars. Mrs Sedge was at the door to greet them.

"Welcome to our Home," she said as they got out of the car. "Do let me show you around. We like to think we provide our Guests the chance of Gracious Living in their Sunset Years."

"That's what it said in your brochure." said Sally.

"If a thing's worth saying, it's worth saying twice," said her ad man husband.

Mrs Sedge led the way into a large room, nicely furnished with chintz upholstered armchairs. One elderly gentleman cackling over a children's cartoon programme on television was the sole occupant. "This is the lounge" she said, stating the obvious.

"Not many loungers," remarked Myron, doing the same.

Mrs Sedge gave him a sidelong look. "Most of our guests are still getting up. They have breakfast in bed and then they often settle down for a little extra nap. If you came along in an hour's time when we serve coffee and biscuits you would find it very busy in here."

"The joint jumps." said Myron. Wimpole gave him an icy stare.

They proceeded through the dining room, the kitchen (our kitchen is open to view at any time) and the sun lounge, the hairdressing/chiropody suite, the activities room, where paintings by the guests were displayed around the walls. "Children's paintings." remarked Myron who was rewarded by a swift kick to the ankle by his wife. "They're done by the inmates" she hissed.

"OK, O.K., I'll button up," was Myron's reaction.

"Good!" said Sally, tight-lipped.

Mrs Sedge led the way back to the conservatory. "I'm afraid I can't show you the actual room we have free. Mr Gladwyn has not called yet." Before they could ask who Mr Gladwyn was and why his absence prevented them seeing the room Matron appeared on the scene bearing a tray laden with cups and saucers. "Tea?" she said brightly.

"Oh God!" muttered Myron. "I'm going to drown in the stuff!"

"Or I suppose you'd prefer coffee, being American." said Matron quickly.

"Ah, Matron!" said Mrs Sedge, helping her put down the tray. "Meet Mr and Mrs Lillywhite. They are thinking of filling our vacancy. I'm not sure if you have met Mr Wimpole, our solicitor?"

"I have not had that pleasure, so far." said Wimpole archly.

"Pleased to meet you." replied Matron coldly.

"And how is Mrs Eglington taking it?" Mrs Sedge asked Matron She explained "Mrs Eglington is the twin sister of the lady who has just passed away."

"She seems to be bearing up, in fact," Matron paused, "in fact she seems quite cheerful. She told me she never liked her sister, and now she's free to enjoy life."

"I'd take that with a pinch of salt, Matron." said Mrs Sedge.

"Oh I do, I do. I don't think we shall be seeing Mrs Eglington going on a cruise round the world just yet."

"Well do keep an eye on her, won't you Matron. She may be a touch hysterical. You never know how people take bereavement. It may not have sunk in yet."

Matron took herself off while Mrs Sedge poured the tea. They sat round a coffee table nibbling biscuits while Wimpole raised the subject that was on everyone's mind. "Mr and Mrs Lillywhite must be asking themselves what all this luxury costs."

Mrs Sedge gave them a figure, adding "That price is all-inclusive, except little personal items like toiletries,"

Myron did some rapid multiplication in his head, came to the wrong answer and could not help himself saying "fuck me!"

There was an awkward silence. Mrs Sedge filled the gap. "I know we are not the cheapest home in the district, but bear in mind that the best needs be paid for."

Myron opened his mouth, saw his wife looking at him and shut it.

Sally had already made up her mind. "What about the practicalities. How do we get my aunt in here?" she asked, and then added "and when?"

"I would be happy to make all the arrangements." said Wimpole. It is only a matter of hiring a car. I will go myself this very afternoon to escort her here and make sure she is settled. Will that be in order, Mrs Sedge?"

Mrs Sedge indicated that it would be quite in order. By the time Wimpole had got himself to Wolverhampton, collected the old lady and brought her back, Mr Gladwyn would have taken Mrs de Havilland's body away, and the room would have been cleared and cleaned ready for its new occupant.

"What about her clothing?" asked Sally. "I don't suppose she has got much at the hospital."

"Perhaps Mrs Wimpole could see to that side." said Myron , thinking that if they had to spend time looking through Sally's aunt's home and sorting out her bits and pieces they could kiss their holiday goodbye.

"There is no Mrs Wimpole." said the lawyer. "I dare say a member of Mrs Sedge's staff would be able to deal with her clothes and things. I would of course attend to the sale of the house and contents in due course."

"That would be very kind." said Sally.

"All part of the service, dear lady."

"And all on the bill, I'm sure," thought Myron. This lawyer was a rip-off merchant if ever he saw one.

Sally thought the same, but reckoned even a champion fraudster would find it hard to make much of a dent in ten million dollars.

Mrs Sedge was already considering her next move. There were still the Primes in the queue waving their company's money. Who would be next to pass over to a better world? Mr Tubbs or Miss Caraway? It could hardly be Mrs Eglington. That would hardly be fair, so soon after she had lost her sister.

Janice came in and interrupted her thoughts by announcing the arrival of Mr Gladwyn.

There was really no need for her to announce him. Mr Gladwyn strode into the room, and went straight up to the Lillywhites, saying "I'm so sorry to hear of your sad loss."

Myron looked at Mr Gladwyn and blinked in surprise. "Who....?"

"Of course," said Mr Gladwyn. "You don't know me. I'm the undertaker. Don't worry, we'll take care of everything. You just have to tell me what you want."

"Excuse me, just what do you undertake?" asked Sally.

Mr Gladwyn was stuck. Words like body, morgue, bury and grave had long vanished from his vocabulary. Did these people really want a blow by blow description of his activities? Then light dawned. The woman had spoken in an American accent. "I am a mortician." he announced. "I am here to arrange the removal of the deceased."

Sally's mind was still in the hospital at Wolverhampton. "Someone might have told me my aunt was dead!" she cried.

Mrs Sedge, who had been discussing details with Mr Wimpole suddenly latched onto what was going on and came over. "Your aunt is perfectly all right, Mrs Lillywhite. Mr Gladwyn assumed, quite wrongly, that you were the bereaved party."

"I'm sorry. Stupid mistake." mumbled Mr Gladwyn.

"Quite," said Mrs Sedge, giving him a look that said all too clearly "speak when you're spoken to, otherwise keep your trap shut". Don't worry, Mrs Lillywhite, Mr Wimpole will be taking care of everything. Be assured your aunt is good hands."

"I'd like to see her before we go home." said Sally.

Wimpole joined the conversation. "You wanted to see something of Britain, I believe. May I suggest you take time to do that, and then come back and satisfy yourself your aunt is comfortable before you go back to the States?"

"Settling in is sometimes a difficult time, especially with Alzheimer's patients," put in Mrs Sedge.

"Sounds good to me, said Myron."

"I'll run you back to your hotel," suggested Wimpole.

As they left they overheard Mrs Sedge talking to Mr Gladwyn.

Burial or cremation?" he asked.

"Mrs de Havilland was alone in the world...."

"Ah. That'll be cremation, then." assumed Mr Gladwyn"

Mrs Sedge managed to finish her sentence".... apart from her sister who lives here."

"Burial then. With all the trimmings." Mr Gladwyn couldn't help rubbing his hands.

There was a finality in Mrs Sedge's voice as she answered. "No, Mr Gladwyn, cremation. As soon as you like. And keep it simple."

Mr Gladwyn's hands stopped in mid-rub and fell to his sides. . "Right you are then. I'll let you know as soon as I've got a slot at the crematorium."

"A slot. Yes, do that." said Mrs Sedge distractedly as Gladwyn went to summon his assistant. She was still applying herself seriously to the question of who was going to be the next candidate to move over to provide a vacancy. Whoever it was, it would be doing them a kindness, really. It wasn't as if they were actually enjoying life at The Poplars, were they?

When Mrs de Havilland's corpse had been removed and her room got ready for the transfer of Sally Lillywhite's aunt from St. Hagwina's hospital to The Poplars, Mrs Sedge was able to retire to her flat for a bit of rest. She made herself a cup of tea, sat back in her armchair and contemplated the events of the day. She had been up very early and hadn't stopped for a moment. There was always such a lot to do when a Guest departed.

She finished her tea and picked up the newspaper. She read a couple of items but found the words dancing in front of her eyes. "I think I'll have a bit of lie-down" she told herself, but as soon as she got her shoes off and settled herself on the sofa, the telephone rang.

It was Janice. "I've got Mr and Mrs Prime in reception. They want to know what the chances are..."

Mr and Mrs Prime..... In her sleepy state Mrs Sedge could not remember who they were and then it came to her. "Tell them to be patient, no don't, just tell them as soon as there is a vacancy I'll let them know, and don't disturb me for the next hour unless the place catches fire."

Mr Tubbs or Miss Caraway. It would have to be Mr Tubbs. With his tar-coated lungs he was finding the business of breathing harder and harder. Why, he would most likely be happy to be cured of the habit. But then it would not be long before his habit carried him off, saving her the bother. It had better be Miss Caraway.

Having made her decision she relaxed into sleep.

Avril and Eddie Prime drove away from The Poplars in a state of mixed gloom and indignation. Avril spoke first. "At least she might have come out to see us. Just letting that kid fob us off. Not what you expect from a high class place."

Eddie tried to calm her down. "Maybe she was busy. One of her patients might have been dying or having a fit or something. They had room at Limes Court, didn't they? Maybe Mother should go there."

"You didn't see the room. If she was my mother I wouldn't even consider it. It was tiny, dark and dirty, more like a cupboard. There wasn't room to swing a cat. And the smell….."

Eddie pulled out to overtake and then thought better of it. "I think Mother's cat-swinging days are over."

Avril smiled. Eddie was never angry for long. "I don't know why, but something tells me we won't have to wait long before there's a vacancy at The Poplars."

Eddie took his hand off the steering wheel and squeezed hers. "Well, darling, since I'm off to the States next Sunday, if we haven't got her in somewhere by then, I'll have to trust to your good judgement."

Sally put his hand back on the wheel. "Seems like you don't have a choice, darling. You'll just have to rely on me to get rid of your mother somehow or other."

Eddie grunted. Get rid were not words he would have used about his mother, but then Avril's own mother had got rid of herself with a massive overdose of her sleeping pills. It turned out she had been saving them up for months. But Avril's mum had been clinically depressed for years.

He had to admit it. He got exasperated with his mother from time to time, so how much harder it must be for Avril, who was with her all day, every day. Even he occasionally thought it would be better for everybody, including herself, if his mother was no longer around, but knocking her off? Surely not.

He glanced over at his wife, serenely staring at the passing scenery. No way. Helping people to depart from this world just wasn't in her nature. His imagination was running away with itself.

And what was Avril thinking? She was telling herself "I'm not waiting for someone to die at The Poplars. That way I'm going to be stuck here with the old woman while he lives it up in L.A. One way or another she's got to go. And soon. Even if I have to get rid of her myself."

Maureen Sedge stood by Miss Caraway's bed and looked down at the old lady. She was sleeping peacefully. In a few moments, Mrs Sedge told herself, she would be sleeping even more peacefully.

Mrs Sedge hesitated. Would she be better doing this to Mrs Eglington? She was being sentimental worrying about Mrs de Havilland and Mrs Eglington, two sisters, presenting themselves at the pearly gates one after the other. A bigger worry was that they would be listed in the Register of Deaths suspiciously close together.

Surely that was nothing unusual. Old people's homes were where you went to die, after all.

She really ought to be standing by Mrs Eglington's bed. Mrs E. hardly knew what day of the week it was, why, she even forgot her own name from time to time. It would be a merciful release for her.

So what was she doing in Miss Caraway's room? Why should it be Miss Caraway who was going to create a vacancy? She might be ninety-three years old, small and frail, riddled with arthritis, but still sharp and alert. A devil at the poker table, if she could find anyone prepared to play with her. She deserved to live a few more months.

And then she remembered. Mrs Eglington had a pacemaker which would have to be taken out before she was cremated. Miss Caraway did not, so she would be disposed of quickly and with the minimum of fuss. It would have to be Mrs Caraway.

Miss Caraway started to snore. Somehow that decided Mrs Sedge. She stepped up to the bed and gently pressed the spare pillow she had taken from the wardrobe onto the old lady's face and waited until she stopped breathing.

Miss Caraway hardly struggled at all.

CHAPTER SEVEN
Mr Tubbs Lights Up

Mr Tubbs woke up. His post-prandial nap, as he liked to call it, was the highlight of his day. He reached out to the bedside table for a cigarette and then remembered smoking was not allowed in the house. As soon as he lit up the smoke alarm, Mrs Sedge's spy in the ceiling, would start shrieking, lights would start flashing all over the house, and Matron would come rushing in with a bucket of water to throw over him.

Clutching his unlit ciggy firmly between his lips Mr Tubbs rolled off the bed and shuffled his shoes on. Transferring the precious cylinder from lips to fingers he pulled his sweater over his head, and then replaced the fag in its rightful place. Making sure his matches were safely in his trousers pocket he tottered to the lift, which was waiting for him for once. He waved the unlit cigarette defiantly at Janice as he went past and took himself out onto the terrace where he was allowed to smoke.

He inhaled deeply and gratefully as he started his afternoon stroll which consisted of a ponderous perambulation round the circular path which surrounded the lawn. It was ponderous partly because of Mr Tubbs prodigious weight and partly because his walk was timed to finish back at the house at the precise moment when the virgin white cigarette had burned down to a tiny stub.

He was half way round when he felt a raindrop fall on his bald head, and then another and another. The very elements were conspiring to spoil his smoke. Mr Tubbs looked around for shelter and his eyes lit on Sam's shed. He made his way over to it and was relieved to see it was not locked.

Mr Tubbs stood in the open doorway looking out at the rain and listening to it hammering on the roof. He puffed away contentedly.

He finished his cigarette and stood there wondering how long it would be before the rain let up enough to allow him to get back to the house. His sciatica was starting to bother him, and he was desperate to get the weight off his legs.

If anything, the rain seemed to be getting heavier. There was a flash of lightning. Mr Tubbs counted the seconds before the thunder rumbled. Seven seconds equalled seven miles. No chance of lightning hitting the shed, then. The wind changed and rain began to blow into the open door. Mr Tubbs retreated inside and pulled the door to. He found himself an old crate and lowered his bulk onto it.

After a while he felt the edges of the crate digging into his flesh. He got up and pushed the door open a crack. The rain seemed to be getting even heavier. Thinking thoughts about Noah's Ark Mr Tubbs retreated and looked for something more comfortable to perch on to relieve the pain in his legs.

Apart from the crate there didn't seem to be anything.

The pain was getting worse. He rested his right leg on the crate, which seemed to relieve the agony a little. Then he realised that, using the crate as a step he could heave himself on to the bench which Sam used for potting plants.

He perched his body gingerly onto it. That was better. It seemed to bear his weight all right. He drew his packet of fags out his pocket; there was just one left. He might as well smoke it; nothing much else to do until the rain let him go back to the house. He lit the cigarette and wriggled a little further onto the bench for greater comfort.

The bench collapsed under the extra weight, precipitating him onto the floor, at the same time knocking over the can where Sam stored petrol for the mower. All would have been well had the lid been properly screwed on. Before Mr Tubbs' confused brain could realise what the smell was, a spark from his cigarette had ignited the leaking petrol.

It was Matron who raised the alarm. She happened to look out of the window and saw flames and smoke coming out of the shed. By the time she and Sam got there the roof had burned through and the deluge had put the fire out.

Amidst the smouldering remains they found Mr Tubbs, only slightly singed, but quite dead.

Soaking wet and bedraggled Matron limped back to the house. Mrs Sedge was on the telephone to Mr Wimpole. She overheard her saying. "I thought I'd better let you know right away, since she was one of your clients."

She saw Matron and cried out "What on earth's happened to you? You're soaked!"

Matron could not believe her ears. Surely the woman had heard about the fire. She panted "Mr Tubbs!"

"What about him?"

"He's dead."

"He can't be. I saw him on the terrace having his daily smoke half an hour ago."

Matron finally realised Mrs Sedge had no idea what had happened. Somehow no-one had told her about the fire. She rapidly put her in the picture.

"How awful. Has anyone phoned the fire brigade?"

"There's no need. The rain has put the fire out."

"But how did the shed catch fire?"

"I don't know. I saw it from the window. Smoke was coming from the shed. By the time I got there it was all over. He was quite dead."

"And you're sure the fire is out?"

"Quite sure. I haven't moved him. There was no point. He was dead." Matron was beginning to shiver from the cold and shock.

Mrs Sedge was telling her to go and get her wet clothes off and have a hot bath when she realised Matron did not know about Miss Caraway. It would sound odd if she was not told immediately. She said. "Don't go for a moment. There's more bad news. Violet found Miss Caraway dead in bed. I phoned Dr Mingus but he's out on a call. I'm waiting for him to phone back. Now I suppose I'd better get on to the fire brigade."

Matron main thought was of getting her wet clothes off and getting warm again, but she said "Why? The fire's out."

"There'll have to be an investigation how it started."

"My guess he was smoking and set light to something."

"Most likely. Now you go and get those wet clothes off. Go on."

"Poor Miss Caraway," Matron told herself as she went upstairs. "We had a little chat this morning and she seemed a hundred per cent. I wonder what it was. Heart attack, I suppose." But she was too interested in getting out of her wet clothes and under a hot shower to give Miss Caraway more than a second thought.

Mrs Sedge had already phoned Mr Gladwyn on his mobile. As luck would have it he was not far away picking up the body of a retired dustman who lived in the village. He got to The Poplars in less than ten minutes but had to wait for the doctor before he could take Miss Caraway away.

Doctor Mingus and the fire brigade arrived at much the same time. The doctor went first to the burnt out shed to confirm that Mr Tubbs was indeed dead, he imagined from smoke inhalation, but did not want to commit himself. He then went to have a look at Miss Caraway, and in her case had no hesitation in completing a death certificate which declared her death had been due to old age, heart failure and arterial degeneration.

CHAPTER EIGHT
Stubble Goes to Lunch

Detective Inspector Eric Stubble had never known business so bad. What had happened? Were the local villains on strike? Had every single Dununder baddie gone on holiday? Was there some massive Criminal Convention on some Costa in Spain cooking up new ways of entertaining the population and keeping highly-trained sleuths busy?

Surely he had not finally got every crook in the district safely under lock and key and worked himself out of a job?

Stubble sat at his desk twiddling a pencil and wondering what the world was coming to. Even the paperwork was up to date, the in tray empty, the out tray bare.

Awful pictures crossed his mind. Stubble back in uniform helping children across the road, Stubble advising householders about the best locks to keep out burglars, Stubble lecturing the Women's Institute about the unwisdom of putting their handbags in their shopping trolleys.

It occurred to him that if he had nothing to do that meant he was unemployed. Not possible. There was no such thing as an unemployed policeman. You just didn't get redundant coppers queuing up at the job centre. They suffered a worse fate. They didn't get the heave-ho and go and sign on like honest citizens; they were found something pointless to do.

He looked at his watch for the twentieth time that morning. Ten past twelve. In five minutes he could decently go across to the Hanged Highwayman for a spot of lunch and a bit of a wet. Better that than sitting in the canteen listening to the happy chatter of the clerks and number crunchers who seemed to infest County Headquarters.

It had been different back in the old Central Police Station back in town, where there would always have been someone happy to go out for a lunchtime drink, but the old nick was a nightclub now. A bloody nightclub. An economy measure, they called it. Dununder Central Police Station, a solid red brick building that had successfully kept the peace of the city for over a hundred years, was sitting on a prime piece of real estate, they reckoned, so why not sell it and relocate its personnel to the big new Undershire County HQ building out on the bypass? More efficient, having County and City under one roof and think of the capital it would release for Operational Improvements!

Well, he hadn't noticed any Operational Improvements. All he'd got out of it was a computer. Bloody thing. Half the time it didn't work. What was wrong with your old-fashioned notebook? OK, it wasn't linked into CCR and DVLA and all those other interesting initials, but as far as he could remember his notebook never suffered from a low battery or went down. And there had always been plenty of bad lads to fill its pages.

The times were out of joint. Now where had he heard that? Very true. Dununder had never run out of villains before. The local criminal classes must be losing their touch.

Or maybe he, Stubble, was losing his.

He hauled himself out of his chair and took himself off to the Hanged Highwayman on the other side of the by-pass wondering what the world was coming to and working out the number of years he had to go before he retired.

The pub was fuller than the detective would have liked. He looked around the early lunchtime drinkers but could see no-one from the station. Not that he knew many of the County people. Most of them weren't even coppers; just civilian back-up staff.

He called to mind the day he had happened to look out of the window of the old Central nick and saw a pickpocket hard at work. He had rung down to desk and the man was hauled in before he could count his takings. You couldn't get an easy result like that today. If he looked out of his window now all he could see was a small paddock with a single gloomy-looking horse tethered to a miserable tree.

There was only one seat at a table free. He put his jacket on the chair and asked the other occupant of the table to keep the place while he ordered his food and got himself a drink. The other, a lean cadaverous man with a face dominated by a droopy moustache nodded his assent. Stubble sensed there was something odd about the man, and when he came back from ordering his Ploughman's he realised what it was. The man's black suit, black tie and white shirt stuck out in the pub like a bicycle at a motor show.

Stubble felt some words of sympathy might be called for. "Lost someone?" he asked.

The man looked startled. "Not that I know of. Should I have? No-one told me if I did." was his puzzling response.

"Sorry," said Stubble, "I thought...... well, the black tie and all that."

The other man's face creased into a smile. Stubble noticed he had froth on his moustache. "True enough. I have just come from a funeral, and I'll be going to another this afternoon. It's my job. I'm an undertaker." He extended a hand. "Joe Gladwyn, Gladwyn's Funerals".

"Stubble shook the outstretched hand. "Funny our paths haven't crossed Mr Gladwyn. I'm in the police. The name's Stubble, Eric Stubble. I'd have thought we might have had some clients in common."

Gladwyn took a draught of his beer. "I've heard of you, but, like you say, we've never happened to meet. Sheldon's seem to get most of the police work, being opposite the station, well, they used to be before it moved. We don't grudge it them. At the moment we've got more business than we can cope with."

"Wish I had." complained Stubble. "All the villains have decided to go straight all of a sudden. Can't understand it."

"Don't worry," said Gladwyn, putting his empty glass down in a meaningful sort of way, "business is like that. It comes and it goes."

Stubble's Ploughmans arrived, and he took the opportunity to ask Gladwyn what he wanted to drink He was glad of his company, any company.

"Much obliged," said Gladwyn. "I'm on Guinness, black being my favourite colour." Stubble got up to get the drinks. When he came back Gladwyn went on with his conversation as if he had not been gone.

"It's all go at the moment, like I said. Lot of old people popping their clogs."

"I suppose it's what they do. Old People. Die." said Stubble, wishing he hadn't.

"Gladwyn did not seem to notice. "Seem to be spending my life up at The Poplars. They've had spate of resignations, sorry, that's what we call them. Sort of joke. We collected there twice yesterday. Bit of excitement. Old feller burnt himself to death. Went for a stroll round the garden, started to rain. Remember that storm came on sudden yesterday afternoon? Poor feller took shelter in the garden shed. Must have decided to have a fag. No-one told him they were keeping petrol there. Whole shed went up in flames, him with it."

"Not very nice."

"Funnily enough," said Gladwyn "It hardly showed on the body. That rain was so heavy it put the fire out almost immediately, but not before he'd become extinct. He wasn't even charred, just lightly smoked.

Stubble, a pickled onion half-way to his mouth, suddenly lost his appetite and put it back on the plate.

"Sorry," said Gladwyn. "When you spend your whole life close to death you have to make a joke of it, else you'd go doolally."

"I suppose we do the same," said Stubble, forcing himself to go on eating, "difference is we don't meet dead people every single day like you. This old man, I suppose there'll have to be an inquest."

"Done already. He was at death's door, lungs shot. Worked with asbestos all his life, and smoked like a chimney. He might have gone any time. Very quick post-mortem. Had a heart attack, the certificate said. We're cremating him this afternoon."

Stubble hurried through the rest of his lunch and drank up his beer. Suddenly he wanted to get back to work. His copper's nose told him there was something here worth looking into, and Stubble's nose had never been known to be wrong.

He took his leave of the undertaker and hurried back to the station.

Avril was ironing Eddie's shirts ready to be packed when Janice phoned to tell her that a place had become vacant at The Poplars for her mother-in-law.

She finished the shirt she was working on, carefully switched off the iron and called a taxi. While she was waiting for it to arrive she went upstairs to check on her Eddie's mum. The old lady was happily watching children's television, singing along with the children on the screen, a song about woodpeckers.

Avril said "I've got to go out for about an hour, mummy. Will you be all right?"

"Of course I'll be all right," the old lady assured her without looking away from the screen. "Haven't I been looking after myself for eighty-four years?" She waved Avril aside. "Look at that little devil; if he doesn't stop pecking away he'll have that tree down!"

The front doorbell rang. Avril said "that'll be my taxi – I won't be long." She shut her mother-in-law's door behind her and ran downstairs to open the door to the taxi driver.

Her business at The Poplars did not take long. There were no formalities to be gone through apart from signing a couple of forms and a direct debit. She was presented with a list of things incoming guests needed to bring with them, like clothing and medication, pictures of loved ones, prayer books if religious, and anything to which the guest might be attached. "You'd never believe how many teddy bears we've got in here," matron told her. "Oh, one thing, your aunt's....." Avril corrected her.... "she's my mother-in-law."

Matron apologised. "Sorry – I'm mixing you up with someone else. Your mother-in-law's clothing needs to be labelled so it doesn't get mixed-up in the laundry."

She saw from Avril's expression that this had not been done. "Don't worry, we can do it here." She saw no point in adding "for a small charge." Money was clearly not a problem with these people.

The relief was evident in Avril's voice. "So we can bring her in any time. As early as this evening?"

"Certainly. The Guests have their supper at six, so if you could bring her along about seven, and give her something to eat beforehand?"

"That will do nicely."

Avril ran down the steps of The Poplars and leapt into the waiting taxi in a state of high elation. "California here we come!" she sang out loud.

"That'll cost you! It's well outside the county boundary, but I'll be glad to take you so long as you pay up front, no problem." said the taxi driver with a laugh, which brought Avril down to earth. She started to think about practical considerations, like how to break it to her mother-in-law that she was going into a home.

She need not have worried. When the taxi got to her house the front door was wide open. Thinking the house must have been burgled she ran through every room of the house. Nothing seemed to be missing, and then she realised what it was that had gone. Her mother-in-law.

She was about to pick up the phone to call the police when there was a ring on the bell.

It was the taxi-driver reminding her that he would like to be paid, and couldn't wait all day. It was then she remembered how she had rushed out of the house forgetting to pick up her purse in her excitement when she heard there was a vacancy at The Poplars. She'd left it on the kitchen table and the old woman must have taken it. She was walking round with all Avril's money, her credit cards, everything.

The taxi driver was sympathetic. He waited while she phoned the police who took a few details and said they would keep a good look out for the old lady, but so far no-one had reported anything. "What was she wearing?" they asked.

Avril described the old lady's clothes and promised to bring a picture of her over to police HQ right away. The taxi driver obliged. When she pointed out she had no money he laughed and told her: "I know where you live, love, so if you don't pay me you really will get your house burgled! Driving's just my day job."

At police HQ a rather ponderous policeman took for ever to fill in a voluminous missing persons form. "If you can give us the numbers of your credit cards," he remarked when he came to that section, "then we'll have her as soon as she uses one."

Avril had to confess she didn't have any of the numbers. Her husband dealt with all that side of things.

"Perhaps you'd like to phone him, madam."

Eddie hated being disturbed at work, but this was an emergency. She could hardly describe her relief when she was put through right away and heard his voice.

She hesitated. Now she had him on the line she wasn't sure how to break the news.

"You won't believe this."

"Astonish me."

"They've got a place at The Poplars for your mother."

"Super! When can they take her?"

"Tonight, but..."

"But what? What's the catch?"

She hesitated again, and then plunged in the deep end.

"Your mother's vanished." She was going to say escaped, but changed it to vanish, which sounded even worse after she'd said it.

"That's all I need. What happened?"

"They phoned from The Poplars. I nipped over there to get everything sorted out, and when I got back she'd gone, and Eddie..."

"Yes..." she could almost hear him thinking what is my daft wife going to tell me next?

"She's taken my purse with all my credit cards and everything."

"Is that all?"

"What do you mean all! She could be out there somewhere spending thousands!"

"Unlikely. I don't think mother knows what credit cards are."

"Surely you should cancel them? Anything can happen."

"No way. I'm going to need those credit cards next week. If I cancel them it will take a fortnight to get replacements, if we're lucky."

"You don't seem to be worried about your mother."

"No, I'm not. She'll come home when she gets hungry. Glad to hear she's got a place at The Poplars. That's a relief."

"I could go round town and start looking for her."

"No darling, you go home and stay there. If she comes home or someone finds her they need to contact you there, not have you wandering all over the place."

"I can't even pay the taxi...."

Eddie began to sound testy: "Look, Avril, I've got a lot of work to get through before I go. Tell the taxi driver I'll pay him when I get home. Just go home and make yourself a cup of coffee, sit yourself down and wait for the telephone to ring. Bye."

Back at the house she waited for the kettle to boil and asked herself why she was getting so het up. It wasn't her mother who had wandered off, it was his.

She was Eddie's mum, after all. You'd think he might be a bit more bothered. She had never been that keen to have the old woman live with them. There hadn't been any alternative at the time. They certainly didn't have the money to pay for care, but this job in America had changed everything.

But Eddie. The funny thing was he didn't seem to be worried about his mother being missing. It was almost as if he'd been hoping she would wander off.

Back at the station Stubble sat himself down and made a list. Stubble liked making lists. The best way to get what you had to do nicely organised was to put everything down on a clean sheet of paper.

It wasn't a very long list. It read:

Registrar
Coroner
Nursing Homes

He sat looking at for a little while and then he added:

Crematorium.

First stop had to be the Registrar. He picked up the phone and then put it down again. Better go over there and have a look at the book. The Undershire Registry had not yet been computerised; they still recorded Births Marriages and Deaths in big old-fashioned ledgers. Stubble liked that.

It made sure, Stubble reflected as he left his office, that the Registrar could read and write. He ignored the lift and went down the stairs, partly because he thought going up and down stairs would help keep him in trim, and partly because the old station hadn't had a lift, so he had never got into the habit. When he got to the ground floor he found was some sort of a commotion going on in Reception.

An old lady in a massive state of indignation was being gently restrained by a policewoman. She was shouting "Should be locked up, they should. It's them you should be arresting, not me. You don't know your jobs. It's profiteering, that's what it is. They're black marketeers, so why don't you arrest them? Selling oranges openly, like that! It's disgusting! And how did they get here? That's what I want to know. Oranges don't grow in this country! Our sailors risked their lives getting them oranges here. I'm going to write to Mr Churchill!"

Stubble stopped for a moment to see the show.

"And the price! Twenty-four pence each! The most I used to pay before the war was tuppence. And why don't they call it two shillings?"

"If you'd only sit down quietly and tell me your name and address, then we could sort everything out and take you home," said the WPC.

"I've told you my name, over and over. You must be either deaf or stupid," expostulated the old lady. My name's Martha and I live at Lavender Lodge in Gordon Street.

"What number Lavender Lodge?"

"What do you mean, what number? It hasn't got a number. It's a big house called Lavender Lodge. "

Stubble had to hand it to the WPC. She was showing no sign of exasperation. "Lavender Lodge is a block of flats, dear, so we need a number. Do you live alone, Millie?"

"Of course not. There's Alec, only he's in Burma and he's not coming back, and Susie and Mary and Edward. And then there's Evie, she's the maid. There used to be Miss Barr, Edward's governess, but she had to go when she got married, so Dad sent him off to boarding school."

Stubble began to understand what the old lady was talking about. He went over and said "We've got a bit of our tea ration left. I think we could spare you a cup, Mrs..."

"Prime, Mrs Martha Prime, pleased to meet you Mr..."

"Stubble, madam, Detective Inspector Stubble, pleased to make your acquaintance. He turned to the policewoman." Please get Mrs Prime a cup of tea, in a cup, a china cup with a saucer. Understand?" The old lady was obviously reliving some sort of wartime experience and the sight of a polystyrene cup might upset what little mental balance she had left.

Martha Prime was still in full flow. "Little Edward's never seen an orange, nor a banana. Did you say you're a detective? Well, they were selling bananas too, now I come to think of it. There's something very fishy about that shop!" She suddenly gathered her open raincoat protectively about her. "You're all in it together. It's a conspiracy. He sells black market fruit and you arrest anyone who objects. Well, I'll tell you one thing. He's not going to get away with it and neither are you! I'll see to that!"

The young WPC was back with a cup of tea in a cup and saucer as requested. Stubble offered it to Mrs Prime. "You drink this while we get things sorted out. If he is selling black market fruit I'll send a constable down right away to pull him in., don't you worry, my dear. Before I do, though, I've got to check the facts. A few shops have got special licences to sell oranges and bananas, you know, for hospitals and places like that. This young lady is new to the force so she doesn't know as much as she should do about the rationing regulations. In fact I'm not one hundred per cent sure about them myself. I'll just go and check the details about oranges and bananas. I won't be a moment."

He went to the nearest computer and looked to see who had been reported missing that day. Sure enough there she was: Mrs Martha Prime, 92 years old, 14 Leamington Avenue, phone 367865, missing since that morning. He picked up the phone.

Avril Prime put the phone down. So the police had got the old woman. Thank goodness she was going into The Poplars. She rang Eddie and was told he was in a meeting so she left word with his secretary that everything was all right, and went off to Police HQ where she found her mother-in-law amusing Stubble and a couple of WPCs with the stories of wartime life that Avril had heard so many times before, often the same story repeated over and over again.

Stubble detached himself from the party and took her to one side. "Has she done this before?"

"No. She's been all right up to the last few months, but I think there's something wrong with her mind. She's going back to her childhood."

"Was she a child in the blitz?" asked Stubble.

"No. She married in 1937. They had three children, twin girls and one son, Eddie, that's my husband. She lost her husband, that's Eddie's father, in the war. She got married again, but they had no children. Her second husband, that's his stepfather, died about ten years ago. She came to live with us, oh, it must be two, no, nearly three years ago."

Stubble was sympathetic. "It must be very hard for you. Have you thought about residential care?"

"She's going into The Poplars tonight."

Stubble felt his nose twitch.

Avril remarked. "I must say they found her a place very quickly. I was told there was a long waiting list. Maybe we are a special case; you see my husband's been promoted. They've given him a very important job in America. We're all going to go and live in Los Angeles. We couldn't take the old lady, of course, so we had to get her into a home as quickly as possible."

Stubble's nose began to sniff in earnest.

"Did they say they expected a vacancy soon?"

"Well they sort of hinted."

The nose went into top gear. Stubble said: "Well, I'm glad everything's turned out so well for you. Would you like me to run you and your mother-in-law home?

"Oh, I couldn't put you to so much trouble."

"No trouble at all. I was going in that direction in any case, and being in a police car will make it less likely the old lady will do another runner, won't it?"

She laughed at this. "Oh, all right then, if you put it like that."

As they drove home Stubble mentioned casually, "They say the Poplars is quite pricey."

Avril agreed. "Definitely. We're very lucky. Eddie's firm are going to pick up the bill, since they're sending him abroad, so we don't have to worry about the cost. To be perfectly honest we would have found a place in a home for her earlier if we could have afforded it. Funny how quickly a place came free so soon after we told them Eddie's firm are paying. I thought they said there was a waiting list. Maybe they gave us priority because of it being urgent because we've got to go to the States."

As she prattled on about America Stubble told himself it had definitely been a good idea to run Mrs Prime home.

He dropped Mrs Prime and her mother-in-law off, declined a cup of tea, and hurried away to get to the Registrar's office before it closed.

With twenty minutes to go he got there, parked on a yellow line, flashed his warrant card at a traffic warden who was lurking ready to pounce, and ran up the steps to the Registrar's office.

He was soon studying the heavy ledger in which the Registrar had written the details of every death in the district in old fashioned copperplate script. How long before someone would find out and insist on installing a computer?

Bingo! Four deaths at The Poplars in just over a fortnight. Three of them in the last three days. He listed them in his notebook.

Mrs Edna Angela Gellatly, 79 years old,

Mrs Freda Josephine de Havilland, 90 years old,

Mr Joseph William Tubbs, 82 years old,

Miss Marigold Constance Caraway, 92 years old,

All residing at The Poplars care home. All died of heart failure except Mr Tubbs who was listed as dead of smoke inhalation as well. All certified dead by Dr Albert Mingus, the last three notified by Augustus Wimpole, solicitor.

He thanked the Registrar who was locking filing cabinets, closing windows and in other ways hinting that she wanted to go home, thanked the traffic warden who had kept an eye on his car, and drove back to his flat.

It was only when he got there that he remembered he had the decorators in. They had closed all the windows before leaving, and he was almost knocked over by the reek of paint when he opened his front door. He opened the windows to let the smell out, reflecting that it was most likely toxic, and every breath he took was taking a minute off his life, but the influx of fresh air didn't seem to make much difference to the smell.

He packed a few overnight things, locked all the windows again and took himself off to the County Hotel for the night, wondering if the bill would be covered by his insurance policy.

While he was eating his solitary dinner he could not help overhearing the conversation of an American couple at the next table. They seemed to be tourists discussing where to go next. They had determined to visit Stratford and Oxford and then make their way to London.

The man was worried about booking hotels. "You get ripped off in a big city like London" he was saying. "I've taken us a room at the Hilton. I don't dare tell you the room rate."

"So what," the woman said, "Wimpole's paying."

Stubble pricked up his ears. That name rang a bell. Wimpole, respected Dununder solicitor. Wimpole, who had notified three of the deaths he'd just seen listed at the Registrar's. What did Wimpole have to do with these two tourists, and why was he paying for them to stay at the London Hilton?

"Wimpole isn't paying, honey," the man was saying. "Lawyers don't pay for anything. We are. Well to be precise, Aunt Edith is. It's all coming out of her money. The seniors' facility, the air fare, the bill for this hotel, our trip round England, you don't seriously think it's all paid for by dear old Mr Wimpole out of his own pocket, do you?

Stubble's nose gave a sniff when he heard the words seniors' facility. Could that be The Poplars?

He glanced over to the next table. They were eating their sweet and would not be sitting there much longer. He leaned over and said "Excuse me."

The woman looked up from her Eton Mess. "Pardon me?" she said suspiciously.

"I could not help hearing you are touring round England, and wondered how you came to choose Dunder. It's a lovely little city, but we don't get many visitors, I'm afraid."

"We're here on business, leaving in the morning."

"Have you seen much of Dunder?"

"Been too busy." The man's tone said "piss off."

Stubble persisted. "I could give you a quick tour if you'd like?"

"We ain't interested." growled Myron. "I'm going to complain to the management – tour guides touting for business while we're eating your meal, what sort of cockamamie deal is that?" This last remark was addressed to his wife, but loud enough for half the dining room to hear.

"Oh, I'm not a tour guide," said Stubble. He nearly added "I'm a policeman," but stopped himself in time. He explained about his flat and how he came to be staying at the hotel. "I'm at a loose end this evening. It would be my pleasure," he concluded.

Sally graciously accepted his offer before Myron could dig up another objection. She said: "Well, if you're sure you've nothing better to do this evening, it would be nice to be shown round by someone who actually lives here. Right Myron?"

Myron grunted a reluctant agreement. He was still sure there was a catch in this deal somewhere. Nothing was for nothing in this world.

He was right, in a way, but all Stubble wanted was information.

Mr Wimpole was working late. Living alone he had no need to keep to regular working hours, and he was expecting a lady.

Promptly at eight o'clock the bell rang and he went to the door to admit her.

"Dear Mrs Sedge, do come in," he said, ushering her into his private office. "May I offer you a cup of tea? Coffee? Or maybe something a little stronger? Sherry perhaps?"

"That would be very nice, Mr Wimpole." she said, taking her hat off and placing it on the old fashioned hat stand in the corner. "A drop of sherry would be very welcome after a hard day. Dry, if you have some."

"Of course, I remembered you like it dry," Wimpole said as he went to the escritoire in the corner which doubled as a drinks cabinet.

They settled down and got down to business while they sipped their drinks. Wimpole opened the batting. "Mr and Mrs Lillywhite are off on their travels tomorrow."

Mrs Sedge started. "But we've just taken in Mrs Lillywhite's aunt, Mrs Clarence. Who's going to pay her fees?

Wimpole could hardly believe his ears. Did the woman not trust him? "I shall be responsible for all the financial arrangements, do not fear, dear lady. The Lillywhites are setting up a trust fund to look after Mrs Clarence, which naturally I shall administer."

Mrs Sedge put her empty glass on his desk. He understood perfectly, refilled it and went on. "The Lillywhites want their aunt to have the best possible care." He stopped to top up his own glass and repeated, "the best possible care, and they are prepared to pay for it. They wish to pay over and above the usual scale of fees at The Poplars to ensure she gets the best."

"That's interesting, Mr Wimpole. I have been thinking for some little time now that we ought to offer that little extra for the more discerning client. At a premium, of course."

Wimpole looked at her over the rim of his glass. "I don't suppose you have worked out any price for this... little extra?"

"Not as yet. It would have to be substantially more than our standard tariff to make all the extra attention worth while. You have no idea how costs are going up all the time."

"Oh, I do, I do, dear lady. Only too well. I was going to suggest putting fifty per cent on top of your usual charge."

"Seventy-five." snapped Mrs Sedge.

"Oh, I think that is a little too much," said Wimpole. "I don't think the market would bear it."

"Well, I have to think of your part of the cost, Augustus as well as my own expenses. Our arrangement...."

"Wimpole smiled. "...would not apply in this case. I shall be administering the trust, you understand."

Mrs Sedge decided the time for plain talk had arrived. "You'd get your cut straight from the trust. Is that what you're saying?"

Wimpole simpered "I'm not implying anything, just leave the details to me. It should prove advantageous to all parties concerned."

"I'm sure it will be. I know I can trust you to do the right thing. It's always a pleasure doing business with you, Augustus."

"And with you, Maureen. Now, shall we have another sherry before we get down to the serious business of the evening?"

"You'll be the ruin of me, Augustus," she said holding out her glass.

" Don't tell me you don't like being ruined," he said as he filled it.

"Been looking forward to it all day." she said as she slipped off her shoes.

"How old did you say this cathedral was?" asked Myron Lillywhite.

"The building we are in is relatively recent. It was built between 1562 and 1584." Stubble told him.

"You call that recent?"

"The original cathedral fell down, you see. It is said the masons felt they were underpaid so they skimped on the mortar. It was built with stone from Dunnder Castle. The castle stood on the same site from 1094 to 1230.

"I suppose that fell down too." said Myron.

"Funny you say that. It did, but not because of a fault in the construction. You won't believe this, I'm sure."

"Go on, try me," said Myron.

"There was an earthquake." said Stubble knowing the reaction this would get.

"Nuts. I don't believe a word. You don't have earthquakes in Europe."

"Oh but we do. Nothing like the sort of earthquakes you have in San Francisco, of course. We have them quite frequently here, usually just strength two or three –enough to make a cup or two drop off a shelf as a rule, but this one seems to have been a little stronger. It coincided with a wet autumn, according to Henri de Chartres, he was a scripter, we would call him a secretary nowadays I suppose, to Geoffrey le Lapin, who was given these lands by William the Conqueror in 1067. Henri's journal can still be seen in the cathedral, by application – they keep it locked away. It seems the Under burst its banks and flooded the city, the water affected the foundations and it just wanted the earthquake to knock it over"

"So why didn't they rebuild it?" asked Sally.

"No idea," said Stubble, whose stock of local history was sold out. "All I know is they built the cathedral instead.

An attendant approached. "The cathedral will be closing in five minutes time, so if you…."

As they made their way to the door Stubble suggested he took them over to the Cock and bought them a drink.

Myron's mind was elsewhere. "The Cock?"

"It's an old coaching inn. The London Mail used to stop here to change horses."

In the gathering dusk they strolled through the cathedral close.

"Look at all those polished brass plates. There's one on almost every house." remarked Sally.

"Mostly lawyers' offices, Sally," explained Stubble. You often find lawyers near a cathedral. It dates back to the days when the church was much more powerful than it is today."

They stopped to examine one of the brass plates more carefully. It read: "Wimpole and Wimpole." Stubble looked up at the first floor window where the light was still on. The lawyer was working late. Lucky Wimpole, so busy he had to work overtime. Did he get time and a half for it? Stubble wondered.

His musings were interrupted by Sally saying "Wimpole and Wimpole, that's our lawyer." She went on to tell Stubble about her aunt in some detail.

Stubble listened very carefully. A rich old lady no longer able to look after herself and alone in the world apart from her niece who lived in America. Someone who had to rely on Mr Wimpole with his Power of Attorney to find a place for her in an old people's home. And the old people's home turned out to be The Poplars. All very interesting. Well worth an evening with this couple and the price of a round of drinks.

It was all so interesting he never noticed that the lights going out in Wimpole's office, nor Wimpole himself coming out of the building shortly afterwards and getting into his car with a woman.

In any case, since he had never met her, he would not have recognised Mrs Sedge.

Sam was not unduly upset when they told him his shed had burned down. He had been clearing out a blocked drain on the other side of the house and had missed all the excitement.

That poor Mr Tubbs. He hoped it had been quick. They said he wasn't burnt to death; had a heart attack, fell over and got his lighted fag mixed up with the petrol Sam kept for the mower. Sam was sure he always made a point of screwing the lid on the can nice and tight. He must be getting forgetful in his old age.

Mrs Sedge had been quite definite it wasn't his fault. She had told him the insurance would buy him a nice new shed, and he could go into Dununder and buy new tools and a new mower and anything else he wanted because the insurance people would pay for them as well.

He had spent best part of the afternoon ordering them. He hadn't realised, until he made a list, just how many bits and pieces he kept in that shed.

There hadn't seemed much point in going back to The Poplars when he had finished. On an impulse he had gone to the pictures. Some film about a divorce in America. It wasn't much good; in fact he had slept through half of it. Perhaps if he'd stayed awake he'd have understood it better.

He'd come out and gone to an Indian restaurant for supper. You always got nice big portions at the Star of Bengal. He'd done himself proud, onion bhajis to start with and then a chicken tikka, and a couple of bottles of Cobra. Mrs Sedge had told him he could buy himself supper. On the insurance company, she'd told him. Sam burped contentedly.

He glanced at the cathedral clock. Half an hour before the bus back was due. He could go and wait at the bus station; on the other hand he could go and have a quick pint. The Cock was a nice quiet pub. That would do.

He was standing at the bar on his own when Stubble and the two Americans came in, but they meant nothing to him until he overheard them talking about The Poplars. He edged closer to see if he could hear what they were saying. It seemed the Americans had a relative who had just got a room at The Poplars. She must be taking the place of poor Mr Tubbs. It seemed a long way to come to get shot of your old mother. Maybe they thought if they stuck her the other side of the Atlantic she wouldn't be likely to find her way back, and they'd have an excuse for not going to see her, like so many as dumped their old relatives at The Poplars and never came back, well maybe at Christmas, but otherwise forgot about them.

Someone put the jukebox on which prevented him from hearing any more. He finished his drink and took himself off to catch his bus. On the way to the bus station he passed a parked car which looked like Mrs Sedge's. He stopped and looked at it. It was the car he washed and polished every Friday, definitely her car, even got the same number plates.

Perhaps she would give him a lift back. No, the mean old cow would never do a thing like that. Anyhow, Sam told himself, he'd be happier going on the bus.

CHAPTER NINE
Stubble's Nose Twitches

D.I. Eric Stubble was on the Coroner's doorstep first thing the next morning only to discover he was away on holiday.

"I don't know if I can do anything to help...." Mrs Phibbs, the Coroner's clerk, surveyed him through enormous glasses that had been the fashion five years before. "If it's an inquest, Mr Seeley from Overton is filling in while he's away. Mr Tandell's gone to Tunisia." She added inconsequentially.

Stubble had always wondered about Mrs Phibbs. How could such a scatterbrain get and keep a job in the Coroner's office. Mr Tandell the coroner was a stickler for precision. Many a time he had pulled Stubble up over a minor discrepancy, so how did he put up with the chaos Miss Phibbs subjected him to daily? Maybe he was having it off with her. Neither of them seemed the type, but that didn't mean anything.

Anyway, his absence suited Stubble well. If there were any beans to spill, Mrs Phibbs was the lady to spill them. He assured her he had not come about an inquest, merely wanted to check on a few recent deaths.

There was no big solid ledger at the Coroner's office. Miss Phibbs sat herself at her keyboard and asked what precisely he was looking for.

Stubble told her what key words to search for: The Poplars; Wimpole; Mingus. As an afterthought he threw in Gladwyn the undertaker and Mrs Sedge. If any of those had given evidence before the coroner, or had any dealings with his office, they would show up on the database.

Gladwyn showed up quite often, that was to be expected from a busy undertaker. Wimpole appeared a couple of times, but the Poplars only once, in connection with Mr Tubbs.

Stubble thanked Miss Phibbs, who said she was only too pleased to help, and went on his way.

Mrs Sedge was looking through her accounts. She noticed the Forsytes had not paid for the final month of Mrs Forsyte's mother's care.

She was about to put a statement with a "please" sticker on it into an envelope, when she had second thoughts and picked up the telephone.

Charlie Forsyte covered the mouthpiece and shouted to his wife "It's the bloody nursing home. They want paying for the last month your mother was in there."

"Tell them we haven't got it. Tell them to sue."

"We don't want that."

"No, of course not. Neither do they." Mrs Forsyte was made of sterner stuff than her husband.

"What shall I tell them?" asked Charlie.

His wife put down her newspaper with a sigh, came over and took the telephone from her husband. "Is that you, Mrs Sedge? How nice to hear from you. Are you well?" she cooed.

Mrs Sedge's reply was evidently brief and to the point.

Mrs Forsyte put up a strong defence. "Your bill for the last month mother was in The Poplars? I'm afraid we do have a problem. Probate you know. I believe this happens quite often. Until that's sorted out we can't touch any of mother's money. It's frozen."

"How long? I don't know. You know what solicitors are like. They do take their time, don't they? We'll just have to be patient, won't we?"

Mrs Sedge put the phone down, telling herself that if she believed that she'd believe anything. When her own mother died the solicitor had insisted that all outstanding debts were paid before he even started work on the estate. She remembered him telling her that a lot of people think they can cheat their creditors by dying on them, and how wrong they were.

She wrote 'bad debt' on the bill and sat mulling over what Mr Wimpole had said last night about Mrs de Havilland's will. The old lady had left everything to The Poplars Retirement Home, 'in appreciation of the devoted care I have received in the last years of my life.'

It turned out that her estate came to a total of £1200, all of which would go to Mr Gladwyn for disposing of her mortal remains. Mrs Sedge had been puzzled. Mrs de Havilland's bills had been paid regularly, by Wimpole. She had asked him why he hadn't warned her that the old woman had barely enough money left to keep her at The Poplars for another month.

Wimpole had explained that the bills were paid for by a long term care plan which was basically an annuity. This had stopped the moment she died. He had advised Mrs de Havilland against taking it out, but she had insisted. She said it would mean she would never have to worry about money as long as she lived. It would have been a good deal if she had lived to be a hundred, but as it was the Undershire Mercantile Insurance Company had made nearly ninety thousand pounds out of the deal.

Mrs Sedge had remarked that she would willingly look after any old lady for as long as she lived in exchange for upwards of ninety thousand pounds in advance. Why should any silly old insurance company get involved?

She knew that some of the residents of The Poplars were well off. The thought of them leaving everything to charity like Mrs Gellatly, or worse still, undeserving relatives, the sort who never visited or even sent a card to their old people on their birthdays; when their money could have gone to The Poplars, made Mrs Sedge's heart beat a little faster and gave her brain considerable food for thought. Gave it a gourmet meal, in fact.

"I never had the privilege of knowing Henry Allardyce," intoned the clergyman in a voice that told Stubble and everyone else in the chapel that he had used this formula hundreds of times.

There were only half a dozen mourners. Not the right word. Most of the people who had come to bid farewell to Henry Allardyce were, like himself, people who happened to be at the crematorium and had been dragooned into attending the service for appearance's sake.

Stubble wondered if he was the only one present had actually known the man who lay in his coffin on the discreetly concealed conveyor belt. Old Henry had been a frequent visitor at the Station.

He had been a Chief Petty Officer in the navy who had never been able to settle down into civilian life after his discharge. He'd ended up collecting trolleys in a supermarket until arthritis put paid to that. He'd spent the rest of his life alone in his little council flat building model battleships out of matchsticks until the arthritis had started to affect his fingers. After that he'd taken to dropping in at the station for a chat when the loneliness got too much for him. "I'm only really happy when I'm among uniforms," was what he told the desk sergeant every time. He always got a cup of tea and a welcome from coppers who wondered what would happen to them the time came for them to draw their pension. As someone had remarked to Stubble "He's clean and polite, which is more than you can say for most of our visitors."

And here was old Henry being sent off, in death as he had lived, alone. He deserved better. The padre droned on, his mind on his lunch, while Stubble stared up at the curiously ornate ceiling of the chapel.

The vicar, or whatever he was, came to "and now we say farewell to our friend....." there was a pause while the man looked at his notes to see who his friend was, Stubble wondered if he ever got it wrong, "Henry Allardyce, in the sure and certain hope........" Stubble's mind wandered again. How many cremations did they do every day? What did it cost? Did they burn the coffins or send them back to the undertakers to be recycled? Was there a fiery furnace the other side of the curtain?

At last Henry's coffin slid along the conveyor belt and through the curtain to his eternal home, and everyone got up to go. The manager of the crematorium noticed Stubble among the mourners and came over.

"What brings you here, Mr Stubble? Did you know Mr Allardyce?"

"As it happens, I did, but I came on business."

"Business is it? What can we do to help the forces of law and order?"

Without thinking Stubble asked the question which had been in his mind a few moments before. "Do they go in the fire right away?"

The manager looked around to see if he could be overheard. "As a matter of fact, and strictly between you, me and the gatepost, they don't. Wouldn't pay, you see. We may be council owned but we have to show a profit." He stopped what looked like what was going to be a discussion of the economics of the disposal of the dead and said "Surely you didn't come out here to ask that?"

"No, just curiosity. What I came for was the names of the people you have..." he was going to say burned, but changed it to "dealt with, in the last few weeks."

"No problem. Come over to the office and I'll do you a print-out."

"Even death's got computerised," mused Stubble. "I suppose the computer turns on the furnace or whatever it is when there are enough bodies in the queue." He examined the print-out and asked "Mr Joseph William Tubbs and Miss Marigold Constance Caraway. They were cremated last week."

The manager contradicted him. "No they weren't, the disposal unit broke down last week. A software fault.

So it was a disposal unit and, as Stubble had surmised, it was computerised.

"We only lit it again this morning. We're just getting it up to minimum heat. We've got a whole week's work to get through, the engineers only sorted out the problem just in time; you see we don't have refrigerated storage here."

But Stubble wasn't listening. Two Poplars corpses were still intact, "I'd like a post mortem on those two. Can you return their bodies to the mortuary?"

"I'd have to have authority."

"You'll get it."

"Murder?"

Stubble was tempted to say "that's for me to know and you to find out" but contented himself by saying "could be." Before adding "I'll be back just as soon as I've got the Authorisation."

"Funny," he told himself as he drove away. Old Henry Allardice, Mr Tubbs and Miss Caraway. I'm thinking of them as if they were -still with us, which they most decidedly are not. Otherwise I'd not be on my way to get a Court Order at this moment.

He was soon on his way back to the crematorium bearing the order to halt Mr Tubbs' and Miss Caraway's cremations pending further post mortem examinations. He felt he was at last getting somewhere. As he approached he noticed a wisp of smoke issuing from the chimney. So the furnace was back in business.

The crematorium manager was waiting for him "Everything's ready for you." he said. "Even loaded them into the van. Give us the papers and they'll be on their way to the city mortuary."

Stubble handed the Court Orders over, signed a receipt for the two bodies, thanked the manager and followed the black van to the mortuary, where he waited outside while the bodies were taken out of their coffins and back into cold storage; taking the chance to phone the pathologist who promised to do the post-mortems the next day.

Then he went home, opened his front door, sniffed, and decided on another night in the County Hotel.

Next morning he set off to plod round the old people's homes in the district, armed with a story about an aged fraudster who might have gone to ground in a care home, so as not to put anyone on their guard. After the fifth home he found himself repeating the story like an automaton. "I need to check your list of residents to see if he's in your home. He's a cunning customer is Slimy Sidney, changes his name as often as he changes his socks. Oh, and could I just know if you've had any recent deaths – he might have slipped out of our hands one last time. If we catch him we'll have to charge him which will be a complete waste of time. He must be in his late eighties by now so I can't see any judge sending an old man like that to prison, but I've been told to try to close the file, and orders is orders."

He met reactions ranging from horror that a criminal might be lurking in their midst, to indignation that the police could think their home accepted crooks, to fascination that one of their residents might be someone with an interesting history. His briefcase was full of lists of elderly people by the time he got to The Poplars, none of which showed anything to excite his interest.

When he got to The Poplars he found Janice in a grumpy mood because Mrs Sedge had reprimanded her, rather rudely. "Stop bothering me with every tiny thing that happens, girl. There's no need to come and tell me the new shed's been delivered. Just tell Sam, so he can start putting it together. Use your common sense, girl!"

So Janice used her common sense when Stubble popped and asked for a list of residents and their comings and goings over the last month. She gave him one which tallied exactly with the list he had got from the Registrar.

His morning's research showed that the Poplars had lost four residents in a little over a week, while all the other homes in the district had suffered one death between them in a month. Could be happenstance, but he doubted it. Back in his office he sat at his desk staring at the list of residents Janice had given him. It was a computer printout showing their next-of-kin, religion and date of admission. It took him only a few moments to notice that at The Poplars, as soon as anyone died they were replaced immediately, often the same day, while in all the other homes installing a new customer could take as long as a month.

He took himself down to the canteen and ate a solitary lunch. As he worked his way through Cornish Pasty and Chips he tried to recall what had happened after his father died. They had done nothing until after the funeral and then it had taken him and his sister almost a month to clear the flat ready to sell it. Of course there were just the two of them, and they had just gone in for an hour or so when it suited them. In old people's homes there was just one room to clear. And what about the new occupants? He'd heard it was not so easy to get old people to leave their homes, even when it was patently obvious they could not be left on their own. Surely the new resident could not be got ready move in the next day, as seemed to be the case at The Poplars.

Back in his office he gulped down a couple of indigestion tablets and phoned Limes Court, which happened to have been the first home he had visited that morning. He remembered the proprietor was a garrulous type. Sure enough, he was very ready to tell Stubble what happened after a resident died. "We have to get rid of their belongings, they always bring a few sticks of furniture with them, we have to give it back to the relatives or store it or get someone to take it away, and then we need to give the room a thorough scrub, the social services insist on that; often we redecorate it. How long between one resident moving out and the next moving in? About a week, I'd say; we could do it in a couple of days if the case was urgent, but it hardly ever is that desperate."

So Limes Court, which Stubble had heard was the cheapest and worst home in the county, took up to a week to take in a new customer, while The Poplars, which was said to be run like a good class country-house hotel, could do the job in twenty-four hours.

Might mean something, might not. Could just be that The Poplars was simply better run, with more staff on hand to cope when a resident died.

The telephone interrupted his ponderings. "Pilbeam here." Dr Pilbeam was the pathologist, plump, portly and pompous. "We're just starting on your two cadavers from the crematorium. You did say they were both elderly, one male one female, didn't you?"

Stubble concurred. "Mr Tubbs and Miss Caraway, that's right."

"Well Mr Tubbs is here all right, but Miss Caraway seems to have had a sex change since she died. I think you had better come and have a look."

Stubble immediately phoned the crematorium. Ignoring the courtesies, he pulled rank.
"This is Detective Inspector Stubble, Undershire Police. There's been a terrible mistake. Please stop all cremations this minute."

"Can't do that." said a slow sounding voice on the other end of the line.

Stubble almost screamed in frustration. "You've got to. I've got the wrong body."

He could almost hear the cogs in the man at the other end's brain grinding away. "You means you ain't got the one you got born with?"

. He seemed to be talking to a simpleton, or maybe a joker. Either way it didn't matter. Sounded like a cleaner or something. Stubble cursed his luck. "Please put me through to the manager, right away. It's urgent.

"Can't."

"What do you mean, can't?"

"They all gone home. Ain't no more bodies for the burning. Furnace is turned off. Cooling down it is. Burnt every last one they did."

"Who's in charge there?"

There was a long pause. Stubble could almost see the man scratching his head. "I suppose I is."

"There must be someone else."

"No. Just I. Ain't nobody else. I be here putting muck on roses. You see. I can't be doing that while there's people here what's mourning people. Wouldn't be right, would it. On account of the smell," the man added in case Stubble had not got the message.

In his frustration Stubble asked again. "You mean they've burned all the bodies?"

"That's what crematorium be for." came back the reply.

"Oh thanks" muttered Stubble as he put the receiver down, "thanks a bundle."

When he got to the mortuary he was met by Dr Pilbeam who told him he had touched neither body, He seemed to think the mix-up was somehow Stubble's fault.

"If you'd gone through the proper procedures we would not have had this shambles," he declared. "Neither cadaver has got an identification tag, and as far as I know no formal identification has taken place."

Stubble forbore to remind him that ordinary citizens dying in their beds among people who know them were not the responsibility of the Police,

The two elderly bodies were pulled out of their drawers for Stubble to look at. A brief inspection showed beyond a shadow of doubt that neither of them could be Miss Caraway on account of both being male.

Stubble checked again. "You're sure these were the bodies you received from the crematorium?"

"Absolutely. Have a look at their toes. Those are our tags. It's the very first thing we check when they come in. These weren't tagged at all. Can't understand it!"

Stubble was puzzled. He looked at the toes. Pilbeam turned the tags round so he could read them.

He peered at the tag on Not Miss Caraway's toe. "*Unknown. Stated to be Marigold Constance Caraway. Ex Crematorium.*" he read.

"Is this some sort of joke?" he asked.

"No." said Pilbeam. "We had to call him something."

Stubble noticed a vacant chair in the corner of the room. He went over to it and sat down heavily. This was a turn-up for the books. Miss Caraway had either been cremated already, or spirited away. Accident or design? How could he tell? One thing was obvious. The mortuary was not the place to look. Why so obvious?

He got up reluctantly and went back to the little group round the bodies.

"Are you all right, old chap?" Pilbeam tried to look concerned. It was not every day a detective came over queer at the sight of a corpse.

"Just tired and frustrated" Stubble reassured him.

"Aren't we all." Pilbeam agreed. "So what do you want us to do with these two gentlemen?"

"Well, you can put Not Miss Caraway back in his drawer for the time being. Go ahead and find out what Mr Tubbs died of, assuming that is Mr Tubbs. I'm going to get over to the crematorium to try and get some sense out of them. Before I go, though, I'd like to have a look at the rest of the bodies you've got here."

Pilbeam was indignant. "What? Check our stock? Don't you trust us?"

"Of course I bloody well do. I have to cover my back all the time. That's why I'm tired and frustrated. If this ends up in court, and to tell you the truth at this moment I can't see much hope of that happening, but we do have to go through the motions; if this ends up in court I can just hear some uppity barrister asking me if there was any chance of confusion in the mortuary," he did what he thought was an imitation of a barrister: "Now, Mr Stubble, did you inspect the rest of the bodies in the mortuary when the mistake was discovered?"

"Point taken," said the pathologist." What have we got in stock, Dave?"

"Just these two and a couple of unidentified, one of each." Dave told him.

"Show Mr Stubble the lady and the gentleman, so he can satisfy the justices, David, " Pilbeam instructed, "and then get yourself ready to help me with Mr Tubbs, if he is Mr. Tubbs."

Stubble took a quick look at the mortuary's other residents, one of whom was labelled, *Unknown female, ex Infirmary* Stubble knew exactly who she was, in fact knew her quite well. "This is old Tillie," he told Dave, "hold on while I think of her surname. 'Tipster', that's it, or that's what she told us."

Pilbeam was in his office, adjusting his bow tie at a mirror Stubble suspected had been put there for that sole purpose. When he heard about Tillie he said "Friend of yours?"

"Not exactly. She used to wander into the old Police Station to get warm when it got too cold outdoors in her sleeping bag. Used to push all her belongings in a pram round the villages. Slept in church porches. Couldn't stand being shut in.

"I checked with Police HQ," Pilbeam insisted, "they didn't know her."

"I don't think they know who I am either," Stubble complained, "not without going to their computers. It was different when we were in the old Musgrave Street Station. We were human beings there. Out on the by-pass we're just so many kilobytes."

"As if we haven't noticed," Pilbeam agreed. "Well, Mr Stubble, you've earned your bread today by clearing up one mystery."

Stubble accepted the compliment graciously. "That's what detectives are for. Always glad to be of service."

"Change the lady's tag, please Dave. *Believed to be Tillie Tipster*. If you'd let us have any other information, Mr Stubble? For our records. Have to cover our backs, just like you."

"Don't ask me, ask UPCoC."

"I suspect that if Undershire Police Computer Centre had taken old Tillie in and given her a cup of tea on a cold night she wouldn't be stiff and cold here now." remarked Pilbeam. "Log on to UPCoC, will you Dave, and see if it knows a Tillie Tipster, and how many sugars she takes, and let's have a cup before we get down to business. Will you join us, Mr Stubble?"

Stubble was tempted, but he reckoned he needed to get over to the crematorium, just in case there was someone there who made sense, so declined and went on his way.

He got there to see a heavily built man with a bushy black beard that covered most of his face in the middle of locking up.

"Excuse me." he said to catch the man's attention.

"It's closed. Come back tomorrow. They comes in at eight."

Stubble recognised the voice of the man he had spoken to on the telephone. He asked "Do you have the home telephone number of the manager?"

"Nay."

"What's his name, then?"

"Gordon, Mr Gordon."

"No idea where he lives, his first name?"

"Nay. What be that to you?"

Stubble pulled out his warrant card "Police. D.I. Stubble. It's important I talk to the manager as soon as possible."

"What you be wanting him for?"

Stubble said "Nothing to do with you, Harry. When did you get out? It is Harry Lamb, isn't it? You had me fooled for a bit with that beard and the phoney accent."

"You never forget a face, do you, Mr Stubble?" said Harry, lapsing into his native cockney.

"It's what they pay me for, Harry."

"I never done nothing. Only done what I was told. Mr Gordon, he said, "You do just what I tells you, no more, no less, and we won't have no trouble. He's been good to me, has Mr Gordon. Gave me this job when I got parole. Got me a place, too. Little house in the Garden of Remembrance. I keeps an eye on things, like, when they all gone home."

"How long were you inside, Harry?"

"Two years seven months and ten days." said Harry. "They said I was a model prisoner. Got maximum remission. Said I was not likely to be a danger to no-one."

That was true enough, Stubble reflected. Harry never hurt anyone. Well, not anyone who was still alive. Harry was hardly one of the world's great brains, but he did have just one talent to help him through life. He was a first-class unwanted body disposal contractor. Concrete overcoats, lead boots, slurry grinders, car crushers, tins of petfood, meat pies, even a shark's tummy; all unlicensed last resting places that Harry was suspected to have organised, but the lawmen only ever got as far as suspicion, never proof. No-one had ever laid a finger on Harry until his luck ran out.

He had disposed of Lou de Ville, born Leonard Dibble, a well known professional longfirm man and serial bankrupt, by the well-known technique of double burial, which involved creeping into a cemetery in dead of night, finding a grave due to be used the next day, digging down a little deeper, dropping the corpse in and covering it with earth so the legitimate deceased's coffin would be placed on top of it. What better place to hide a body but in a grave?

Unfortunately a storm later that night washed away some of Lou's earthy duvet, and when the funeral arrived at the graveside the next day the mourners were greeted by Lou's face grinning up at them. Harry got five years.

And here he was serving out his parole in a crematorium of all places. An ideal place for someone with Harry's skills.

Not just any crematorium, but one in a backwater like Dununder. Could be coincidence, thought Stubble, but unlikely.

As he drove home it crossed his mind that he had met up with three old friends that day. Harry the corpse disposal man, Tillie Tipster who wandered round the county with all her worldly goods in an old pram, and Henry Allardyce, ex-Navy, who died all alone in the world. "Not exactly living it up with the movers and shakers, are you Eric?" he told himself as he drove back to his flat.

Mrs Sedge was burning the midnight oil in her flat on the top floor of The Poplars while her Guests slept more or less soundly on the floors below. Sitting up in bed with a clipboard in one hand, a pencil in the other and a calculator on the duvet she had written LONG TERM RESIDENTIAL CARE PLAN at the top of the page. Then she had taken her calculator and was doing sums with it, realising as she did so that she didn't need a calculator for what she was doing. Under the heading she wrote:

52 weeks at £500 per week = £26,000.

She thought for a moment and then wrote: £26,000 for 4 years = £104,000

She sat staring at what she had written for a little while, looking slightly puzzled, and not a little miffed, until a crafty smile spread across her features and she added:

Plus interest!

She studied her calculation for a little while and then said out loud "The question is how long do they last? I'll have to check in the morning, but I guess two years is about average."

She pondered a little longer and then added, "But what happens if they go on and on? Old Mrs Gabriel was 101 before she died. She was with us for eleven years."

She stopped talking to herself, put the clipboard, pen and calculator on the bedside table, turned out the light, snuggled down under the duvet and told herself it was swings and roundabouts. If the average was two years it meant a lot of people died within a year of going into The Poplars. They would balance out the Mrs Gabriels of this world.

As she drifted off into a contented sleep the thought went through her head that long stay residents could perhaps be encouraged to leave on their last journey before they had used up all the money they had invested in The Poplars Long Term Residential Care Plan. It was a pity they wouldn't live to be a hundred and get their card from the Queen, but that was life. Or did she mean death.

Mr Gordon, the manager at the Crematorium was adamant. "We have a foolproof system here, Mr Stubble. If we get a body from a hospital it's always properly labelled; the hospitals are always worried about mixing up patients and so are we for that matter. The undertaker attaches a label to the coffin, we check to make sure the tag and the label agree before we do anything else. We take off the label on the coffin and the tag from the body just before it goes into the furnace and attach it to the burial authorisation."

It didn't sound very foolproof to Stubble, or knaveproof for that matter. There was a known knave on the premises in the shape of Harry Lamb. He could easily have switched the bodies over. After all, he had been alone on the premises every night since he got out of the nick.

"Are the bodies kept somewhere secure?" asked Stubble.

"Oh definitely," the manager told him. "Kept under lock and key. Especially since we have someone working her who is a criminal on parole."

"You mean Mr Lamb." said Stubble quietly.

The manager was startled. "How did you know that?"

"My job to know things like that."

"Shall I call him in?" asked the manager. "It will mean waking him up. He's partly employed as a sort of night watchman, so he'll be asleep just now."

Stubble reflected that Harry's expertise was getting rid of bodies. Swapping them over, especially bodies that were legally dead, was not really his thing. "No don't wake him up. I'd rather talk to the man who is in charge of the incinerator, if that's what you call it."

The manager said "I'll get Mr Forster." and went out. He returned with a man in spotless white overalls. Mr Forster, it turned out was the man who had looked out Mr Tubbs and Miss Caraway the day before and saved them from the fire.

Stubble asked him if he had opened the coffins to check he had the right people. He got the reply he expected. Mr Forster had just checked the labels. They had been rather rushed yesterday, dealing with the backlog. He remembered they were both very plain coffins, the cheapest sort. Most people liked something a little more respectful.

Stubble made a point of asking: "There were only two plain coffins?"

"Just those two. All the others were better class. That's how I knew they had come from the Poplars – they always use the cheapest."

It was the work of a moment to telephone Mr Gladwyn to find out what sort of coffins Mr Tubbs and Miss Caraway had had. Mr Tubbs had been put into The Respect, which was the bottom of the range, but Miss Caraway had made the arrangements herself, and had been delivered to the crematorium in an Eternity, which was one of their more expensive models.

So Mr Forster had been careless and jumped to the wrong conclusion. It was obvious he had not checked the coffins properly. As he put the phone down Stubble realised Mr Forster was still standing there. A glance at his face confirmed he was to blame. There was no point in taking out his frustration on him, he just said "I won't be taking it any further, but I have to know. You really can't be sure you checked the names on the coffins, can you?"

"Well, sir, I can't be absolutely sure. Yesterday was such a rush, you see..."

Stubble held up his hand to stop the flow of apology and self-justification. "That's all right. We all make mistakes. You'd better get back to your furnace."

Stubble watched Mr Forster trudge across the car park to the building at the back of the chapel which was his kingdom, while he pondered his next move. He hadn't got one. He would just have to hope that sniffing around the affairs of Mr Tubbs, Mrs Gellatly and Mrs de Havilland would yield some sort of lead.

And if they didn't do any good he would still keep an eye on what went on at The Poplars. It wasn't as if he had anything else to do...

He took himself back to his office at Police HQ to find it still a hive of inactivity as far as he was concerned. The local villains were still seemingly on strike.

It wouldn't last. Sooner or later they would be back at work and keeping him busy. In the meantime he had better find out what he could about the deaths of Mrs Gellatly and Mrs de Havilland. What he did about Mr Tubbs would depend on what the pathologist discovered.

Mrs de Havilland had been cremated a couple of days after her death. He wondered if she had been wealthy, and if so, where her money was going to go.

He ran his finger down the list of recent deaths Janice had given him and came to Mrs Gellatly, who had died a little earlier than the others. Was she cremated with the same indecent haste? He ran his finger down the list he'd got from the crematorium manager. The name was not there. He looked again. Still no Gellatly. She must have been buried.

She could be in any of a score of churchyards, but most churchyards are full up these days, so the best bet was the Municipal Cemetery. He phoned them and they had the details to hand almost immediately. A Mrs Gellatly had been buried there. Who was the undertaker? Gladwyns.

Mr Gladwyn the undertaker, who had started Stubble on this whole line of enquiry.

Did they have the names of the next of kin?

No, but Mr Gladwyn would be able to help him about that. Did he want the number?

Stubble fished in his pocket and there was the card Gladwyn had given him in the pub, it seemed like only yesterday.

Well, it was only the day before yesterday.

Mr Gladwyn was helpfulness itself. "No problem at all, Mr Stubble; always a pleasure to help the police with their enquiries. Now what name was it? Gellatly? Plot No. V24. Daughter by the name of Forsyte. Do I know the address? I most certainly do. We keep writing to Mr Forsyte reminding him we need a contribution to the Gladwyn Pension Fund."

Stubble raised his eyebrows "Didn't they give you a tip?"

Gladwyn dropped the levity and spelt it out. "He hasn't paid his bill. Some sort of delay in proving the will, he says. Of course I know that's a lot of tosh. You don't have to go to probate before paying the undertaker. Looks like we're going to have to cut up rough with Mr Forsyte. Don't like doing it, grieving relatives and all that, but a man's got to eat."

Stubble managed to get the Forsytes' address out of Gladwyn after a few minutes being lectured about how Mr Gladwyn would not have gone into undertaking if he had his time over again. He put the phone down and rubbed his ear.

Mr Forsyte would be away at work at this time of day, but Mrs Forsyte, Mrs Gellatly's daughter, might be in. He phoned the number Gladwyn had given him and got the engaged signal. He tried again – still busy. He decided to take a chance and go round to the house.

Mrs Forsyte was in. A harassed looking woman in her forties who looked well due for a trip to the hairdresser.

She was less put out than he expected when he announced himself and showed his warrant card. "Come in," she said "I suppose it's about the bills."

This was a bit of luck. He was wondering how he could get round to the money side of things without putting her on her guard, and she had led him straight to it.

"Well, partly," he said "it must be a great worry to you."

"Will we have to go to court?" she asked.

Better still. Going by the book he should have told her at that point that the bills were a civil matter of no interest to the police. Instead he said "We always try not to let things get that far, Mrs Forsyte. Would I be out of order if I asked you to make a nice cup of tea? I'm sure you like to have one yourself."

He could sense her relief. It was almost tangible. She most likely thought she would have the cuffs on by now. The old 'we're on your side, really you know. Just trying to sort everything out' routine seemed to be working like a well-oiled machine.

She disappeared, into the kitchen he supposed, shutting the door behind her. He got up and looked round the room. Nicely furnished, some expensive looking nick-knacks on the mantelpiece. The latest television in the corner. Carpet could not be more than a couple of years old. Any of it paid for?

His thoughts were broken into by the muted sound of her voice. He eased the door open and found he could hear her clearly. She was on the telephone to her husband, he guessed. She was saying "The police are here, Charlie, about the money."

Shit. The husband would know he wasn't interested in the debts. Now she would be on her guard. It wasn't going to be an easy ride after all.

He closed the door and went back and sat down. When she brought the tea in he went on as if he had not overheard her, changing tack slightly. "The public always think we like getting convictions. We don't. It wastes our time getting the evidence together, going to court. Our job is to prevent crime, which why I'm here. We suspect something underhand is going on, a criminal conspiracy, involving... well, it would be best if I didn't tell you who might be involved until we know a little more. You may be innocently involved which is why I've dropped in to talk to you, informally but in complete confidence, of course. I'm not taking any notes, and I must ask you to tell no-one at all about this conversation, until it comes out into the open."

Mrs Forsyte nodded. "I think I understand. Can I talk to my husband about it?"

Stubble smiled as he said "The law says I can't stop you but I'd esteem it a favour if you didn't. The fewer people who know at this stage the better. We don't want to put the naughty lads on guard, do we?"

She sipped her tea and said "I see."

Stubble asked if she could spare him another cup, and went on "This is a little delicate. I hope you don't mind me asking some rather personal questions. Your late mother....."

She nodded her assent.

"I wonder if you would be able to tell me what the funeral cost?"

She knew exactly, and gave him the figure.

"Excellent. To be paid to the undertakers in due course. Was anyone else involved, financially, I mean. Any other bills connected to the funeral?"

"No-one. Oh, yes, I think Charlie gave a tip to man who drove our car."

"Hmm. Stubble tried to look disappointed. "That's all. Sorry to have troubled you at a difficult time. Oh, there is one other thing."

She was gripping one hand with the other. Wanting the interview to be over but afraid to say so.

"I see she was buried. Most people seemed to be getting cremated these days. I think I should prepare you in advance, even though it may never come to it." He paused, as if not sure how to go on. "There's no easy way to say this. We may have to exhume your mother. As I say, it is not very likely, but you need to be warned so you can come to terms with it."

He watched her eyes. No trace of a tear. No reaction at all really.

He asked, a touch brutally. "Were you very close?"

"Not really. She was away a lot when I was a girl. I spent the holidays with an aunt mostly."

"You went to boarding school?"

"Yes. St. Angela's."

"That can't have been very nice for you."

"On the contrary, it was the happiest time of my life."

"Why were your parents away?"

"They were geologists. Spent their lives going all over the world looking for oil. My father was a freelance, my mother worked for a big American oil company."

"That must have been well paid. I suppose she left you well provided for."

Suddenly it all came out. "Not at all! We got hardly anything. She was a hard woman. I shouldn't say it, but my mother was a bitch, a hard hearted bitch. She should never have had a child. I was just an unwelcome interruption to her career. She was quite well off so you'd have thought she'd have left some money to us. Not her, she left all her money to the Geological Society. I'll never forget what she said when I got married. She said: "Now you've got a husband, he can look after you.""

Now the tears came. Tears of self-pity. Stubble waited patiently until Mrs Forsyte managed to compose herself, thanked her for the tea and took himself off.

So Mrs Gellatly had not been short of a penny. Had she been killed for her money? Upsetting for the murderer to discover everything had gone to charity. Who might have killed her? Her daughter and her son-in-law were obvious suspects, but Mrs Forsyte's body language said otherwise. She hadn't reacted at all to his suggestion they might have to exhume her mother's body. Who else might have done it? Someone at The Poplars? But why? Was she paying her care bill? Did they knock off customers who got into arrears? He realised he was wandering off into the world of the preposterous.

But then when all the rational explanations had been exhausted the stupid one sometimes turned out to be the truth.

Could be that she hadn't been killed at all. Mustn't jump to conclusions. People do die in old people's homes. An unfortunate fact, but a fact all the same. But why so many all at once at the Poplars? Something smelt, but what?

Stubble scratched his nose. He could not stop it sniffing, however baffled he might feel.

When he got back to police HQ there was a message on his desk that Dr Pilbeam had called. Stubble phoned him back without a great deal of expectation. He was right.

"Your Mr Tubbs. I could call it suicide but I'll have to settle for heart failure. Could have happened any time the way that man must have lived. From the state of his cardiovascular system I'd postulate the man wolfed down greasy food all his life. His lungs were solid tar and his airways were almost blocked. His liver was a superb specimen, of advanced cirrhosis. There was a touch of smoke in the lungs, fresh smoke that is, but he could only have taken a couple of breaths before the heart finally packed up. The fact is this gentleman smoked ate and drank himself to death. I'll send you the full report if you need it,

Stubble thanked him and told him not to bother, but Pilbeam had not quite finished with him.

"Mr Stubble, do you think there is any chance I could get to keep the body. My students would die to get their hands on a specimen like this."

For a moment Stubble's brain conjured up the students using poor Mr Tubbs in one of their Rag Week stunts, and then he remembered that Pilbeam was the visiting lecturer in pathology at the university.

"I suggest you get in touch with Mr Tubbs's solicitor, or his relatives, if he had any."

"Who are they? Do you know? Can you find out?"

"Sorry, Doctor. Too busy. Try Wimpole's in The Cathedral Close. They do a lot of work for The Poplars. Perhaps the people at The Poplars could tell you if there is any family."

Pilbeam said "Thanks." Stubble heard the unspoken "for nothing."

Charlie Forsyte came home with the news that the police had phoned him asking if they could have a look at his mother-in-law"s bank account.

"What did you say?" asked his wife.

"Told them to go ahead, of course. What does it matter to us? Or to her, come to think of it, now she's dead?"

"Don't you think I should have been the one they asked? She was my mother after all."

She had expected him to say something like, he hadn't thought, he was sorry, of course it was for her to say. Instead he went ape.

"What the fuck has it got to do with you!" he screamed. "The old bitch didn't leave us anything, so where do you get involved? Eh?"

He was pouring himself a drink and stepped toward her. She flinched, thinking he was going to crack the bottle over her head. "I'm the one who's been trudging in and out of bloody lawyers' offices trying to get some sort of case together so we can get hold of your bloody mother's money while you sit here all day doing fuck all except wring your hands."

"If you'd asked me..." she said lamely.

"I didn't ask you because you're not likely to be any use. You've never been any use!" with which he walked out of the room. She heard him tramping upstairs.

She decided the best thing was to act as if nothing had happened. She went into the kitchen and put a light under the potatoes and peas, lit the grill and put the chops under it. Then she sat down and started to weep.

She heard him coming down the stairs. He stood in the kitchen door observing her for a few seconds and then announced he was going out.

She lifted her head and sniffled. "Where."

"None of your damn business."

He staggered home some towards midnight and fell asleep on the sofa.

In the morning he showered and arrived for breakfast as if nothing had happened. She made his coffee, boiled his egg as she had done every morning since they had been together. When she ventured to say "nice morning" he just glowered at her.

After he had gone to work without a word to her she phoned police HQ.

"Mr Stubble?" she asked when she was put through to him. Cynthia Forsyte here. If you want to dig up my mother, it's OK by me," she paused and then said, quite quickly, "I shall be going away for a few days, not sure how long, but I'm sure my husband will be able to help you if there's anything you want to know."

Stubble thanked her, wondering what had prompted the call. Maybe his asking her husband about the bank account. Something not right about the Forsytes, he was certain.

What he hadn't seen any point in telling her was that it was unlikely her mother would be exhumed, because the local villains seemed to have called off their industrial action, ended their vacation or whatever had kept them quiet and were back at work. The night had produced two burglaries and a ram raid, and news was coming in of the hijacking of a security van while it was delivering cash to the Post Office in the city centre, all of which had priority over what was, after all, only a vague feeling that something fishy was going on at The Poplars.

The matter of the suspicious deaths at The Poplars would have to be put in the pending tray for the time being.

PART TWO

CHAPTER ONE
Sam Finds a Skull

A year or so later an invitation to a charity concert at the stately home of Lord and Lady Scorpion arrived at Wimpole's office, addressed to Augustus Wimpole Esq, and friend. He asked his close friend Mrs Sedge if she would like to accompany him and the pair, after tea and listening to an indifferent string quartet, all in aid of a deserving cause, found themselves strolling through the grounds of Scorpion Hall.

Going through a doorway in search of a little privacy they found themselves in a walled garden where neat beds of assorted vegetables were quietly thriving. A gardener materialised from behind a row of beans and got into conversation with them.

Wimpole observed that the garden seemed to be producing far more vegetables than Lord and Lady Scorpion could eat, at which the gardener explained that some of the garden's produce was consumed by the staff and visitors, but most of it was sold to local hotels and restaurants to help with the upkeep of the Hall.

This set Mrs Sedge thinking. If Lord Scorpion could save money in this way then surely Sam could grow vegetables in the grounds of The Poplars to help feed the Guests and keep costs down. When she put the idea to Sam he was enthusiastic and immediately set about clearing the nondescript shrubbery by his newly built shed to make a vegetable plot.

When he had dug over the patch he had selected for planting, he started to mix in compost from the heap he had made from the grass cuttings and kitchen waste the previous year. At the bottom of the heap he dug up a bone and then another and then another. He was tossing the bones to one side and happily thinking he was excavating some sort of dog's treasure trove until he uncovered a skull when it dawned on him that he was digging up a human skeleton.

Mrs Sedge was in the kitchen sampling the Irish stew that was going to be served to the Guests when Sam burst in brandishing the skull. A kitchen hand took one look and fainted. She would have fallen into a vat of soup had chef not knocked her to the ground, at the same time shoving Sam and the skull out of his kitchen.

"It only wants the Food Hygiene people to see that thing in here and we are deep into the shite" he roared while Mrs Sedge backed him up by screaming "Get out!"

Unfortunately in his haste chef pushed Sam out of the wrong door. Instead of ending up back in the garden he erupted into the Guests' lounge where he managed to trip over and drop the skull. It rolled across the carpet and ended up at the feet of Mr Gadsby who had played for Aston Villa in his youth. He instinctively kicked it into touch, which happened to be Mrs Canter's lap. She was in the middle of putting on her glasses to inspect it when Sam arrived, grabbed it and clutching it like a rugby ball ran off to his cellar where he felt safe. He sat on his bed panting and wondering what to do next. One thing he was sure of. He was going to get the sack. Mrs Sedge had been very very angry with him.

Sam's employment prospects were the last thing on Mrs Sedge's mind. She was in a state of some panic. Surely all the bodies had been safely cremated? Where had this skull come from? Wouldn't Gladwyn have said something if any of their clients had been incomplete? Perhaps it was an old skull, a relic of some forgotten war or accident or something; nothing to do with her. Forcing herself to appear calm, but unable to control a trembling hand, she phoned her best friend.

Mr Wimpole instantly switched from lover to lawyer. His curt instructions calmed her down a little. "Phone the police. Just tell them your handyman has found a skull, then stay where you are. When they arrive be sure to say nothing, absolutely nothing. You have no idea how the skull came to be in your garden. That's all. Right? Don't touch anything. I'm coming right over. With luck I'll get there before they do."

He drove like the wind but Stubble got there first. He happened to be in the vicinity when the call came through, and it took him less than a minute to get there. His nose had been right all those months ago. Something fishy had indeed been going on at The Poplars.

He bounded up the steps into Reception and asked Janice where the skull was.

Janice, who knew nothing of the goings-on in the lounge, took him for a stray nutter. "You're looking for a skull?" she said, wondering how to get help.

"I was told a skull has been found on the premises," Stubble insisted.

Janice repeated his words back to him hoping it would humour him. "A skull has been found here?"

"Yes. A skull. I'd like to speak to whoever is in charge."

Janice was only too pleased to do as she was asked. She called up to Mrs Sedge's flat and was relieved to hear she would be down immediately. "It's a man about a skull," Janice told her, so she would know there was a problem.

"Ask him who he is?"

Janice did so. "Detective Inspector Stubble" came the reply.

"Ooooer" said Janice, remembering his visit a year ago.

Mrs Sedge arrived and Stubble got straight to the point. "I'm told someone here has found a human skull"

Mrs Sedge nodded. "Sam, that's our odd-job man, came into the kitchen with it."

"Can you show me the way to the kitchen please?"

"It's not there now. I told him to take it away."

Stubble saw this was not going to be easy. "So where is it now?"

"I don't know. He could have taken it anywhere."

"Think where he might have gone, please madam." said Stubble, taking deep breaths to preserve his equanimity.

"I don't know. He ran off. I was only concerned to get it away from a food preparation area. The hygiene regulations, they're very strict you know." Mrs Sedge kept glancing at the front door, hoping Wimpole would arrive soon.

"You must have some idea where he's gone." insisted Stubble."

"I really don't know."

"Please try to think."

Mrs Sedge spent a few moments trying to look as if she was racking her brains and finally said "He's got lots of little hidey-holes round the place, out in the garden, in the attic, in the boiler room. We'll have to search ....."

Janice broke into the conversation. "I think I saw him go down to the cellar. He was in a bit of a hurry."

If looks could kill, Janice would have been struck stone dead by Mrs Sedge.

"How do we get into the cellar?" asked Stubble.

Mrs Sedge was desperately trying to think of a way of stopping him going down there when Wimpole arrived.

Stubble greeted him warmly. "Ah, Mr Wimpole, I thought you might be along. Mrs Sedge was just going to show us down to the cellar."

Down amongst the old furniture they found Sam sitting on his bed clutching the skull. He was staring straight ahead and saying over and over again. "I dug it up. I dug it up."

Stubble got a pair of latex gloves out of his briefcase and put them on before he went over and gently eased the skull out of Sam's hands. Sam was looking round his visitors as if they were the inhabitants of a bad dream, come to get him for some awful crime. He knew only one thing: it was all his fault.

"Where did you find it, Sam?" asked Stubble gently. It seemed to break the spell.

Sam spoke. "Compost heap."

"Where's that?"

"Behind me shed."

"Would you like to show us?"

"What about the skull?" asked Mrs Sedge. "I'd rather the residents did not see it."

"Is there a lock on the cellar door?" asked Stubble

"Yes"

"Then we can leave it here"

The little party followed Sam to the compost heap. The other bones were just where Sam had tossed them. Stubble took one look, before calling Police HQ.

Then he told them he would have to wait until help arrived and in the meantime no-one was to leave the premises. "There will be a lot of our people here shortly. We will be erecting a tent over the site. Have any of you any idea whose remains these could be?"

All he got were blank looks.

A couple of residents approached, their curiosity aroused. Stubble went into the routine he had used so many times, "There's nothing to see here. Please go away." The residents ignored him. "It's bones," one observed. "People are so untidy these days," the other commented.

Mrs Sedge gently took one of the old people by the arm and led her away. Wimpole followed her example with the other. Stubble was relieved to see a uniformed constable approaching across the lawn.

Leaving the policeman on guard he went back into the house. He waited until the Scene of the Crime team arrived and then headed back to his office. There was no point in hanging around when the SoCO people could get on with their business perfectly adequately without him. He would be better employed getting out the file he had started when his suspicions had been aroused months before by the unusual spate of deaths at The Poplars.

The records on the file showed four deaths and four disposals, three by cremation and one by burial. There were ways of checking that they corresponded, not infallible in the case of the cremated ones, bearing in mind the confusion he'd discovered the year before, but an exhumation would definitely tell him if Mrs Gellatly was in the right grave or otherwise. It looked as if his carelessly uttered threat to her daughter, Mrs Forsyte, a year ago might have to be carried out.

Whose was the skeleton in The Poplars' garden? Stubble went into pondering mode about the remains Sam had dug up. The skull still had its teeth which would be some help in identification. It was most likely someone connected to The Poplars but he must not jump to that conclusion. It was improbable that it was an outsider, but then again it could be. And who had buried it? People who wanted to get rid of bodies usually did it in a wood where they were unlikely to be seen digging, or somewhere where they thought no-one would ever look. Under a flower bed in their own garden was surprisingly popular. Never in Stubble's experience in someone else's garden. But why bury it in a shallow grave in the home's grounds where it was almost certain to be discovered? Under a compost heap of all places. It pointed straight at Sam, which was a good reason for looking elsewhere. If Sam had buried the body there he would never have dug up the bones, let alone brought one into the house.

He stopped day-dreaming and tried to focus his thoughts. People at The Poplars divided into three groups: residents, staff and visitors.

The body was most probably one of the residents. There must be all sorts of reasons for getting rid of an old person. It just could be a visitor, but why would a visitor be buried in the grounds? Could it have been a staff member? He would have to ask if anyone had left suddenly without giving notice; if there had been any serious quarrels. After a few minutes thought Stubble came to the conclusion there was not much he could do until the forensic boys and girls gave him an idea how long the body had been lying under the compost heap. Knowing whether male or female would narrow the field a bit.

It would also help if they could give him an idea about the cause of death, but he wasn't sure if they could help him there. It all depended how long the body had been in the ground and how much Sam the gardener had disturbed it.

There had not been so much excitement in the Guests' Lounge for ages as the old people's musings paralleled Stubble's.

"Coppers crawling all over the place. I came here to get some peace and quiet. Might as well be back in the nick," remarked Mr Stacey who had spent a lot of time in cells at various locations before his heart started to give him grief.

"It could be any of us lying out there in the garden." said Mrs Briggs just to cheer everyone up.

"We're all going to help the police with their enquiries," an excited Miss Blenkinsop kept repeating.

"Will we have to give evidence? Go to court?" quavered Miss Dawson.

Mr Simms sat in his seat by the window reciting "Alas poor Yorick" over and over again.

If they all hadn't been so busy someone might have noticed Sam creeping past carrying his suitcase. There wasn't much point,

Sam reckoned, in waiting to be sacked. He might as well go of his own accord.

Matron knew nothing about the discovery what was left of Miss Bonnie's body. She was away attending the funeral of her Aunt Agnes in Edinburgh.

The interment was taking place on a bleak hillside near the airport in a light drizzle. From time to time the proceedings were drowned out by the drone of aircraft taking off. When the service was over everyone hurried to find shelter. Except Matron.

She lingered among the tombstones reading the inscriptions, most of them of little interest, but occasionally she came across one with a touch of humour or human interest like "constant companion of her husband" which Matron guessed meant she never left the poor man alone. One William Thompson had "gone to God's heavenly garden". Now what had he done with his life?

The drizzle turned to rain and she tore herself away and hastened after the others. It would never do to miss the drinks and sandwiches which were waiting for them in a room above a pub round the corner.

Up in her flat on the top floor of The Poplars Mrs Sedge and Mr Wimpole stared across the garden at the taped-off burial site. The grave itself was covered with a sheet. On the lawn a couple of sweating policemen were sorting out the rods that would form the framework of a tent to replace the sheet.

"Do they have to do that in full view of the Guests?" asked Mrs Sedge.

"I wouldn't worry about your residents. Best bit of excitement they've had for ages," said Wimpole. "You've no idea who it is down there, or who might have put them there?"

"None at all." She guessed what was in his mind. "I've always been most careful. All our dead are accounted for, don't you worry."

"Did you get a good look at that skull?" he asked. He put his arm round her shoulder.

She shook him off. "Not just now, Augustus, I'm not feeling like it." She shuddered. "Seeing that skull's shaken me up."

"I managed to get a good look at it. It looked quite fresh to me. No chance it was someone left over from the Civil War or anything like that."

Mrs Sedge wondered where a solicitor got his knowledge of dead bodies from. Was it something they did as part of their training?

"I don't like the look of that detective." she remarked.

"Oh Stubble? He's all right, well, as far as a policeman can be all right. Bit of a plodder. Perspiration rather than inspiration. Not one of nature's brightest sparks. I'm afraid you're going to see quite a lot of DI Stubble."

"Where do you think he will start? Will he talk to everyone in the place?"

"Very possibly. I'd be surprised if he didn't start with Sam, he's the one who found the body."

"Perhaps we'd better have him up and tell him what to say."

"Which is what? Not a good idea. Assuming you know what to tell Sam to say, even Stubble will sense he's been coached."

Mrs Sedge said gloomily: "It won't do The Poplars any good. We have a reputation to keep up. Hardly going to be helped by finding a corpse buried in the garden."

Wimpole did not know what to say to that.

The policemen on the lawn finished sorting out their rods and took them over to the grave where they started slotting them together.

"I've changed my mind. Perhaps I had better have a word with Sam," said Wimpole.

Mrs Sedge phoned down to Janice to ask her to send him up. A few minutes later Janice rang back. "I can't seem to find Sam, Mrs Sedge. I've looked in the cellar and gone round the garden, well, as far as I could with all those policemen there. I even looked in the kitchen, and I can't find him anywhere."

"Oh, he must be somewhere around. Sam has a knack of hiding himself away whenever he's wanted," said Mrs Sedge quite unfairly. "Just let me know when he appears."

Wimpole was still staring out of the window. "What do we do?" Mrs Sedge asked him.

"Absolutely nothing for the time being" he replied, "but I'd love to know whose bones are lying down there."

Back at Police HQ, Stubble would have been happy to know the same. It would not tell him who put the corpse there, but it would be a start. Could it be some stranger heaved over the wall from outside and buried in dead of night, perhaps with the intention of damaging the good name of The Poplars? Stubble realised his imagination was running away with him again. The most likely thesis was that it was the body of a resident or perhaps a staff member. Why would anyone want to kill a visitor and bury him in the grounds of the home?

It should be easy enough to trace a missing resident, assuming the home kept proper records. The same with staff members. There should be lists of who arrived and who left in both cases. No point standing here in his office staring out of the window at the miserable horse who lived in a paddock behind Police HQ. She wouldn't tell him anything, even if she was an English-speaking horse. DI Stubble went in search of his car and drove off to The Poplars.

Wimpole saw him arrive, park his car carefully, lock it and make his way into the house.

"There he is." he remarked to Mrs Sedge.

"Who is?" she asked. She had been asking herself what had happened to Sam at that moment.

"Our friend Stubble. He's just driven up."

The phone rang it was Janice telling Mrs Sedge that Mr Stubble was downstairs wanting to see her.

"We'll be right down," she said, checking her hair in the mirror.

Sam was sitting on the upper deck of a 323 bus as it meandered from village to village in the general direction of Gloucester. He had been lucky to catch it; the bus ran only ran twice a week.

Gloucester was a big place. There'd be lots of buses there. He'd be able to get one going to Bristol. Bristol was a port. There'd be ships there going all over the world. Sam reckoned he'd be able to stow away on one. He'd tell the captain he was there as soon as it was safely out to sea, of course. Perhaps he could work his passage. He looked round the bus and saw he was alone, so he got out his purse and counted his savings. There was enough there for a little while. He could even go up to London. See the sights. There were all sorts of things he could do.

Then he realised he had been silly. He should have let Mrs Sedge give him the sack, so she would have had to pay him his wages up to date, and maybe a bit on top, but at the time all he wanted to do was get away. He had got all mixed up, what with the skull and all those bones and everything.

When he got off the bus in Gloucester he found he had to wait forty minutes for the Bristol bus. He perched himself on his suitcase and waited patiently until it came. When it arrived he hauled his suitcase up the stairs – there was more chance of being alone on the top deck and Sam liked being alone. As the bus drove out of the station he looked down and saw the roof of a police car, white with a big number on it, driving past.

It was only then that it came to Sam that the police might be after him. The quicker he got on that ship and out of the country the better.

"If there's anything we can do to help your investigations, we will be only too pleased." simpered Wimpole. "I imagine you'd like to talk to Sam first." Stubble surprised him by asking "Sam? who's Sam?"

"Sam, our gardener/handyman. He's the one who found the body." Mrs Sedge told him.

Stubble apologised. "The man with the skull. Sorry, I had forgotten his name. There's no need to talk to him for the moment. What I'd like is your residents' records." Mrs Sedge heaved an inward sigh of relief, but Wimpole immediately felt something was not going according to plan. Why did he want to see those records? "Those are surely confidential," He felt it best to raise an objection.

So Mr Bloody Wimpole was going to be as obstructive as possible, was he? Stubble glanced at him and said "I'll waste some time applying for a warrant, if you'd like. The magistrates love being called away from their suppers, don't they? I'll be sure to mention your name."

Wimpole knew when his bluff was called. "I shall want to be present when you examine the records"

Stubble laid it on with a palette knife. "Of course, Mr Wimpole. You can even examine my notes, if I make any. I'm sure your assistance will be invaluable."

"We keep the records on computer." said Mrs Sedge.

If she thought this would faze Stubble she was wrong. "All the better. All I want is a list of the residents for the last five years with dates of arrival and departure. I imagine you could print that out in no time at all."

Wimple nodded his agreement to Mrs Sedge.

"No problem," said Mrs Sedge. She disappeared into the office leaving Stubble and Wimpole awkwardly staring at each other. "I'll just go and see how the lads are getting on in the garden, and let them know I'm here," said Stubble. "I'll be back in a couple of minutes."

Wimpole, left alone, started to pace up and down. Janice interrupted his thoughts by remarking "Awful, isn't it."

He looked at her as if she was an interesting bit of wildlife that had just crept out of a hole in the skirting board. He said "Yes" and walked to the open front door. Stubble was coming back across the lawn. The two policeman were staggering towards the grave bearing the cover to go over the frame they had erected.

Mrs Sedge arrived with a few sheets of paper just as Stubble returned.

"Here they are: all the Guests listed by date of arrival and date of departure, just as you asked, and the staff records are here in this file."

"Computers. Aren't they wonderful," said Stubble. "Is there somewhere I can sit down and study this data?"

Mrs Sedge showed him into the dining room. He sat himself at one of the tables and started to study the list Mrs Sedge had given him. Wimpole stood watching him for a moment and then sat down opposite him. A moment later Mrs Sedge joined him.

Stubble looked up "There's no need for you to stay, but if you wish to, I don't mind. You may be able to help me if I come across something I don't understand."

The three of them sat in silence, only the ticking of the grandfather clock Mrs Sedge had put there to give prospective residents and their relatives an impression of solid old fashioned comfort could be heard.

Stubble was busily checking off residents who had come and gone. Every now and then he noted the name of someone who had not left The Poplars to go to hospital or directly to the next world.

Most of these had gone to other old people's homes, most probably because The Poplars did not suit them or because they needed something cheaper. Each time he came to one of those Mrs Sedge was able to recall where they had gone, which he noted. They would all have to be followed up.

When he finished he took a fresh piece of paper and listed those names without ticks, or notes, which would in theory correspond with the current residents of the home. He pushed his chair back and stood up.

"Not my job, but someone's got to do it," he told Wimpole and Sedge. "I usually give my sergeant routine jobs like this, but she's on sick leave. Now, Mrs Sedge, I'd be grateful if you would let me have a list of your current residents."

"Are you suggesting...." said Wimpole.

"I'm suggesting nothing. I'm just getting on with boring detective work. Leaving no stone unturned, no avenue unexplored. Usually a complete waste of time until bingo! something doesn't look right. Then the old bloodhound goes sniffing around in earnest." Stubble peered at the carpet as if expecting to see a trail of bloody footprints and then asked Mrs Sedge "You've no idea who the body could be, then, Mrs Sedge.

Wimpole intervened. "You have already asked my client that question."

"Quite right. I already did, didn't I? It's been a long day. Sorry, sorry."

Without saying a word Mrs Sedge went out and returned a minute or so later with the list of residents. Stubble sat down again and went on ticking.

When he had finished he stood up. "That was a stone I didn't need to turn over. Your records tally exactly. Ninety per cent of my time is wasted, you know. If only I had a way of identifying the other ten per cent I'd find life a lot easier. Next job is to talk to your residents and staff. I'll have to interview them all, I'm afraid. I imagine that will be part of the ninety per cent wasted time as well, but routine, routine, routine. Drives you mad, but it's got to be done"

Wimpole coldly smiled his understanding.

"They'll be wanting to lay the tables for tea." said Mrs Sedge

"Is there somewhere else we could go?" Stubble asked.

"I suppose there's the conservatory, but there's no light in there."

"That's all right," Stubble reassured her. I'll just make a start now and come back in the morning. While you get the conservatory ready I'll just go and have another look to see if they've found anything interesting down in the garden."

Matron's nephew saw her to the train. No-one outside the immediate family had recognised her, or if they had, they hadn't said anything. Not that she looked like her pictures in the newspapers. She was older for one thing, and she had made an effort to change her appearance. She had put her hair up and now that she needed to wear glasses she had deliberately chosen heavy frames. She'd kept her mouth shut too, which had been a help; she had just uttered conventional pleasantries, said nothing that might have given the game away.

He could not say he was fond of his aunt. There was something unsettling about her. Nothing he could put his finger on. Perhaps it was because she guarded her tongue so carefully. And of course the knowledge she had done something. He wasn't sure what it was; no-one in the family ever spoke of it directly; just vague hints.

He shuddered as he got into his car. Someone was walking across his grave his mother had told him that meant. And now she was in hers. He'd never see her again. Alone in the car the emotions he had kept in since her death overwhelmed him and he broke down in tears.

Sam emerged from the bus station in Bristol and looked about him for some sign as to which way to go to get to the docks. Seeing none he decided to walk downhill, since he reckoned it was unlikely they would be at the top of the steep street he could see in the distance. Eventually he came to a wide river and walked along it for some distance without seeing any sign of a ship.

He stopped a passer-by and asked how far it was to where the ships were. The man looked quizzically at him for a moment and then said "Fair way, mate. You won't see any ships until you get to Avonmouth."

Sam plodded along, his suitcase weighing heavier with each step he took until he came to a bench, placed there in memory of one Jack Dyson who had loved the view. Grateful to Jack Dyson, whoever he was, Sam rested his weary bones on it. After a while he began to doze off. He woke up when raindrops began to fall on his head. He blinked and saw a bus approaching.

It would at least be dry inside the bus, so he hailed it and got on.

"Where to?" asked the driver.

"Where you going?" asked Sam, still stupid with sleep.

"Avonmouth."

"That'll do me," said Sam.

As he paid his fare he asked if the bus stopped anywhere near the docks.

"Right outside the dock gates, sailor," said the driver. "I'll give you a shout when we get there."

Sam dozed off again but the bus driver forgot to call him and only noticed he was still there when he got to the terminus. "Never mind," he said "you just sit there and you can get off when we pass the docks on the way back. I'll make sure to tell you this time."

There was no need. Sam moved to a seat near the driver to make sure he did not get carried back into Bristol. All the same, the driver called out "next stop, sailor," louder than Sam would have liked, as they approached the gates. He got off and sat in the bus shelter uncertain what to do next. The dock was guarded by heavy iron gates which slid to one side when a vehicle went through. Sam noticed the drivers all showed some papers to the gatekeeper sitting in a little hut outside the gates. Anyone who approached on foot had to show their documents before being admitted by a small side gate.

Sam was wondering what papers he ought to be showing, or whether he would have a better chance of climbing over the fence somewhere away from the gate when he heard a deep voice asking "Hallo, mister. Looking for a berth?"

He looked up to see a tall deeply tanned man with close cropped grey hair looking at him. He wore what looked like naval uniform. His sleeves boasted four gold stripes and his cap badge bore an anchor superimposed on a map of Africa surrounded by gilt palm leaves.

Sam nodded. He was feeling utterly weary and bed sounded an excellent idea. "Yus." he confirmed.

The naval officer stretched out a wiry hand and said in the accent of the deep south of the United States: "Captain Roger Dade of the good ship '*Largesse.*' Been here refitting and now I'm looking for hands. Let's see your ticket.

Sam held out the bus ticket he still had in his hand.

The captain looked at it and then studied Sam quizzically. "Not a sailor, are you?"

Sam nodded wretchedly.

The captain ordered Sam to stand up. Sam did as he was told and found the captain staring into his eyes, and then sniffing his breath. Once again he studied Sam in silence. Then he said "Want to go to sea, no questions asked?"

"Yus." replied Sam.

"We got a deal," said the captain, "shake on it." and Sam found his hand being gripped in the captain's powerful fist. "I'll have you aboard in no time at all. Just keep your mouth tight shut, OK?"

CHAPTER TWO
Mrs Bonnie is not Herself

Stubble found nothing to interest him at the bottom of the garden. Dr Pilbeam the pathologist had come, given his view that the bones had not been in the ground more than a couple of years at the most, snorted that he was only qualified to deal with flesh and blood, not disturbed skeletons, said he'd do what he could when they delivered what he called "the material" to his mortuary and taken himself off suggesting Stubble might like to get one of the bones carbon dated..

Stubble went back to the house and rang the university archaeology department. The lecturer who answered sounded rather keen to help him and rather let down when she heard what exactly he wanted. Their carbon dating kit was accurate only to the nearest ten years. She believed there might be some slightly more accurate equipment at Cambridge. Stubble thanked her and cursed Pilbeam and his weird sense of humour.

The conservatory turned out to be comfortably furnished with cushioned wicker chairs, which he reckoned would put people at their ease. He spread his lists over a table and asked Mrs Sedge to send in her residents in alphabetical order.

Twenty minutes later his head was going round. He had only seen two old ladies. Mrs Adams seemed to think he was a government official trying to take her pension away, and Mrs Arthur had regressed to her youth which by her account had been somewhat busy. He told her several times that that would do, but Mrs Arthur persisted in going into pornographic detail. When she went on to suggest he accompanied her upstairs to her room for some slap and tickle, as she put it, he had to ask Mrs Sedge, who had taken it upon herself to sit in on the interviews to see fair play, to take her away.

"Who's next?" he asked, consulting the list Mrs Sedge had given him. "Mrs Bonnie. Let's have a word with Mrs Bonnie?"

Mrs Sedge went away and came right back. "She's not down in the Lounge. I'll go up to her room and see if she's awake. You won't want to wake her up yourself, will you?"

"Certainly not." agreed Stubble, wondering why Mrs Sedge would even think he would.

Mrs Sedge took herself upstairs and went along to Mrs Bonnie's room. It was locked.

"That's funny," she said out loud to herself. They can't lock themselves in from the inside and in any case fire regulations forbid these doors to be locked. The lock must be faulty. As if I haven't got enough on my hands just now. Thank goodness Matron gets back tonight. I suppose she does have to go to a family funeral, even if I can't spare her."

While she was talking to herself she was selecting the master key from the ring she carried at her belt. The lock was not faulty; the wards slid back easily and the door opened with no trouble at all. Inside Mrs Bonnie was sitting in her wheelchair looking out of the window.

"I'll have to have a word with those girls about locking guests in without my say-so," Mrs Sedge said, still talking to herself, "come on Mrs Bonnie. I've got a nice policeman downstairs wants a chat with you."

"What?" said the old lady.

"A policeman!" shouted Mrs Sedge. She didn't remember Mrs Bonnie being deaf. It seemed her hearing had deteriorated.

When they got downstairs Mrs Sedge introduced Mrs Bonnie and warned Stubble he would have to speak up because she was rather deaf.

"Deaf? Who says I'm deaf?" said the old lady

"Good afternoon Mrs Bonnie!" said Stubble in a louder than usual voice.

"No need to shout!" she said "I'm not deaf. I'm not Bonnie either!"

Bonnie is not what I would call you myself, Stubble thought, looking at the wizened old woman. She seemed to be getting terribly agitated. Was he wasting his time talking to all these daft old women?

"Just a couple of questions, Mrs Bonnie," he started.

She did not let him finish. "Are you stone deaf, young man?" she shouted. "I keep telling you I'm not Mrs Bonnie.

Stubble looked across to Mrs Sedge who spread her hands in mystification and said "If you're not Mrs Bonnie, dear, then who are you?"

No doubt Mrs Bonnie would now announce she was the Queen of Sheba or Joan of Arc. He supposed it was not uncommon for feeble-minded old people to have that sort of delusion. This one didn't. She said indignantly "I'm Millie Borland. Always have been. Always will be. I can't understand why everyone in this place has suddenly started calling me Mrs Bonnie. Get it into your head – the name's Borland, Mrs Millie Borland."

Stubble ran his finger down the list in front of him. No sign of the name Borland on it. He looked across to Mrs Sedge again. The expression on her face told him all he needed to know. She was even more astonished and puzzled than he was. Wimpole materialised out of nowhere and put his hand on Mrs Sedge's shoulder. He whispered something in her ear. Stubble did not need to lip-read to know what it was. He might as well have held up a placard saying "keep your mouth shut. I'll do the talking!"

"You seem to have a resident you don't know about," Stubble remarked mildly.

Wimpole said "Would you mind if I had a word with my client in private?" Stubble motioned them out of the room. If this was Mrs Borland, then what had happened to Mrs Bonnie? Stubble got up and looked out of the window. The tent was now up. The sun was setting. The Scene of Crime team seemed to have packed their bags and gone home. A lone constable was standing guard over the grave.

Could those bones out there belong to Mrs Bonnie?

The train rumbled over a bridge. Matron sipped her coffee and checked her watch; she'd be back at The Poplars well before midnight at this rate. No point in arriving too early. She would stop somewhere and have a meal, a couple of drinks maybe, before she went back. Dinner yes, drinks no. She was going to need to have all her wits about her.

She fished in her handbag for her bank statement and looked lovingly at the balance yet again. Who would have thought a year ago that she'd have so much money? She folded the statement, put it back and drew out her airline ticket to New York and back. She'd had to buy a return ticket to get into the USA, but once she was there she was sure she'd have no trouble getting a green card. Nurses were in great demand everywhere in the world.

Matron was going to make a new start, in a country where no-one had ever heard of her.

The *Largesse* slid slowly down the Bristol Channel, the lights of North Devon to port and the brighter ones of South Wales to starboard.

In the crew's mess Sam finished his plateful of corned beef hash. "More?" enquired the cook who was sitting opposite him drinking a mug of coffee.

Sam declined the offer; he had already polished off two helpings, and addressed himself to his own coffee.

"Hope you like corned beef hash," remarked the cook.

"Love it." said Sam. "Food's OK on this boat."

"Bit of luck you liking hash," said the cook. He could see Sam hadn't caught on. "Because you'll be getting it day in day out." he felt obliged to make sure his new mate had got the message.

Sam didn't react. "Any idea where we're going?" he asked.

"We say 'headed' the cook told him. Ships don't go any place, they get headed, see?"

Sam nodded.

"I can see this is your first trip. You're a landsman. Sticks out a mile. Well, my friend that is a question you just don't ask. Not on this ship. You don't bother yourself about what sort of cargo we've got below decks neither, and if you happen to notice it don't tally with any bills of lading or manifests, assuming there are any, well friend, you'd best keep your eyes shut as well as your mouth. Last guy who asked too many questions went for a swim.

"Doesn't worry me," Sam told him. "I wouldn't do that. I can't swim, see."

"Oh dearie dearie me!" said the cook, picking up Sam"s plate and disappearing into his galley.

Stubble heard the door open. Mrs Sedge and her solicitor had come back. Right away Wimpole got down to work. "My client does not, you understand, concern herself intimately with the day to day running of the home. She does not know every resident personally. There seems to have been some sort of administrative mix-up."

Stubble looked over at Mrs Borland who was muttering to herself, and agreed. "Happens in the best of families; I am sure you will be able to sort it out quite easily. All you have to do is discover how Mrs Borland comes to be here and what has happened to Mrs Bonnie. Then let me know." He turned and looked out of the window at the grave again. It should be easy enough to establish whether it was Mrs Bonnie down there in the garden by reference to her dental records. But of course the skull was not with the rest of the body. It was in the cellar.

He looked at his watch and decided he had had enough for one day. "I don't think I need keep any of you any longer. I'm sure this lady" he indicated Mrs Borland, "would like to go back to her room, and I need my supper, as I imagine you do. I'll see you in the morning."

Wimpole and Mrs Sedge breathed a joint sigh of relief. He gathered up his papers, put them in his brief case and made for the door. Then he turned and said "Oh, before I go I'll need key to the cellar. That's where the skull is, isn't it?"

They stiffened. Mrs Sedge asked "Will you need us to come down there with you? I hate it down there."

"Don't worry, dear, I'll go with the officer." said Wimpole.

"Dear" was it then? Stubble made a mental note. He said "By all means, Mr Wimpole. You may be able to help"

Stubble went out to his car to get a large plastic evidence bag and returned to the house. Wimpole led him down to the cellar. Stubble put his pen through one of the skull's eye sockets, deftly dropped it into the bag and sealed it. "Nice to have a solicitor watch me do that," he remarked brightly, "it means there's no chance anyone will accuse me of switching skulls when we get to court."

Wimpole merely grunted.

The taxi dropped Matron at The Poplars just after ten o'clock. She was surprised to find Mrs Sedge manning the reception desk.

"Ah Matron," she said. "I'm so glad you're back. We've had the most terrible day." Matron made sympathetic noises wondering what had been so terrible. "Sam dug up a body in the garden yesterday morning and we've had the police here ever since. The idiot brought the skull into the kitchen, it was awful, one of the Guests started playing football with it and then Sam took it down to his cellar and sat there holding it until the police arrived."

Matron felt the blood rising to her face. She got a tissue out of her handbag and blew her nose, then said "How dreadful!"

But Mrs Sedge had not finished "But that's not the half of it. It seems Mrs Bonnie isn't Mrs Bonnie, but an imposter. The police are talking to everyone, of course, and when I went to get Mrs Bonnie her room was locked and there was this woman inside who said she was called Mrs Borland. Naturally the police are suspicious."

Matron felt icy claws probing her heart. She forced herself to keep calm and control her panic.

"I don't suppose Mrs Bonnie could have started to call herself Borland?" Mrs Sedge theorised. "Do we have her maiden name anywhere in her records? Perhaps she has started to revert to her youth or something."

"Could be." said Matron feeling like a hunted animal, "Old people do sometimes do that sort of thing."

"Well, you have a talk to her in the morning. Perhaps you can throw some light on the mystery. Oh, I'm so glad you're back, I can't tell you. What with running the home and dealing with the police all on my own, I'm quite exhausted."

On that Matron could agree with her. "Me too. Travelling does not agree with me. I'm ready for bed."

"Off you go then. It's going to be a long day tomorrow."

"Too right," thought Matron. She said aloud "Good night then," turned on her heel and went to her room before Mrs Sedge could say any more.

Mrs Sedge spent a sleepless night worrying. About who had put the body in the grave in the garden, about possibly having another murderer besides herself at The Poplars. About who this woman in Mrs Bonnie's room was and where had she come from. About why the room was locked. Then there was Stubble. Once a detective started sniffing around who knows what he might uncover?

She need not have worried about Stubble, who had gone off at a tangent and was not going to appear until after lunch. He too had woken up in the middle of the night and not been able to get back to sleep. Turning the case over in his mind he had suddenly had an idea. He got up and got out the telephone book. There were only three Borlands in the book. He went back to bed and dropped into a deep dreamless sleep.

In the morning he dialled the three numbers. As might be expected the last one was the right one. Lucy Borland picked up the phone. "Mrs Millie Borland? She's my mother-in-law .....Yes, she's in The Poplars; she's very happy there.....The Police? Is anything wrong?"

Stubble reassured her and arranged to see her at work that morning. It turned out she had got a job at the garage where he got his car serviced. When he got there he recognised her immediately. She took him to their small canteen and made him a cup of coffee. He apologised for taking her away from her work.

"They can spare me for a few minutes," she said. "I hope this is not going to take too long."

"Me too. We're both busy people." he noticed she was avoiding his eyes. Nearly everyone involved in this case seemed to do that. No doubt she was wondering what she had done wrong.

Suddenly she turned and faced him, like an animal at bay. She said "Now, what is this all about?"

He asked. "Does the name "Bonnie" mean anything to you?"

"Not a thing." .

The Poplars have your mother down on their books as Mrs Bonnie, Mrs Wilhelmina Bonnie."

"Wilhelmina, what a funny name."

"It's Dutch, or German. No Dutch or German connections in your family?"

"No, why?"

"It was quite popular years ago. I just wondered if Bonnie might have been her maiden name, or whether your mother had any close connections with the name, because that is what the people at the home are calling her."

"I don't understand."

"Nor do I." Stubble reached for the sugar. "I thought you might be able to give me a clue."

"Sorry, I can't help you."

"Just a couple more questions and then I'll be off." He could almost feel her relief. "When did she go into The Poplars?"

"About eighteen months ago. We were pretty desperate, I can tell you. We thought there would be quite a wait to get her into a place like that, and we had money problems at the time, but she went in almost immediately. It seemed someone had just died on the day we got in touch with them, so they had a room vacant. Mother went in the same day. I suppose the dearer places have shorter waiting lists. They were very accommodating about the payments too. We were very pleasantly surprised."

Stubble pricked his ears up. "How much does it cost a week?" he asked.

"You'd have to ask my husband – he pays all the bills."

"What time does he get back from work?"

"He gets in rather late as a rule. About seven o'clock. He does a lot of coaching after school. He has to, to help pay mother's care."

Stubble asked her if he could come round to their house that evening, and took himself off with a distinct feeling that he had made progress, although in which direction he could not be sure.

His next stop was the dentist. He stood in the waiting room watching the fishes. Why did dentists always have aquaria in their waiting rooms? Did they think it calmed the customers, or was there some mystical affinity between teeth and fish?

"You might as well sit down," said the receptionist." He'll be a little while; he's in the middle of a wisdom."

"Middle of a wisdom?"

"Tooth. They're the devil to get out. The patient is booked in for half an hour, but he's been in there already for three quarters."

There was crash from the surgery. The receptionist hurried inside but came out a moment later smiling. "It's out. Came out so suddenly Mr Graveney overbalanced and hit his head on the instrument trolley. Everything's all over the floor. The autoclave will be working overtime. We've just got to stop the bleeding and tidy Mr Lett's mouth up a bit and then Mr Graveney will be with you.

Stubble nodded. Somehow he did not feel like opening his mouth. A dull ache started up somewhere around his upper right molars. He sat down and tried to interest himself in an old Good Housekeeping, not very successfully.

Eventually a man emerged, looking calm and undamaged. Stubble assumed he was the dentist until he sat down and suddenly looking queasy, wrote out a cheque which he handed to Stubble before he took himself off keeping his mouth tight closed. Stubble glanced at the cheque and asked himself why he had not gone into dentistry.

Mr Graveney the dentist staggered out a moment later followed by his nurse. Blood was pouring down his face.

She sat him down and soothed his ego while cleaning up his face

"Don't know why you didn't come straight to us," the dentist told Stubble once the nurse had pronounced him out of danger and he had accepted the cheque. We handle nearly all the old people's homes round here. The residents can keep their own dentists, of course, but a lot of them are in no condition to say who they want. Mostly plate work, of course. By the time you are old enough to get into one of those places you haven't got many of your own teeth left, which is why I recognised the dentition immediately. It must be Mrs Bonnie. She has all four opposing original front incisors. Very rare in someone as old as she is.

"Was." Stubble did not trouble to wrap it up.

"Oh dear, she was such a nice old lady." the dentist went on. "Very placid temperament."

Stubble reflected that her temperament at the moment was as placid as you can get. He said "You're sure?"

"As sure as I can be from what you've just shown me. How did she die?"

"We don't know that yet."

"Convey my sympathy to the family, won't you, although I seem to remember her telling me she didn't have any relatives left. When's the funeral? I might go; she was the sort of patient you remember, we got quite friendly."

"I'll let you know," said Stubble, wondering if he ought to make an appointment to have his own teeth checked out. "Thanks for all your help. One of my officers will come round and take a formal statement for the record."

He drove straight to The Poplars where he asked to see the accounts; he wanted to check whether Mrs Bonnie or Mrs Borland, or perhaps both of them, were paying to be resident at the home.

Mrs Sedge demurred. "I don't think you should look at the accounts without Mr Wimpole's say so," she said.

"Get him on the phone," said Stubble tersely. The Sedge and Wimpole partnership was beginning to get on his nerves.

Mr Wimpole had no objection to his checking the accounts, provided Mrs Sedge was present and that was all he was looking for. Wimpole knew that any attempt to stop Stubble or delay him would look very odd in court.

He soon found what he was looking for. Mrs Bonnie was partly funded by the local authority and partly by a small annuity. Both payments were bang up to date. On paper Mrs Bonnie was still quite alive. There was no mention of a Mrs Borland. As far as the home's accounts were concerned she did not exist.

"So Mrs Bonnie is Mrs Bonnie," remarked Mrs Sedge, even if she does think she's someone else. "Old people sometimes come out with the strangest things. I wonder where she got the name of Borland from?"

Stubble said nothing. There no need for Mrs Sedge to know he knew the answer to that question.

She in turn didn't think there was any need for Stubble to know, since he hadn't asked, that Matron had come back.

After a solitary dinner at the Star of Bengal, Stubble drove to the Borlands' semi on the outskirts of the city. Their house was newly painted with a carefully tended front garden. The sight of it depressed him. Everyone seemed to have a cosy settled existence except Eric Stubble.

The Borlands were waiting for him, with the best tea service on a trolley and a freshly baked cake on what looked like an antique cake stand but was probably repro.

"It's about your mother, Mr Borland," Stubble started when he had got the cake, one of the stickier sort, out of the way.

"What's she done?" asked Borland facetiously.

"Drunk in charge of a wheelchair," said Stubble hoping to put the man at his ease. A joke, however weak, often helped bring out facts that otherwise lay hidden.

Borland played up. "She hasn't got a licence, or insurance, either."

Stubble leaned forward. "I want to check the payments for her care."

"I pay them every Sunday afternoon. Give Matron the money as arranged. She says we are one of their promptest payers."

"Do you keep their bills?" asked Stubble, knowing the answer in advance.

He was right. Borland said: "They didn't send any. They said there was no need since I had already paid."

"You have the cheque book stubs, or your bank statements?" asked Stubble.

Borland frowned. "What is this? I thought you said you were from the police."

Stubble reassured him. I'm nothing to do with the Inland Revenue, if that's what you're thinking. I take it from your reaction to my question that you paid Matron in cash?"

"Drew it out of the cash machine every Sunday on the way to The Poplars. I've made a special arrangement - it's above the bank's daily limit." He went to a drawer and drew out a file of bank statements. "See, once a week."

Stubble cast his eyes over the statements for form's sake and handed the file back. "When do you expect to see your mother next?" he asked Cameron Borland.

"We go every Sunday afternoon."

"Could you come to The Poplars right now?"

"To see my mother? She'll be asleep most likely."

"Doesn't matter. I just want to make sure she is your mother; there seems to be some sort of mix-up in their records and it's getting in the way of our investigations."

Mr Borland looked up. "Investigations?"

Stubble hesitated for a moment. Was there any reason not to reveal what he was looking into? "It's a missing person enquiry. One of the old ladies has gone AWOL and there seems to be some confusion as to which one."

"Only too pleased to help. I'll get my coat on."

At The Poplars they went straight to Mrs Borland's room. The old lady was in bed but not asleep; there was a night light by her bedside. Cameron went straight up and kissed his mother.

"You're very late, son," Mrs Borland complained.

"That's all I need to know. Thank you" Stubble said softly. "I won't stay. " He closed the door quietly as he left.

Mrs Sedge put the phone down. Her hand was trembling. She grabbed hold of it with the other one to stop it shaking.

"Bastards!" she shouted to the empty room "Shit!" she yelled, "Fucking scumbags!" she howled.

That was the third such call she had had that day. No bloody confidence, no trust in other people. That was what was wrong with the world today. Everyone assumed the worst at the slightest whiff of suspicion. No smoke without fire, they said, and took their relative off the waiting list. Just like that! They didn't want to hear her side of the case. Oh no! They assumed that just because a body had been found in the garden, something that could happen to anyone, she was doing away with her guests.

Who knows how it came to get there? Could have been dumped over the wall, might have been there for years and years, before she bought the place. Maybe it had been murdered by someone who had a grudge against her, so they could bury their victim in her garden.

She poured herself another glass of brandy. How did they think she could make a living running this place, if she kept knocking off her customers? She needed their money. Didn't anyone understand that? In a moment of honesty she remembered she had actually killed a couple of them. Well, she hadn't actually killed them, just helped them on their way into the next world. She filled her glass again and inspected the bottle. It was nearly empty; one of the staff must have been at the brandy. She'd have to mark the bottle before she went to bed.

She looked at the clock. No point in phoning Wimpole at this time of night. She was beginning to have her doubts about his usefulness as a solicitor anyhow. All right for run of the mill stuff, but when the going got tough he didn't seem to have too many answers. She should never have gone to bed with him, but she was flesh and blood, wasn't she? As far as his performance went he wasn't exactly Casanova. Not by a long way. Maybe something to do with his professional ethics? Perhaps a solicitor is like a doctor, not allowed to have sex with his clients. Bit of a turn off, thinking about that while you're doing it.

Funny, her glass was empty. She didn't remember drinking anything. Stupid bloody glass. Something else didn't know what it was doing. She picked it up ready to throw it at the wall. Serve it right. Better not. Nowhere to put me brandy if I smash it. Fill it up instead. Nice glass. Glass not meant to be empty.

Oh buggeration. Now the fucking bottle's empty. Everything's empty. Everything in the whole world. Empty. Better phone Wimpole after all. Need advice. Lots of advice. He knows all about empty. No...... let's have a little nap first.

Stubble was lying in bed watching television with half an eye. He could afford to relax a little, now he knew for certain that the body in the garden was Mrs Bonnie and the one in the bedroom Mrs Borland. It was just a matter of finding out how she came to be dead, which Pilbeam and his boffins would do, and who put her there, which would be down to him.

Had Mrs Sedge killed her? All those deaths in one week last year pointed in her direction. Maybe The Poplars worked on the basis of a quick turnover. Was she getting them to leave their money to her and then doing them in? Such things had been known to happen in the best of families.

Was Mrs Sedge on the resurrection game? Keep the dead alive on paper and go on taking their pension and any subsidy the local authority pays to look after them? Could be murder, could merely be fraud. He was betting on fraud.

Of course it was only a hunch, but hunches were what he was good at. His bloodhound nose had sniffed him to Detective Inspector rank.

If that was the case, then the next question was how many old people Mrs Sedge was managing to keep alive as far as the home's books were concerned while their mortal remains mouldered in their graves.

It might mean digging up the grounds of the Poplars, and any other likely spots where she might have hidden her clients. There could be dozens. Hundreds. That Wimpole, funny old character; Stubble's nose said he was implicated in some way. When they mixed the bodies up at the crematorium last year, was that a simple mistake? Maybe not. Worth having a sniff around there too.

Stubble drifted off to sleep. His faithful nose snored happily. It looked as if it was going to score again.

The television wondered why it bothered.

CHAPTER THREE
Wimpole is woken up

"Come over, I need you!" Mrs Sedge sounded urgent. Wimpole sensed a touch of panic in her voice.

"But it's past midnight. I was in bed asleep."

"Are you telling me you're only interested in me during working hours?"

"Oh, I thought you were calling in my professional capacity."

"Silly boy!"

Wimpole's feet were cold. He was still half asleep. He had stubbed his toe getting to the telephone. This was not the sort of thing he had in mind when they had started their relationship. Sex in the office or in bed after a pleasant evening together was one thing. Being yanked out of said bed in the middle of the night by a woman panting for sex was something else.

"Can't it wait until tomorrow?" His feet were freezing. Why hadn't he put his slippers on?

"It won't be the same then. You're not going off me, are you?"

"Of course not." Liar. He had been celibate from the time he got divorced until Mrs Sedge came along and he was beginning to wish he still was.

"Well, are you coming over or not?"

"I've got a headache. I think I've had too much to drink." He desperately dredged up excuses.

"It's the woman's job to have the headaches."

He really did not want to have to get dressed and drive out to The Poplars. This was not turning out to be the discreet affair he had planned at all. He'd have to find a way to get out of this situation. Even if it did mean losing a client. He had been a fool mixing business with pleasure.

And then his hormones took charge.

"Give me twenty minutes. Can you wait that long?"

"For you, I'll wait all night." She laughed. He forced himself to laugh back.

He really must get a telephone installed upstairs in the bedroom, he told himself as he plodded up the stairs.

It took him more than twenty minutes for him to dress, put his teeth in, find his car keys and drive to The Poplars. When he got there the place was in darkness. He was just wondering if he was in the middle of a dream when the door opened and Mrs Sedge's finger beckoned him inside. There was just enough light inside the house for him to see her putting her finger to her lips as she led him upstairs on tiptoe. He followed, his heart racing in anticipation of the delights awaiting him once they were safely behind the locked door of her flat. There was life in the old dog yet.

He had thought she would drag him into straight to her bedroom, so when she pushed him into an armchair his mind started to explore exceptional delights. She went to the drinks cabinet and poured him a stiff whisky, saying "You'll need this."

He was not so sure. He had had a couple just before going to bed which perhaps was why he had this headache, which seemed to be getting worse. He was also wishing he had pulled on a different pair of trousers. These were much too tight. He tried to wriggle into a more comfortable position and in doing so managed to spill some of the whisky onto his fly.

He put the glass down and stood up. That was a little more comfortable.

Mrs Sedge was standing not too far away, also holding a glass. He moved towards her. She backed away and said "You'll feel like sitting down when you hear what I'm going to tell you. Drink up! You'll need that too. I need your help."

Suddenly his trousers were not tight after all. He lowered his gangly frame onto the arm of the chair, and sipped his drink. He glanced at his watch and realised he had not put it on. There was a clock on the mantelpiece, and he made a mental note: Consultation commencing at 1.20 a.m. He was damned if he was going to work the night shift without charging at least double time.

She said "I had three cancellations today."

"Three cancellations?"

"Three people phoned and asked us to take their relatives off the waiting list."

"Why?"

So this was Wimpole, her astute lawyer. "Because of the body. It's going to be in the paper tomorrow, but the word's getting round already Would you want your mother in an old people's home where they dig up bodies in the garden?"

"Only one body, and there's no proof it's got anything to do with you."

"I know. But that's not what they're saying. One of the cancellers actually used the word corpse. They're talking mass murder out there. God knows what's going to be in the paper tomorrow."

Wimpole racked his brain. This was something completely outside his experience. He was only a humdrum country solicitor, after all. He heard Mrs Sedge plead "what should I do?"

"Do? Refute the rumours. I'll get an injunction first thing in the morning to stop them publishing." As he said it he realised he could not. No judge would stop a newspaper publishing the fact that the police were investigating a body found in a shallow grave in someone's garden, and no paper would be fool enough to so much as speculate who had put it there. There was nothing he could do, but he had a pretty good idea Mrs Sedge was not going to take that for an answer.

"How do I refute the rumours?" she asked.

"Issue a press release saying you have no idea how it came to be there. You say your gardener found it. Perhaps some word from him. Come on, I'll help you draft it and I'll drop it into the Sentinel office on my way home."

Home. How he longed to be there. He said "Get your gardener. He may be able to throw some light on this affair."

"He'll be asleep."

"Wake him up." he was beginning to lose patience with Mrs Sedge.

She went off to get Sam. Wimpole sat there wondering if he could slip away while she was gone and then realised that would not do him any good. She knew where he lived. He turned ideas for the press release over in his head without coming up with anything very convincing.

She burst into the room. "He's gone. He's not there. Sam's vanished!"

Even worse. The world would quickly jump to the conclusion this Sam character was underneath his own cabbage patch. He composed a lame press release suggesting that the body found at The Poplars could have been buried over a hundred years ago and ten minutes later was back in his nice warm car and heading for his nice warm bed. Delivering the press release could wait until morning. The Sentinel didn't come out until after lunch. After a decent night's sleep he might think up something better.

Stubble normally breakfasted on a mug of instant and a bowl of cereal, but today felt like something more substantial. He took himself off to Greg's Café and treated himself to their Full English breakfast complete with extra toast, and several cups of coffee. Feeling thoroughly benign he drove to County Police Headquarters.

Even finding the car park full of the cars belonging to admin staff who never moved from their desks, leaving no room for an honest detective who needed his car at a moment's notice, did not dispel his good mood. He bounded up the stairs to his office on the fourth floor two steps at a time, to the amazement of file-carrying civilian staff waiting for the lift, and strode into his office. He flung the window open and called a cheery good morning to the miserable horse, who ignored him as usual, and sat down and went through the pile of paper which had accumulated on his desk overnight.

Most of it was copies of memos that the clerks on the floors below had diligently distributed to all and sundry to make sure no-one could complain they had not been told what was going on. Underneath the pile of bumph he came to what he was waiting for.

Dr Pilbeam had been, for once, concise and to the point.

The skeleton had been in its shallow grave for a maximum of two years, most probably less. He was not able to state cause of death due to the condition of the body resultant on its being buried uncoffined very close to the surface which had resulted in an accelerated decomposition but he could discern no signs of violence, nor traces of suspicious substances. He would hazard a guess, and only a guess, that death could have been due to any number of possible causes associated with the advanced age of the subject as evidenced by the condition of the bone tissue which showed distinct signs of advanced osteoporosis. The deceased appeared to have been a female between eighty-five and ninety-five years old. In the absence of any other evidence he had to conclude the deceased had very possibly died of a problem associated with advanced senility.

Stubble translated: No violence, no poison. Mrs Bonnie had most likely died of old age, which tallied with his own opinion. The question now was what had Mrs Sedge, and possibly Mr Wimpole, been up to.

There was no point in checking their bank balances, although he would, for form's sake. That brace of vultures would surely have salted away their profits in nominee holdings somewhere. The lists of residents would be useful, but who was to say Mrs Sedge had not been taking in residents for cash, no questions asked and nothing in writing. Mr Borland paying cash to Matron every week pointed in that direction. He didn't know much about the economics of ageing but somewhere he had heard that old people had to pay for their care until they only had a little money left, when the Council took over. Perhaps Mrs Sedge was in the habit of keeping them until their money ran out and the local authority took over when she bumped them off without bothering to notify anyone. The local council could go on paying for dead pensioners for ever, in theory.

If the people at City Hall were as competent and vigilant as the ones on the floors below him at County Police HQ, they'd never notice the overpopulation at the Poplars. Such people were simply not programmed to see the wood for the trees. Not their job.

No. Wimpole and Sedge would not take that risk. They were much too cunning. They most likely kept the dead alive for a while, say a year, and then let City Hall know the old person had died, having taken an extra year's cash.

Stubble pondered his next move. He could go on trying to get something out of Sedge and Wimpole, or he could dig up the garden. Digging up the garden would mean going to the Chief Constable who would need to be convinced there was murder involved before authorising the expense, and on the basis of Pilbeam's report there was no murder.

He went over to the window and stared at the miserable horse for some time. Then he called the Chief's secretary. The Chief would be able to give him a few minutes right away as long as he was brief, since he was off to a rotary club lunch.

Stubble did not take up much of his boss's time. When he came back to his own office he had the satisfied look on his face of a man who has got exactly what he wanted.

Sam leaned over the rail of the good ship *Largesse* and wished he had never been born. It was the first time he had been to sea. His only knowledge of it was from films where ships sailed across calm blue seas while their passengers had fun above and below decks. It was lies, all lies. The reality was a lot of greenish water which was anything but calm, a freezing cold wind, the ship moving up and down all the time and his stomach heaving, even though all he had ever eaten in his whole life must by now have come out of it.

He became conscious of someone standing behind him. He turned and saw it was a black man, well over six feet tall and broad to match. If the gods were kind he had come to throw Sam over the rail and end his misery.

No such luck. "Not to worry, friend," said the man. "Nelson always felt like that first couple of days at sea. You'll get over it, but I think you'd be better off in your bunk below."

Before Sam could protest he was picked up like a baby. "Name's Joshua Benin," said his carrier. "Joshua I was baptised and Benin is where I was born."

"Sam" Sam managed to get out before another bout of retching.

"Are you saved? That's the big question." said Joshua.

Sam groaned. He wasn't saved – he was lost.

"Soon as you feel better you and I are going to have the greatest pleasure men can have together."

Sam was in no condition to protest he wasn't that sort of bloke. Then he heard Joshua explain "You and me are going to read the Good Book together. My friend Samuel, your New Life starts this minute. I just know you want to put all that sinning and hatred behind you." He deposited Sam gently on his bunk and covered him with a blanket. "Just you lie there and let the good Lord take you in His arms."

Sam closed his eyes in despair. If the Good Lord was holding him why couldn't He keep still? When he opened them again Joshua had gone. He closed his eyes and drifted off into troubled dreams in which grinning skeletons rose unbidden from the ground.

Stubble opened his notebook in an officious sort of way. "I need to interview your staff. Will it be inconvenient if I take them in alphabetical order? I shouldn't need anyone for more than a few minutes."

Mrs Sedge said: "We are very busy, you know."

"I quite understand, but it's got to be done. Now, if you could get, who's first? Phyllis Andrews, can you get her down here, and when I've finished with her she can fetch the next on the list, so I won't have to bother you again."

Mrs Sedge went off to get Phyllis Andrews and warn her to keep her mouth shut. As she went up in the lift she remembered she had not mentioned Sam's disappearance to Stubble. "Never mind," she told herself. He's a policeman – it's his job to find out things like that."

As he sat waiting for Phyllis Andrews to appear Stubble heard the sound of a helicopter hovering over The Poplars.

The Chief had moved quickly. The infra-red photos they were taking would soon reveal all recently disturbed soil, it might even display traces of any body buried in the garden. Assuming there were any other bodies, that is.

If the helicopter's camera revealed anything there would be no need to waste police time digging. This Sam character could do it.

Augustus Wimpole put the tips of his fingers together and stared at them. He was in a hole. There must be a way out. His first instinct had been to ask Mrs Sedge to take her business elsewhere. He could tell her it was to put the police off their track.

No good. If anything it would attract attention to him. Of course they did not have to know that his firm had stopped working for her, well….. they would not find out for a while. When they did he could explain that he suspected something at The Poplars was not as it should be and decided to put clear blue water between his practice and the retirement home.

It wouldn't wash. They would start going over everything with a fine tooth comb. Best to go on acting the simple solicitor who had his vague suspicions but no evidence, not enough to go on. He might even tell them he was waiting until he had enough solid facts to go to the police with.

And then there was Mrs Sedge. There was no fury like a woman scorned, and if she thought he was backing out of their relationship, who knew what she might do? If only he had kept her at arm's length. He had been tempted and he had fallen. He would have been better off going to a brothel. He had heard whispers that there was a high class establishment in Dununder. As it was he had done the ultimate unethical act and screwed a client.

It hadn't been all that wonderful either. He had thought it might be better with an older woman, one who knew a trick or two, but to be honest it had not been worth it. It had been just like doing it with his wife. Nothing like the mind-blowing experience the books he kept in the locked drawer in his desk said it should be.

An awful thought crossed his mind. She might be pregnant. Surely not. She was too old. Could the police tell he had been having relations with his client? DNA or something? Wimpole shivered.

How to put them off his scent and on to hers. That was the question.

He suddenly realised the telephone had been ringing for some time. He answered it. It was secretary announcing his eleven o'clock appointment.

"Send him in."

Act normally. Carry on as usual. It was all he could do.

"Tina Watkins, she's the last," Stubble said out loud to the empty room as Tina, a plump rosy-cheeked kitchen assistant closed the door behind her.

It had to be done, but interviewing the staff had thrown up nothing new. They all said much the same. Old people came and went; they just cared for them, fed them, washed them, took them to the toilet and befriended them. Eventually they died. That's what happened in old people's homes, didn't it? He asked each one if they had any reason to be suspicious. None. Were they present when any of the old people died? Occasionally they were.

Could they say which ones? He got varying answers to that question, nothing that struck him as being out of the ordinary.

There was only Sam left to question and Sam seemingly had done a runner. Stubble notified HQ, telling himself the system should not have too much trouble locating him, if Sam was the simple soul Mrs Sedge said he was.

Pity about Sam not being there. He'd rather been relying on him to dig up the grounds of The Poplars if the helicopter found anything worth looking into. With Sam absent some coppers would have to do the digging instead. The Chief would not like the effect on his budget and would be sure to give him a lecture about Managing Manpower Resources, as if Stubble had not read the book too.

He took himself off to the registrar just as he had done the previous year, and then to the crematorium, where again the pattern emerged that most old people from The Poplars got cremated very quickly. There hardly ever seemed to be any relatives at the funeral.

When he got back to his office there was a call from the helicopter cameraman. The prints would be along in the morning, but in the meantime Stubble should know that there was nothing unusual in the grounds of The Poplars except what appeared to be a Roman Road running straight under the house itself and traces of a small building, a cottage or something similar, beneath the drive. The only piece of ground recently disturbed was the grave site, which of course he already knew about.

He phoned his bank manager to ask if there was any way he could find out where The Poplars bank account was and had a piece of luck. The Poplars account was right there. Not only that, but the manager immediately suggested Mr Stubble would like to drop in to discuss his overdraft. Perhaps he could come over right away.

Stubble didn't have an overdraft. For a moment he wondered what the manager was talking about and then the penny dropped. He was discreetly helping the police with their enquiries. Stubble guessed there was something about The Poplars account which had aroused the manager's suspicions.

"I hope you don't mind me leaving you for a few minutes. One of the cashiers has got a little problem. I reckon it will take about a quarter of an hour to sort out. Perhaps you'd like to watch the TV while I'm gone," suggested the manager.

For a moment Stubble wondered what the man was talking about and then twigged that The Poplars account was visible on the computer monitor. He sat down and ran his eyes over it. There was nothing unusual on the page the manager had left open. Regular transfers into the account of the monthly residents' bills, and numerous payments out, no doubt for the upkeep of the home. He scrolled up to the previous month and then the month before that. Then he struck gold. A single sum of £104,000 had been paid in and the same amount paid out about a week later. There were several previous occasions when the same thing had happened.

When the manager came back Stubble asked him if he knew where that £104,000 had gone.

"We only have the cheque number and the amount, so I can't really help you, but I'd hazard a guess it went to Mrs Sedge's private account."

"Is that held here?"

"Sadly no. She has a small account for her personal expenses, but I would imagine she has an offshore account, or some other way of keeping funds out of the revenue's sight"

You mean there's something funny going on?"

"That's up to you to decide."

Stubble suspected the bank manager's readiness to break the rules only went so far, but he pressed on. He asked "Do you have any idea why those large sums came into the account in the first place."

He was right. The reply was not terribly helpful. "No idea. We just take the money in and pay it out. It's just figures to us, not money as you people on the outside see it. We do try to keep an eye on what's going on, though, especially when large sums are involved. I remember all the transactions were payments by individuals, as opposed to corporate clients. My guess is that they could be lump sums from residents. I asked myself could they be gifts "in appreciation of wonderful care." Old people can be manipulated, you know."

Stubble nodded. "If they were gifts, though, they would not all be for the same amount, would they?"

"True," said the manager. "We check the signature carefully on any cheque for more than ten K. It's routine. These were always in order."

Stubble asked "Don't you have to report large movements to the treasury or something?"

"Since the beginning of the year, yes."

"And there have been no big sums coming in since that date? Would I be right?"

"You would. I imagine that if she has been getting any large payments they have gone straight out of the country."

"How would she do that?"

"Get paid in cash and take it abroad in a suitcase. Fly somewhere like Zurich and pay it in there, or if she gets a cheque, send it to an agent in a tax haven, like the Cayman Islands. He'll make all the arrangements to make sure it isn't traced back to her, for a price of course. There are all sorts of ways of laundering money, illegal of course, but you'd be surprised how many people, and what sort of people, indulge in it."

"Which means whoever paid her had to go to their bank and draw out over a hundred thousand pounds. Doesn't that look suspicious?"

"Of course. But proof of nothing."

After a half-hearted attempt by the manager to sell him life assurance Stubble left the bank feeling like a man whose overdraft has been written off. He felt he was making progress at last.

His euphoria was short-lived. When he got back to police HQ it was pouring with rain. The car park was full and someone had parked in his clearly marked space so he had to put his car in the pay and display car park round the corner. He looked round to grab his raincoat off the back seat to go to get his ticket, and saw it in his mind's eye hanging from its hook on the back of his office door.

It was a saturated Stubble who found a note on his desk telling him the Chief Constable wanted to see him at 0900 the next morning

The Chief Constable was positively avuncular. "Come in Eric, come in. Sit you down. Cup of coffee?" He brandished a coffee pot. "One of the privileges of rank - not having to drink the ghastly stuff that comes out of those machines."

Stubble was immediately on his guard. When the Chief put on the 'we're all mates here' act it usually preceded some sort of roasting. He was much less dangerous when he was in one of his incisive, efficient man-on-top-of-his-job moods. Stubble asked himself yet again what he had been summoned for; it certainly was not to discuss coffee. He accepted a cup and awaited whatever rocket the Chief was about to fire at him. It was not long in coming.

The Chief smiled and said "The Compost Heap Corpse, as our friends in the press are calling it, how's it going?"

Stubble launched into a full account "We've established that the body was a Mrs Bonnie, a resident of The Poplars who died about a year to eighteen months ago of natural causes, as far as forensic can tell. I'm trying....."

The Chief suddenly interrupted him "I've had a complaint. Someone at the Rotary Club. They say you are harassing Mrs Sedge, the owner of the nursing home. If this Mrs Bonnie died naturally, isn't that the end of it? Why are you spending so much time on this case?"

So that was it. Hadn't he noticed a little Rotary badge on Augustus Wimpole's lapel? He protested "Hardly harassing her. I've been talking to the residents and staff, checking there are no more bodies buried in the grounds of The Poplars and trying to find out how the body came to be there. All routine stuff."

"Why?" The Chief wasn't usually this slow on the uptake.

Stubble told him. "Because Mrs Bonnie isn't dead."

The Chief took the opportunity to wax sarcastic. "If she isn't dead, why are her bones lying in the garden?"

Stubble explained patiently. "She's only dead in fact, not on paper. No death certificate; her annuity is still being paid and the local authority are still helping to pay for her care. The lady who Mrs Sedge says she thought was Mrs Bonnie, occupying her room, turns out to be a Mrs Borland."

"I see." said the Chief in a tone that implied he didn't.

Stubble wearily went back to the beginning. "Last year there were a series of deaths at The Poplars which aroused my suspicions. I investigated but didn't find anything concrete. There was something not quite right there but until this body turned up it I couldn't start a formal investigation."

"Been doing your usual poking around, have you, Stubble? Your famous nose at work again?"

Stubble smiled and refused to rise to the bait. "Yes sir. There seem to be various financial irregularities which I am following up."

"I don't like it," said the Chief. "You need help. This is a job for a team, not a lone wolf like you." Look at this. He handed over that afternoon's Dununder Sentinel and Guardian. The headline shouted COMPOST HEAP CORPSE, POLICE BAFFLED.

"Doesn't look good. What am I to tell them? Something along the lines of every available officer working on the case, or do you think 'one of my best men is poking around trying to find out what happened' sounds better?"

Good sign, Stubble reflected. In almost every case he'd handled the boss got itchy just before all the pieces fell into place. Every time he had had to stop him sending in a mob of hobnail-booted coppers to scare everyone concerned into a wall of silence.

He had an idea. He said. "There's been a development. The gardener who found the body has vanished."

It worked like a charm. The Chief grinned from ear to ear and poured more coffee into Stubble's cup as a reward. "So that's it. Just got to find him and the case is closed. That's what I like to hear!"

"He won't get far" Stubble almost blushed as he uttered the cliché. He was sure Sam would turn up; just as he was sure Sam had nothing to do with Mrs Bonnie's death and burial. The man simply wasn't bright enough. Most likely he'd been scared off by the sight of blue uniforms. But he had bought him, Stubble, time. Time to really find out what had been going on at The Poplars. The longer it took to find Sam the happier he would be.

But he wasn't listening to the Chief who was saying: "Jolly good, Stubble. Another result for the nose, eh! I'll tell the papers we have a suspect. The quicker they're shut up the better."

That sounded good. Let them think Sam did it and the real culprits would be off their guard. He grinned back at the Chief Constable and lied. "Just got a few loose ends to tie up once we catch him and that'll be that."

"Glad to hear it," said the Chief, picking up his phone to signal the meeting was at an end, "I'll make a note that you'll be back at your desk for some real police work on Monday."

Stubble wondered what it must be like to be the Chief, spending your days reading unreadable reports and worrying about manpower and budgets, as he went back to his desk, got out his thinking pad and made another list.

Four dead in one week last year.
More cremations than burials.
Always cremation if no relatives.

Mrs Bonnie under compost heap. Natural causes.
Why? By who buried?
Mrs Borland in Mrs Bonnie's place.
Suddenly room for Mrs Borland.
£500 a week. Cash.
Mrs Bonnie dead. Still paying fees?
Borland pays £500 weekly to matron. Goes to Sedge?
Big payments in and out of Poplars account. Why?
Wimpole. Shifty!
Sedge. Shifty!
Sedge - Wimpole. Connection?
Smells like fraud. Offshore payments. Fraud squad? ????
Where Sam the gardener?

Why had he kidded the boss the case was almost closed? He could walk away, he supposed. Mrs Bonnie dead of natural causes, Sam buried her in the garden because... why? Did he bury the old lady or was it someone else? Even Sam, simple soul that he was, would not confess to doing something he hadn't done when they caught up with him. The man was patently too honest. The whole Poplars thing stank and it was his job to clean it up. He stared at the list hoping for inspiration until it dissolved into a blur. Nothing came. Stubble was stuck.

He went down to the window and stood staring at the miserable horse. A light drizzle was falling and the horse had taken shelter under the tree, but it still looked very wet.

Stubble pondered what it must be like to be that horse. All it ever seemed to do was stand in the field. Surely someone must own it. Did it have a name? Eeyore, perhaps? Definitely an eeyorish sort of animal.

He was wasting time, worrying about a horse he did not even know. What did he care about its name?

Name! Something he had noticed but not really taken in. Matron. A woman with no name. Everyone called her Matron.

He must be getting tired. Of course the woman had a name. He pulled the list of staff out of his briefcase. Miss Juanita Standish. He had used it that very morning when he had asked the Strathclyde people to see if they could contact her. And then gone back to calling her Matron, just as Mrs Sedge and everyone at The Poplars did.

Two missing persons. Juanita Standish and Sam Clodd. And he had paid no attention to either of them. Persons who disappear in the middle of an investigation usually have something to hide. He had been too fixated on Sedge and Wimpole.

Feeling much more positive he fed their names into his computer. Nothing. Neither name appeared on that massive list of villains. There were six Standishes, but all were men, and no Clodds. There was an S. Clodde but his first name was Simon, several driving and taking away convictions. Could not be the same person since he was marked deceased the year before.

Stubble slumped into his chair. He seemed to be getting nowhere.

He forced himself to concentrate on Matron. Juanita Standish. Not many Juanitas about. Well, not here. In Spain maybe quite common. Should he notify the Spanish Police?

Was she Spanish? He had never met her, so had no way of telling. Mrs Sedge would know.

He picked up the phone yet again.

Mrs Sedge was relieved he was asking about Matron. The heat was off her, by the looks of it. Yes, of course she had references for Juanita Standish. Would he like to see them? She was about to say good-bye and put the phone down when she decided the best thing would be to come clean. Get Stubble on her side. He'd find out soon enough if he was sniffing around Matron.

She said "She had a past, you know..."

As she expected, he said he would be right over.

"You might have told us about Miss Standish before now," said Stubble as soon as he saw her. "It would have saved us a lot of trouble, and time."

Mrs Sedge poured out the tea. I didn't know you were interested in her," she said innocently.

Stubble thought of the list he had just been making. Shifty Sedge! "Show me the references and tell me all about the lady."

"For a start," began Mrs Sedge, "She's Mrs Standish. Her qualifications are in her maiden name of Robinson. I've no idea why she didn't trouble to get new certificates when she got married. That's what most people do."

"Not really a criminal offence. You said she had a past."

Mrs Sedge was not to be tempted to give him a straight answer. "A lot of girls use their maiden names for work. It's quite common. If they're known round the hospital as Nurse Smith, then they think it could be confusing if they suddenly turn into Nurse Brown. And of course these days a lot of people live together and don't bother to get married."

"What did she do wrong?" asked Stubble impatiently.

"She was at Addenbrookes. You've heard of it?"

Stubble confirmed that even policemen had heard of Cambridge's famous hospital.

"She was on the intensive care ward as a trainee."

"I thought you said she was Registered Nurse?" interrupted Stubble.

"Being registered is like a first degree. You have to be qualified for the specialities, like intensive care, theatre, pediatric, geriatric, psychiatric and so on to get promotion."

"I see. What did she do?" asked Stubble seeing Mrs Sedge about to go off on another tangent.

"Her boyfriend came in as a patient. She cut off his oxygen supply as a result of which he became a virtual vegetable. She said it was an accident, of course. The tube came undone and she didn't notice. She said the alarm didn't go off, but they tested it and it was working perfectly. She was had up for negligence and struck off. She was lucky not to be charged for attempted manslaughter if you ask me."

"Hang on a moment," said Stubble. "You said she was married. If he was her boy-friend did she marry him?"

"A virtual vegetable? That would be crazy."

Stubble reflected on the crazier things he had seen in the time he had been on the force but said nothing. He nodded to her to go on.

"They had been childhood sweethearts, boy next door and all that, and everyone assumed they would marry, which they were going to do, and then he stood her up. Jilted her at the church porch. There was talk that he was gay."

"I take it she married someone else?"

"On the rebound. On the surface her husband was everything a woman could want, good looking, good job, well, actually he was policeman, tipped for a top job one day." Mrs Sedge could resist the temptation to smirk.

"What went wrong?"

"He was a sadist. Beat her, enjoyed humiliating her, made her life a misery."

Stubble's memory began to stir. He vaguely remembered reading about the case. He said "That was some years back, five, six, seven years ago? I did hear about the case, if it's the same one. Didn't he go to prison?"

"Five years. Killed someone in a pub brawl. Said the man was making advances to his wife."

"What about her?" Stubble said by way of getting his questioning back on track.

"She wasn't prosecuted or anything like that, no real proof, but of course she couldn't go on working as a nurse. Some say she might have disconnected the boyfriend's tube to get back at him for making her marry the other man, but even if it was carelessness, they didn't feel they could trust her, even as a domestic. It wasn't easy for her to get another job, not with everyone in the profession knowing about her."

Stubble asked the obvious question. "Why did you employ her, if you knew she was struck off? She could easily make the same sort of 'mistake' with one of your residents."

It occurred to him that she might say it didn't matter so much with old people who are at the end of their lives, but she didn't. She said "I'll be very frank. In this business, and I am running a business, it isn't easy to recruit qualified staff. They come expensive if they come at all. When someone who had been registered came along, even if she had been struck off, only too glad to get a job anywhere, I jumped at the chance. As you can see I'm beginning to regret it. She's been with us nearly two years, but I still have my doubts about her"

"Not good at her job?"

"Oh, fair enough. I kept her away from any actual nursing as much as possible. Her duties were mainly supervisory, but even so she made mistakes. What she did while she was off duty was no affair of mine provided she didn't damage our reputation here; I'm told she used to go down to village and get drunk and then, well, they say, she was, you know, available."

"You mean she was promiscuous,"

"That was the word I was looking for. Thanks." She folded her arms to indicate she had said all she was going to say.

That might have been so as far as she was concerned. Stubble had other ideas. "Surely it is unwise to employ a nurse with a record like that?" he asked

"I just told you, she didn't work with the Guests. Her main duties were administrative."

"It doesn't sound like it, if she was called Matron."

Mrs Sedge ran her hand through her hair, a most unfeminine gesture. Stubble sensed he was getting to her. She said "Our old people like these old-fashioned titles. It makes them feel more secure. To be honest it helps sell the place. It sounds good to have a matron, rather than a manager."

To be honest, thought Stubble. *She's lying for sure.*

He said "Well that's cleared that up. All we have to do now is find the lady. Strathclyde Police are on her track. It seems she has been seen in Edinburgh. It's funny – crooks often wrap their lies round a kernel of truth. When you showed me her note saying she had gone to Edinburgh I asked myself if that was just to put us off the scent. Something tells me she's left the country.

Mrs Sedge leaned back in her chair before she dropped her bombshell. "Oh, didn't I tell you? She's back. Came back last night. Shall I call her in?"

Stubble nearly said "You might have told me!" but it would have been a waste of time. Mrs Sedge would only have said "You didn't ask!

When Matron arrived Mrs Sedge showed no sign of leaving the room. Stubble had to ask her to go to have any hope of putting Matron at her ease.

"Now Juanita," he opened, "Can you throw any light on how Mrs Bonnie came to be buried in the garden?

"I didn't kill her!" was the answer he got.

"I didn't say you did." He could see she was about to cry. "All I want to do is to get to the facts. Find out what happened."

She sniffed and blinked back tears.

Stubble ignored them. "If you didn't kill her, who did?"

"Nobody. She was dead when I found her."

"I know. Died in the natural course of things. Old people do that, and then the doctor signs a death certificate and they have a funeral, but not in Mrs Bonnie's case. She missed out on those silly formalities. Just got herself buried in the garden. I need to know why? My Chief Constable keeps nagging me to find out."

Suddenly he got to his feet, strode to the door and flung it open.

"Just passing!" said Mrs Sedge, straightening up.

"Just pass off." he hissed.

"I'll leave the door open, we'll get more privacy that way." he told Juanita as he sat down again. "Now, you say Mrs Bonnie was dead when you found her, which ties in with what our forensic people tell us. What did you do when you found out she was dead?"

"Put her in the wardrobe."

"You put her in the wardrobe?"

"I had to hide the body, you see, because Mrs Sedge was away."

Stubble guessed the story would make sense in the end if he lent a sympathetic ear. He was right. She started to tell her story, slowly, carefully. He sensed she was keeping something back.

"She was away, and those people, the Borlands were desperate to get their old mother into a home, you see, so I gave them Mrs. Bonnie's room. I had to because she didn't pay me."

"Who didn't pay you?"

"Mrs Sedge. All I got was my bed and board and a bit of pocket money. You see, she knew."

He held up his hand. "About Addenbrookes. I know all about that."

It was all that was needed. The flood gates opened. "After that I couldn't get a job. Any job. The case got so much publicity. Even cleaning floors, no-one would have me. I was desperate, and she knew I was. My little flat was being repossessed, I couldn't keep up with the mortgage, and then I saw her advertisement in The Lady, phoned up and she offered me the job. I was glad to get somewhere to live, even if I did get paid a pittance."

"I still don't see what this has got to do with Mrs Bonnie."

She laughed, a thin dry almost scornful laugh. "The money. It was my ticket out of here. The Borlands paid me cash. I only had to get rid of Mrs Bonnie. I couldn't get the doctor and the undertaker in, could I? Mrs Sedge would have known."

"I'm surprised she didn't notice."

That scornful laugh again. "She wouldn't notice if I had put an elephant in the bed. All she cared about was the money and the paperwork, not the actual old people. She calls them her Guests, but they're just money to her."

"But didn't Mrs Bonnie stop paying, I mean, when she was dead?"

"No, that's the thing. The local authority were paying for her, and since they didn't know she was dead they went on paying. I took her body out when everyone was asleep, she was light as a feather, and buried her behind the shed. How was I to know Sam was going to put his compost heap over the top of her?"

"So you put old Mrs Borland in Mrs Bonnie's room, and kept the money her family paid every week for yourself?"

"That's right. It was a chance to rebuild my life, you see. The only chance I had. You must see that."

"I do see, Juanita." He said softly." In fact I'm not sure I wouldn't have done the same in your situation."

"Does that mean it's all right?"

"Not quite. We are going to have to charge you with concealing a death and illegally disposing of the body. If you tell the court what you've just told me I imagine they'll be lenient."

"I'm so glad it's all come out at last."

"You'll have to come with me to make a statement down at police HQ, and I'm afraid I will have to charge you, but you'll be back here within the hour.

That would shut the Chief up. Police not baffled any more. Mystery solved. Case closed. But his nose told him that was not the end of the matter. There was more sniffing for Stubble's nose to do.

When he had taken Matron down to police HQ, charged her, arranged bail and delivered her back to The Poplars with a warning to say absolutely nothing to anyone, he went to City Hall where the finance department proved to be much more efficient than he had expected. They soon had the figures he wanted.

Every resident at The Poplars stopped paying as soon as they shuffled off this mortal coil, except the undead Mrs Bonnie. There she was, enthusiastically drawing benefits until last week, when evidently Mrs Sedge had thought it best to announce her death to the world. He wondered if she was going to give back the money for the time Mrs Bonnie had been dead and drawing benefits. But then what about Mrs Borland? Was she on the public payroll? Better check her out.

Mrs Sedge had seemed really surprised when he told her there was an impostor in Mrs Bonnie's room.

The screen showed no trace of Mrs Borland. But then she hadn't been at The Poplars, on paper, until last week. Surely, though she should be on the list this week. No sign of her.

He asked if a mistake might have been made.

"Not possible," the clerk said. The payments are automatically double-checked by the system."

Stubble scratched his head. "So why wouldn't this Mrs Borland be on the list of recipients?"

The clerk wondered his ignorance. "Maybe because she's got money. We only help people who have little or no savings or assets. Didn't you know old people have to sell their houses before they are eligible to be supported by the local authority?"

"This lady didn't have any money."

"It could be the people at the home haven't got round to putting in a claim yet."

Stubble felt his head going round. Mrs Bonnie, Mrs Borland, Mrs Sedge, Matron, or rather Juanita Standish if that was her real name, a monstrous regiment of women if ever there was. Only one man: Augustus Wimpole, no, two; there was the mysterious Sam Clodd He'd asked some of the staff at The Poplars about Sam and got nowhere. Kept himself to himself, very quiet, got on with his job, didn't talk a lot.

He wondered how far Sam had got.

Sam was lying on a hatch cover soaking up the sun.. The ship was not moving. The glass-smooth sea stretched away to the horizon, as blue as it usually looked on postcards. Everything, not just the engines, seemed to have come to a stop. The crew idled on deck, the captain lay in his cabin fast asleep below, the bridge was deserted.

When Sam asked Joshua Benin what was going on he got the enigmatic reply "the Lord will provide, don't you worry your head, my friend."

Sam got up and peered over the side. It was something to do. A school of small fishes Sam imagined they were sardines, swam past. The cook threw a piece of offal through the galley porthole attracting gulls from nowhere. Well they looked like gulls. Sam didn't know that much about birds and fishes, or bees for that matter.

He went back to his hatch cover, lay on his back and started to fry his front. It seemed the only thing to do.

Stubble nursed a cup of tea in Greg's cafe and tried to tie up the loose ends. Somehow one end always escaped the knot. He knew there was a nasty fiddle going on. Sedge and Wimpole were up to something. Wimpole's complaint to the Chief confirmed that. Was Matron, Juanita Standish, involved, or just an innocent, caught up in whatever was going on? Was her fiddle just a side issue, or part of a much bigger piece of skullduggery?

His head was going round and round. He stared into his teacup, but there was no help there.

Bonnie and Borland. Borland and Bonnie. His nose told him the solution lay somewhere in that direction. The Borlands were paying the nursing home for the room that Mrs Bonnie was occupying, but Mrs Bonnie was dead, so she couldn't be in that room, could she? Simple fraud, nothing else. This Mrs Sedge had claimed benefit for a dead woman. If she was claiming for one resident, then why wasn"t she doing so for more? That was the usual pattern when fraudsters found a way to cheat the system. But then, she didn't know Mrs Bonnie was dead, did she?

Couldn't be fraud, with Mrs Bonnie buried in the garden. Yes it could; no death certificate, no probate. No income tax people sniffing around. No will.

What was he thinking – no will. Of course there must be a will. All old women made wills. It was what old ladies did.

Wills. Easily traceable. They all went through the Probate Office, and they were not even confidential.

More boring legwork. Check the wills of ladies who had died in the last, say, two years and see if any of them left large amounts to

Mrs Sedge or The Poplars. And maybe Mr Augustus Wimpole, Solicitor and Commissioner for Oaths.

And there were those three large sums paid into the bank and then taken out again. If there had been others, after compulsory notification came in, what were they for and where had they gone? How could he find out? Confront Mrs Sedge? His nose told him not to.

He needed help. Someone who knew about the world of figures. An accountant or a banker. The bank manager maybe. No. That gent had already gone as far as he could. Someone totally outside the case.

Then he remembered Ted Batters. Ted was the man to ask. They had been on that course on elementary accountancy together. It had seemed a complete waste of time to Stubble but Ted had said he was going to try for the City Fraud Squad.

He went back to the office and phoned the City of London Police, and yes, DI Batters was there.

Ted was glad to help. Looked like this woman was up to something, especially since the big payments stopped when the law changed. Yes, the bank manager was right. She was most likely taking or sending the money abroad somewhere. That was the problem. It could be in any of a thousand and one banks round the world. His best bet would be to check the accounts of the residents at this old age home, see if any of them had large amounts in the bank and had taken large amounts out, and if so, who got paid, and when.

Stubble told him. About £100,000. He held his breath. Hopefully Ted would say something like: sounds interesting, want us to come in on the case? But he didn't. He just told Stubble the case was outside the City's jurisdiction and in any case too petty to be bothered about.

Stubble put the phone down wondering about a world where £100,000 was petty cash.

Then he realised he didn't know how to trace the bank accounts of the residents in question. He couldn't ask them because they were dead.

But the Probate Office might know.

He'd be happier dealing with a straight murder case. That was more his territory. All this money stuff was confusing..

His nose sniffed and told him there might be a murder or two in there somewhere, even if the death he was actually supposed to be investigating had turned out to be death by natural causes.

CHAPTER FOUR
Matron Slips Away

Three o'clock in the morning. Matron had finished her rounds with Violet who was on night duty. "You'll call me if anything exciting happens," she said as she declined the cup of tea Violet always made afterwards. She had gone up to her room and waited. At four o'clock she picked up her suitcase, opened her door cautiously and tiptoed to the fire escape at the end of the corridor. And stopped. The fire escape went right past the kitchen window where Violet was making her tea. She would have to risk going through the house.

She turned and made her way to the main staircase and down to the hall. The kitchen door was shut, but she could see light under the door. She pictured Violet the other side of it reading Hello as she sipped her tea. Her heart thumping loud enough for someone to hear it, she crept across the hall and released the catch on the front door.

It clicked. To Matron's ears it sounded like a gun going off, but there was no sound from the other side of the kitchen door. She carried her case outside and pulled the door shut. It clicked again and Matron had to resist the temptation to start running.

She walked across the fields into Dununder. It was not the shortest or the easiest way, but a lone woman walking along the road with a suitcase in the small hours would be sure to attract attention, if she didn't get run over by some late night drunk.

When she got to the town she went straight to the railway station and, finding it closed, sat hidden from view on a bench behind a bush in the little park across the road waiting for the station to open. When it did so at five o'clock she joined the early morning long-distance commuters on the first train to London.

Half an hour after Matron had left the building Maureen Sedge pushed open the door of Mrs Kinloch's room. A pillow swung from her hand. A double dose of Mogadon had made sure the old lady was fast asleep.

For a minute or so she stood looking down at her. Most of the residents slept on their backs. Up to now all she had had to do was put the pillow over their faces and hold it there until they stopped breathing. They struggled a bit, but not enough to be a worry. This one was sleeping on her stomach, her head to one side facing Mrs Sedge. She was not going to be so easy.

She pushed the pillow into the sleeping woman's face, put her hand on the back of her head and pressed.

It didn't work. Mrs Kinloch woke up, struggled free, realised what was going on, sat up and started to scream.

A mistake. Her face was not at an awkward angle any more. Mrs Sedge pushed her down, knelt on her legs, put the pillow back across her face and held it there. The old woman's arms pulled at her wrists but she hadn't the strength. With the pillow held against her face her old body was fast running out of oxygen. She struggled as hard as she could, but it was no use.

Mrs Sedge was getting desperate. Someone might have heard that scream and come in any moment. Suddenly the old woman's back arched and her body relaxed and lay still. She held the pillow there a little while to make sure, and then took it off.

To her horror Mrs Kinloch came to life and rolled over to the other side of the bed in an effort to escape. She found herself chasing the old woman to catch her before she could shout for help again.

She caught her arm and swung her round, grasping her in a macabre dance until they both fell over onto the carpet. The old lady had one arm free and Mrs Sedge felt her nails on her face. The old bitch was trying to scratch her eyes out!

She managed to get her hand on the struggling woman's chin. She pushed hard and suddenly there was a snapping noise and the body went limp. Panting, Maureen Sedge got up and stood, resting her hands on the kidney shaped dressing table Mrs Kinloch had brought from home, until she got her breath back.

She stared at the body on the floor. There was no doubt about it, this time the old cow was dead.

She switched the light on and started to tidy the room, she pulled back the bed clothes and hauled the body on to the bed, composed the head on the pillow, and pulled the duvet up to try to make it look as if the old lady had died in her sleep. The eyes stared up at her and shuddering she forced herself to close them. The mouth hung open. She tried to close it, but it fell open again. The head rolled to one side. She propped it back up against the pillow, but as soon as she let go it rolled back.

As she stood wondering what to do the door opened. It was Violet.

She said "Oh, it's you Mrs Sedge. Is Mrs Kinloch all right? I was wondering why the light was on in her room."

Maureen Sedge thought furiously before saying: "I heard a noise as I was passing, and came in. I think she's passed away."

Violet looked at Mrs Kinloch. She said "I'll get the doctor."

"No need for that," said Mrs Sedge, her heart pounding, "I checked for a pulse and she's quite dead. I think she must have had some sort of seizure. There's no point in getting the doctor out of bed. He can't do anything for her now. I'll phone him first thing in the morning." She drew the sheet over Mrs Kinloch's head, trying not to do it too quickly.

"She was such a nice lady." said Violet, wiping away a tear, "It was her birthday tomorrow, I mean today. We baked a cake, with icing and all. Fruit cake, she liked fruit cake."

"How old would she have been?" asked Mrs Sedge for the sake of having something to say.

"Ninety. It would have been her ninetieth birthday tomorrow. Both her sons are coming to the party. Now they're going to come for her funeral. Lord, that is so sad."

Mrs Sedge tried to keep her voice level as she said "Sons? I didn't know she had any relatives."

"She's got two. Alastair and Cameron. Lovely boys they is. She told me all about it. She didn't know where they were, and they thought she was dead. Alastair in Australia traced her with that internet. Then he found his brother as well and it turned out he was in Australia as well, so they all had a family again. Their father was a bad man, came home drunk, beat them all up. She got put in hospital and the boys, they was only little, got put in care. They lost touch with each other. It was only last year they found out what had happened to her. Now they've come all the way from Australia for her birthday and they're going to find out she's gone!"

While Violet had been saying this Mrs Sedge's brain had gone into overdrive. She repeated "there's no point in bothering Dr

Mingus until the morning; there's nothing he can do for her now. Draw the curtains and lock the door, Violet."

"The curtains is already shut." Violet pointed out.

"So they are. We'll just lock the door until the doctor gets here to make sure no-one disturbs the poor lady."

"Shouldn't we tell the sons?"

Why did Violet keep asking all these awkward questions? Mrs Sedge moved towards the door, hoping Violet would leave as well. She said "Not if they're coming later today. I'd rather tell them in person than wake them up at this time of night."

"They must have got mobiles? You could leave a message."

Mrs Sedge had the answer for that one. "Even worse. How would you like to get a voicemail or a text message telling you your mother had died?"

Violet saw the point of this, she said "Nothing we can do for her now. Then she said "Good-bye darling" to the body on the bed and at last left the room. Mrs Sedge followed her out and locked the door behind her.

She went straight up to her flat and called Augustus Wimpole on her direct line.

Augustus was fast asleep and dreaming. The Lord Chancellor's office was phoning to ask him if he would like to take his bar exams so he could take the job of Lord Chief Justice which was being reserved for him, but the telephone kept sliding out of reach. He gradually became aware it really was ringing.

He opened an eye and glanced at the bedside clock. 5.37. He swore quietly to himself.

He heard Mrs Sedge's voice on the answering machine downstairs but couldn't make out what it was saying. Whatever it was it could not be anything that wouldn't wait till morning.

Augustus Wimpole turned over and went back to sleep.

Matron checked in at Heathrow without any trouble, went through immigration, bought herself some duty free scent, a pack of cigarettes and a book, and settled down to read. She was well into chapter two when she looked up and saw that her flight was delayed four hours. She went to the enquiry desk to find out why.

"Technical delay at Bahrain." The woman behind the counter was brusque. "Nothing to be done." Matron wished she had flown British Airways. She would be half-way across the Atlantic by now.

She began to worry. Four hours. That would give them time to find out she was gone and warn the ports and airports. That bloody travel agent. Advised her to book Air India to save a few quid. She tried to go back to reading her book but could not concentrate. She lit a cigarette.

Which is when she saw the two policewomen coming straight towards her.

"Excuse me, madam." said one.

They were always very polite at first. "Yes?"

"I must ask you to put your cigarette out or move to the smoking area over there"

"I'm sorry." I did not realise." Matron hoped her relief did not show.

The policewoman smiled, a friendly sort of smile. "A lot of people don't. Just look out for the ashtrays, there are always ashtrays in the smoking area, and you'll be all right. It's a common mistake. The 'no smoking' signs aren't as obvious as they ought to be."

"Thank you." she said, picking up her things to move.

"Just a minute," said the other policewoman. This one was taller and didn't look as if she knew how to smile. Matron's heart missed a beat. "Did you just buy those cigarettes here?"

"Yes." Now what had she done?

"You seem to have a problem about reading notices. It says on the packet, in big letters, "Not to be Opened in U.K". You are not supposed to smoke Duty Free cigarettes until you leave the country."

"Thank you. I'll be more careful next time."

She heard the policewomen laugh as they moved away. "Half witted," she heard the tall one say. Stifling her indignation she found herself a seat in the non-smoking section and went back to her book.

As she stubbed out her cigarette the thought came to her that there was no way the word could have gone out that she was missing and might skip the country. There hadn't been time. She hadn't been stopped when she showed her passport and those two had only been interested in her smoking. She went back to her book.

A page or two later she started to worry again. The instruction to watch out for her and stop her leaving the UK could be flashed to Heathrow at any moment. Those two coppers would be sure to remember her face.

She picked up her things and took herself off to the toilet, where a succession of desperate ladies wondered what she could be doing in there all that time.

Dr Mingus was quite used to getting telephone calls from The Poplars to tell him one of the residents had died. They always seemed to come while he was eating his breakfast. Fortunately The Poplars was on the way to his surgery, so he could usually pop in, have a quick look at the body, sign the death certificate and be away in a few minutes.

In most cases the deceased had been ill and under his care just before they died, but lately there had been a few where the death had been sudden and unexpected. He hadn't seen this Mrs Kinloch since he had examined her when she arrived some eighteen months ago. He remembered her well. She had struck him as being in remarkable health for an eighty-eight year old. Perhaps he should have checked her over her a little more carefully.

Mrs Sedge showed him up to Mrs Kinloch's room herself. "Matron's away, I'm afraid, so I'm having to do everything myself. I don't know about you, but staff is one of my biggest problems. It's so difficult to get the right sort of people these days."

Dr Mingus wasn't listening to her prattle. He was wondering how long this was going to take. His mind was on a tricky practice meeting that evening.

Mrs Sedge unlocked the door, still talking. "I don't know what happened. We try to look in on every guest at least once a night. As soon as I got into the room I could see something was wrong, she was lying at such an odd angle. When I switched the light on the first thing I noticed was her head sort of lolling off the bed. I think she must have had some sort of seizure."

Dr Mingus moved Mrs Kinloch's head from side to side. His diagnosis was instantaneous. Her neck was broken. He asked "Was she like this when you found her?"

"Yes," lied Mrs Sedge. "I heard a scream when I was at the end of the corridor doing my rounds. I didn't think it was that important – a lot of our old people make noises in the night so I didn't hurry to see what was happening. When I got to the room her head was off the bed, about here," Mrs Sedge pointed to a spot by the side of the bed. "I put her head back on the pillow without thinking after, of course, I had checked her vital signs. It seemed the decent thing to do I now realise that was a mistake. I can't have been thinking straight."

"Hmm" was the doctor's response. The Poplars was proving to be something of a burden on the practice. Its residents tended to be ill more than most, in fact it was on the agenda for the practice meeting. They were always being called out to The Poplars. Too much work for too little reward. Did they really need the occasional perks, the bottles of whisky, the cases of wine, the Christmas hamper Mrs Sedge gave them to ensure that little extra attention for her clients?

He said "There will have to be a post mortem examination." There was no way he could wrap it up.

Mrs Sedge panicked. She said "Is that absolutely necessary?" The expression on the doctor's face told her she should have kept her mouth shut.

"It's the law" said Dr Mingus. "As she hasn't been seen by a doctor in the last fortnight then there has to be a post mortem to determine the cause of death. It's more than a year since I saw her."

Forcing herself to keep her voice steady Mrs Sedge said "I suppose it will be a formality. How long will it take?"

"A day or so. I'll make the arrangements."

"Where will it be?"

"Undershire General, I imagine. I'll let you know. In the meantime please leave the body just as it is, lock the door and don't let anyone in."

Mrs Sedge asked him "Can't Mr Gladwyn take her away? It upsets the Guests to have a dead body on the premises."

"Can't help that," said the doctor. "Do they have to know?"

"I'm sure they know already. You can't keep secrets in this place."

"I'll phone as soon as I get to my surgery and let you know as quickly as I can," the doctor told her, "and I really must go; there's sure to be a queue of patients waiting when I get there."

Dr Mingus shut his bag and said good-bye. He really did want to get to the surgery to see his patients, but the real urgency was to talk to Dr Pilbeam to ask his advice. No way was that a natural death.

As he got into his car he remembered the practice meeting and felt a headache coming on.

"Just touring round?" The US Immigration Service agent was ten minutes away from the end of his shift and had tickets for the Yankees game. The last thing he wanted was a problem that might stop him getting away, so this lady he needed like a hole in the head.

"That's right." Matron told him. "Just looking round the country."

"Made reservations? Booked a rental? Hotels? I need to know a little more, lady." The agent was praying she had.

Matron hoped her nervousness did not show. "I intend to spend a few days in New York and then go to Buffalo to see the Niagara Falls."

"How you going to travel?"

"By Greyhound bus."

"And after Buffalo?"

"A few days in Chicago and then I want to see Seattle and work my way down to California."

"Work? What sort of work?" He was never going to get to the game on time. He'd caught a Brit coming in to work on a tourist visa. She'd have to be detained and there would be countless forms to fill in.

"I do not intend to work." could he hear her heart beating? Was she blushing? "I want to go slowly down the West Coast, stopping as the mood takes me."

"You got any money?"

"About $20,000 in cash."

The agent's eyebrows shot up. "You going to take all that dough on a Greyhound? Rather you than me, lady." He handed her passport back, with a smile of relief. "Enjoy your stay."

As Matron passed through the door marked Exit which led to the Land of the Free he added sotto voce "That's if you get as far as the Port Authority to catch your bus without getting mugged. "

"I can't tell you over the phone," said the lady at the Probate Office for what seemed like the fourteenth time, "You'll have to write in with the details."

"I could fax them over to you. How long will it take if I do?" asked Stubble.

"Depends how many accounts you want to check. A week, maybe more."

"This is a murder enquiry," said Stubble. That usually opened doors.

Not this door. "We're extremely busy" said the lady. "Could be longer."

Stubble put the phone down cursing. There must be another way to get sense out of the Probate people, but why should he have to waste time finding it? Why did he have to get mired in all this financial muck? Nice simple murders were what made the job worth doing.

And then he got a phone call from Dr Pilbeam.

Mrs Sedge picked up the phone and put it down again. She got up, splashed some more brandy into her glass and paced nervously round the room, Maybe it was not a good idea to talk to Augustus. He might be her lover, but he was a lawyer too. Would he stand by her? That was the wrong way to put it. Husbands stood by wives when they were in trouble. Augustus was a lover, or was he even that? How many times had they slept together? They hadn't actually spent a night in the same bed; it wasn't even a relationship, just a sordid little affair. Mrs Sedge suddenly faced reality. As far as Wimpole was concerned she had just been an easy lay.

She told herself to get a grip on herself. Augustus might have had sex with her, but he was still her solicitor. If the post mortem found signs of violence she would have to talk to him. She might as well talk to him now. She picked up the phone again and put it down again.

What was she going to say? "I've killed one of the guests and they are going to do a post mortem." He'd tell her to wait until there was a result. It had been his idea, this long term care scheme. It was all his fault. She wouldn't have started shortening their lives if it hadn't been for him.

He'd deny it .He'd say, yes, the long term plan was his idea, but not the bumping off. Bumping, humping. She giggled hysterically. Augustus wasn't into bumping but he was into humping. Did he do it with all his women clients? Was it legal to do it with a client? Maybe solicitors were like doctors. She could get him struck off. In any case if it got out it would not do him any good. She smiled slyly. Augustus would do as he was told.

She would talk to him. Ask him generally about the law as far as post mortems were concerned. Sound innocent. Tell him The Poplars had never had one before. She sat down and reached for the telephone.

Which rang.

It was the doctor phoning to tell her Mrs Kinloch's body was going to be collected shortly and taken away for post mortem.

As she put the phone down she felt the bile rise in her throat.

A quarter of an hour and two alka-seltzers later the phone rang again. It was Janice calling to tell her the men were there to collect Mrs Kinloch. She dabbed perfume behind her ears, sprayed breath freshener into her mouth to disguise the brandy and went down to the front door to receive them. As she emerged from the lift she managed to convince herself she was walking in a straight and dignified fashion. Two men in dark suits were getting out of a black van which looked just like Mr Gladwin's. As they came into the hall another car drew up. Out of it stepped a familiar figure, Detective Inspector Stubble.

He didn't bother with any polite chit chat, merely announced "We've come to see Mrs Kinloch." Mutely she led them up to Mrs Kinloch's room, unlocked it and led them inside. The two mortuary attendants waited while Stubble looked round the room. Then he said, "O.K. go ahead, but try to disturb the bed as little as possible."

They did their business swiftly and expertly and went on their way. Stubble stayed behind. He still seemed interested in the room, looking here and there, opening drawers and cupboards. Then he peered under the bed. She was about to ask what he was doing when he said in an authoritative tone of voice "Right ho. That's it for the moment."

As she made to lock the door he reached out his hand and said "I'll take that, if you please, and any spare keys you happen to have." She looked up, startled. "He said: I'll be posting a constable outside the door. We have to do that, until they've done the post mortem." He must have seen the alarm on her face because he added, reassuringly, "It counts as suspicious circumstances, you see. Dr Mingus couldn't issue a death certificate because he suspects she had a broken neck. I'm sure it was some sort of accident, but until we can be sure we have to keep the scene clean, as we call it. In other words, not disturbed. The post-mortem will go through as a priority, so the officer should be away by tonight. Please don't worry – it's the regulations. More and more of them, aren't there, getting in the way of ordinary people trying to get on with their lives. Daft if you ask me."

She nodded, not trusting herself to speak and say the wrong thing.

He went on, "If you'd be so kind as to go outside you'll see a young lady constable sitting in my car. Ask her to step up here, will you? And if you could provide a chair for her, and occasional cups of tea, and perhaps a sandwich I'd be most grateful, and I'm sure so would she."

His manner was so breezy and reassuring that Mrs Sedge felt almost cheerful as she went down the stairs.

As soon as he had finished at The Poplars Stubble drove straight to the mortuary, where Mrs Kinloch's body was being prepared for examination. Pilbeam emerged from his office to greet him. "You'll have to do without me this morning, I'm afraid. I'm needed at the Infirmary. I'll leave your cadaver in the capable hands of Dr Who."

Dr William Ho, known universally as Dr Who, was Pilbeam's deputy. He was a short neat man who always appeared to be terribly busy. Stubble had heard it said that Dr Ho did all the work while Pilbeam got the credit.

Pilbeam beamed. "Broken neck, you think? Should be pretty straightforward, Of course you'll be wanting to know how she came to break it, a woman of her age. I imagine a fall. Where was she when you saw her?"

Stubble explained "She was lying in bed with her head propped up on the pillow. "The owner of the rest home where she lived says she fell out of bed. Silly woman put her back again to make her look decent."

Pilbeam moved the head. "And you believed her I'm sure!" He went over and moved Mr Kinloch's head. "Definitely broken. Neck fractures and dislocations don't cause death unless the nerves are affected, which could well be the case in this instance. We'll know when we open her up. She must have hit the floor with some force."

Stubble asked "Would there be any traces of that on the body?"

"Of course there would. There's most likely some sort of mark on her head, she'd have had some sort of lump if she'd lived. He parted the old lady's grey hairs with his gloved fingers. "Good Lord! Some impact. It's broken the skin, and there's blood on the hair. Very interesting."

"Any bruises?" asked Stubble.

Dr Ho answered him. "You won't get them, not if she died immediately. Blood would stop flowing, you see." Unlike Pilbeam, who was wearing his usual tweed suit and trademark bow tie, he was scrubbed and gowned ready for work. "But we'll see what we can find. First of all I'd like to have a look at that neck."

He seized a scalpel and applied it to Mrs Kinloch's neck. Stubble announced that he could do with a coffee and left the room.

He was still drinking it when Dr Ho found him. "Ah. Mr Stubble, come have a look. I think we've found something interesting." Reluctantly, Stubble followed him back to the examination room.

Mrs Kinloch's old body, pitifully naked, lay on the dissecting table. To Stubble's relief it was not cut open. She looked peaceful.

"I've changed my mind, going to leave the neck till last. It's definitely broken. No lesions there. I would say her head was forced back in some way. I was about to have a look at her heart and lungs when I noticed these."

Stubble looked at the old lady's thighs. There were diagonal marks across both, just above the knee. "What does that mean?" he asked Dr Ho.

"Someone or something was pressing on her legs not long before death. My guess is someone was holding her down. She could have been leaning up against something like a table, but she'd have to have had her legs unnaturally wide apart to get the marks in that position. There's something else I noticed. Look at the nails of her right hand."

Stubble looked. Mrs Kinloch's nails were varnished, in a bright purple. She must have been a lively old lady to go about with purple finger nails. The varnish was cracked and some had fallen off and one nail was broken.

Dr Ho told him to look at the other hand.

The left hand was perfect, the nail varnish as if it had just been applied. "What does it mean?" asked Stubble.

Dr Ho said "Nothing. She could have damaged her nail varnish at any time, but it's a clue to something else. Look at this." He picked the hand up. It seemed normal enough, wrist, palm four fingers and a thumb. Stiff, now that rigor mortis had set in. He delicately picked up the end of little finger by its point; nothing happened. He did the same with the next; it was rigid. Then he took the middle finger, which bent back under the weight of the arm. The same happened when he grasped the index finger. It could well be that nail varnish was broken in a fight. I'll be checking the contents of her finger nails, of course."

"Two broken fingers. Old people's bones tend to be brittle. We'll have a closer look to make sure, but my guess is that these were broken just before death."

"You mean," said Stubble slowly, "there was some sort of struggle."

"Precisely. I suggest you go back and have a chat with whoever said they found her. It's only conjecture, but I think this lady was killed, and was fighting back when it happened."

"You don't need me here?" asked Stubble.

"Not at all. We will be going into everything very closely, Mr Stubble, very closely indeed. I will be very interested in the condition of her lungs, for instance, and her heart. And I'll be taking specimens from her finger nails, see if she scratched her assailant. I hope there will be material for DNA. You'll have my full report by the morning." He took up his scalpel again and leant over Mrs Kinloch's chest.

"Thanks," said Stubble, but Dr Ho hardly heard him. The detective was already half way through the door, retching as he went.

Mrs Sedge had been trying to get hold of Augustus Wimpole all day. His office kept telling her that Mr Wimpole was in court. His secretary promised to get a message to him just as soon as ever possible. Yes, she did understand the urgency of the matter. Could she tell him what the matter was? Confidential? Yes, she would certainly let him know.

Mrs Sedge tried Wimpole's mobile, but it was switched off. She toyed with the idea of going down to the court and catching him there, but realised that would only reveal her anxiety. She poured herself a brandy to steady her nerves. It was her third that day, and they seemed to be having no effect at all.

She tried to get on with some routine paperwork, but she could not get her mind to focus.

The telephone rang. It must be Augustus. She grabbed it.

Janice's voice: "Mrs Sedge. Mrs Kinloch's sons are here. I've sat them down with a cup of tea. What shall I tell them?"

Did you put cyanide in their tea? The thought ran through Mrs Sedge's head. She told herself to get a grip and told Janice she would be down in a moment. She gulped down yet another brandy, steadied herself and walked carefully out of the room, closing the door behind her.

She emerged from the lift and walked straight up to Mrs Kinloch's sons. "I'm so very sorry!" she gushed.

"Sorry?" said the elder one, Alastair. "We're in no hurry. It isn't as if you kept us waiting very long."

Cameron, the younger son, sensed something was wrong. He asked "Where is Mother? Is she in her room?"

Mrs Sedge repeated "I'm so very sorry "I'm afraid I have to tell you that your mother passed away in the night." We've been trying to contact you."

Alastair looked at his brother. "She didn't say anything about not feeling well when. I spoke to her on the telephone last night."

Cameron agreed. "Last time I saw her, it must have been about a month ago, she told me how well she was feeling." After a momentary pause he added "and how well she was being looked after here."

Alastair said "Where is she. We'd like to see her."

"She's been taken away. They've got to do a post mortem."

Alastair raised his voice. "God! They might have waited until we arrived. It isn't as if you didn't know we were coming."

Mrs Sedge felt a cold chill creeping down her neck. She didn't want to admit the police were involved. "It was so sudden. The doctor hadn't seen her for months. He said that meant there had to be a post mortem. It's only a formality. He wanted to get it done quickly, before you arrived."

"Well he hasn't succeeded in that, has he?" said Alastair. "Who is this bloody doctor, anyway."

Dr Mingus. He sees to all our guests."

Cameron laid his hand on his brother's arm. "There's nothing we can do to help Mum now, Alastair. They've got to find out why she died, for our sake as much as anyone else's."

Alastair's wrath abated a little. "Where is she now? At the local hospital, I imagine. Can you tell us how to get there?"

Mrs Sedge suddenly realised she had no idea where the body was. Mrs Kinloch was out of her hands, after all, and in Stubble's. "I don't know exactly," she said. "I suggest you ask Dr Mingus, he'll have all the details. Would you like to come into the office to use the telephone?"

She discreetly left the brothers alone in her office while they phoned Dr Mingus. It wasn't long before she heard a shout of "IN THE PUBLIC MORTUARY! THE POLICE!"

A little while later Mrs Kinloch's sons emerged with the news that they had to go down to the mortuary to identify their mother. "It seems they don't take your word for it." said Alastair.

"That woman's been drinking." she heard Cameron say as they went out without so much as a glance in her direction.

Sam stood at the rail and watched the other ship approach. Unlike the *Largesse* it looked old and unkempt. Its sides were streaked with rust. Its funnel was supposed to be green, but red lead showed through where the paint had dropped off. There seemed to be a great deal of activity on its deck.

Suddenly the *Largesse's* PA system came to life. It was the first time Sam had heard it. "Wakey wakey, rise and shine you jolly mariners," cried Captain Dade. Let's have you all on deck. We've got cargo coming aboard. Loosen the hatches, rig the gangplank. Stir yourselves you idle lads!"

Joshua Benin clapped Sam on the shoulder. "Come on Sam, help me get the hatch cover off. The two of them went round the hatch unhooking the line that held the cover in place. When it was free they dragged the heavy canvas to one side and roughly folded it against the ship's rail. Joshua looked towards the bridge and raised his hand. There was a grinding noise and the hatch opened.

Sam looked down into the hold, expecting to see an empty space or crates of merchandise. Instead there were rows of narrow bunks, with hardly any space between them. Joshua found a ladder from somewhere on deck and lowered it on to the deck below.

He explained: "As soon as they're down below we take the ladder away to make sure they stays where they is. Don't want them coming up and making trouble, does we?"

"Who's them?" Sam asked.

"The cargo." said Joshua simply.

"You mean," said Sam slowly, "they, those people over there, are the cargo?"

"Not people, Sam, heathens. It's a cargo of heathens we're taking aboard."

"What for?" asked Sam, thinking that perhaps the *Largesse* was some sort of missionary ship.

"What for!" exclaimed Joshua, "What for! Why to sell to the other heathens. That's what you do with heathens. Buy and sell, buy and sell. You'll see. He disappeared for a moment and came back with a nasty looking cudgel. "Here, take this, you may need it. If any those niggers gets uppity, tap him on the head, no messing."

Sam said "but you're a nigger yourself.!"

"You noticed," said Joshua. "Difference is I'm saved. I'm in a state of grace. They have yet to see the light. See?"

Sam didn't see but he knew when to keep his mouth shut.

A file of black men started coming across the gangway that had been rigged to join the two ships. Every now and again one jumped into the sea, preferring to take his chances with fishy sharks rather than the human ones into whose hands he had fallen. They were ushered into the hold down Sam and Joshua Benin's hatch. When all the men were stowed and the ladder drawn up the captain pressed a button on the bridge and the hatch slowly closed over them. Then women started to file across to the Largesse. They were ushered aft where no doubt there was a similar dormitory.

"I'm off this ship next time we touch port!" Sam told Joshua as they roped down the hatch cover again.

"I don't think so" said Joshua slowly. "You see, Captain Dade likes his crew to stay aboard when we're in port. He don't like people going about talking about our cargo."

"Can't stop me getting off" protested Sam.

"I think he can, I think he can, Mr Sam," Joshua Benin said slowly and sadly. You see, Samuel, if there's any slaves on this ship, it's you and me. We ain't never going to get off this ship, unless you want to jump in the sea like those poor souls just now. Ain't no whale going to swallow them up and spit them out on the beach like ole Jonah."

"Oh my God!" said Sam softly.

"But there is a way to be free." said Joshua, looking up. "My body may be in chains but my soul flies free. My spirit is safe in the arms of Jesus. Come with me Brother, and tread the path to eternal salvation."

"I'll think about it," answered Sam, whose soul was miles away, in an old people's home in far away Undershire.

Matron's body was in New York, but her soul was in Tulsa, Oklahoma. She had just come off the telephone in an internet cafe after seeing a vacancy at a clinic in Tulsa posted on the net. The wording had been a little vague but the lady who had answered the phone had sounded quite positive. When she heard that Matron had an English nursing qualification she had told her Dr Caine would like to meet with her.. When would it be convenient? They had fixed on a date two days later.

"You can bring your resumé with you," the lady had said. Matron wasn't quite sure what a resumé was, but imagined it was a fancy American word for her CV. She stayed on the café's computer long enough to compose a brief work of fiction.

Augustus Wimpole being in Court was not a way of avoiding Mrs Sedge, he really was there until his case finished late in the afternoon. Augustus hated days in court. They nearly always turned out to be a waste of time. There must be a better way to turn the wheels of justice, he told himself as he drove back to the office.

"Any calls? Any crises?" he called out to his secretary as he dropped his briefcase on to his desk.

"Only Mrs Sedge, from The Poplars. She called several times. I think it's important. The police are involved. Something about a body."

"Oh, it's the body in the garden. Most likely they've dug up something. It'll wait until morning, won't it? It's been a long day and I'm feeling tired."

"I'm not sure, Mr Wimpole. She has phoned, let me see," she consulted her pad, "seven times today."

"O.K." he said wearily. "Get her on the line."

"What's up, Maureen?" he asked.

She said breathlessly. "I'm so relieved to hear you. It's the police. They've sealed off Mrs Kinloch's room and her two sons are here and she's having a post-mortem because she hasn't seen the doctor and Dr Mingus says that's all right and I don't know what to do."

"I take it she's dead." he said drily.

"Of course she's dead!" she wailed.

"Have they asked you any questions?"

"Well, not really. Only things like when did I find her and where was she. They said sealing the room was something they always do if there's a post mortem."

Augustus tried to make his pencil stand on its end. It fell over as he told her "I can't see what you're worried about. It's bad for The Poplars' reputation, I suppose but once the autopsy is over her family will be able to bury her and you can forget all about it."

"It was the Long Term Care that did it." said Mrs Sedge suddenly.

"What do you mean by the Long Term Care? A note of alarm crept into Augustus Wimpole's voice.

"Taking their money in exchange for keeping them for the rest of their lives."

"What's that got to do with Mrs Kinloch?"

"She was in the plan. She paid over the £104,000."

Mrs Sedge wondered why Augustus was being so dense. Hadn't they discussed shortening the lives of the Long Term residents over and over again?

She heard him as if in a dream. "Are you trying to tell me you helped Mrs Kinloch out of this world?"

"Well, of course. Wasn't that the idea?"

"Augustus Wimpole's voice was suddenly cold. "Are you trying to suggest I told you to kill your residents after they had given you a substantial sum in exchange for lifetime care?"

"It was your idea!" Mrs Sedge said weakly.

She knew already what his response would be. It was even crueller than she expected. "What a ridiculous notion! That you and I discussed killing your residents? You must be crazy to even think of such a thing!" He spoke each word slowly and carefully, no doubt into a tape recorder or to give his secretary time to write it down.

"What should I do?" she wailed.

"Nothing. Try to keep calm and wait for the police to contact you. When they do, say nothing and call me immediately. Unless of course, you choose to employ another solicitor."

Mrs Sedge slowly put the phone down.

She had never felt so utterly alone.

The following morning Mrs Sedge did not feel like breakfast. She felt even less keen on eating when she heard that Stubble was in the building and had been poking about, asking questions. She did not want to see him but knew she had to act as normally as possible.

"Mr Stubble!" she tried to sound charming. "Back again?"

"Yes, I'm back, I'm afraid. Just a few things I missed last time. I didn't quite finish interviewing the staff."

"I thought you saw everyone except Sam. Any news of him, by the way?"

"Not yet, but I'm sure we'll find him soon. It wasn't Sam I was thinking about. I need to talk to your Matron again. Is she free?"

In her panic the day before Mrs Sedge had not even noticed that a key member of her staff had vanished. Her bed had not been slept in, and there was no suitcase above her wardrobe. No-one had seen her. They phoned Violet, who was just about to go to bed after her night shift, and she confirmed that she had said good night to Matron around two o'clock the night Mrs Kinloch died. She assumed she had gone to bed.

Mrs Sedge was far from angry to learn that her right hand woman had disappeared. She felt a load had been taken from off her back. She told Stubble, trying not to show her relief, "Well, that explains what happened to Mrs Kinloch. I mean it's obvious, isn't it!"

"I was wondering what her motive might have been," said Stubble mildly.

"I think there is something you ought to know," said Mrs Sedge.

"About Mrs Standish's record?" asked Stubble.

"You know?" said Mrs Sedge, startled. She seemed to have forgotten about telling him about her.

Stubble was not inclined to remind her. "We know all sorts of things, Mrs Sedge,"

"She was mad as a March hare, wasn't she?"

"If you say so, Mrs Sedge," he said, trying to get on her nerves. "I'm a little puzzled as to why you employed her if you knew what she'd done."

"She made a clean breast of it at the interview and swore she would never do anything like that again. He was her lover after all. Why should she harm any of these old people?"

"I haven't investigated that yet, but I will," said Stubble. "Before I do, though, I will have to get her back here, so we'll tell the ports and airports to keep an eye out for her, and then we'll circulate a description. We'll find her, don't you worry."

"You've no idea how difficult it is to get qualified staff out here in the country," said Mrs Sedge and then wished she hadn't. The less said the better.

Matron got out of the taxi that had brought her from Tulsa International airport and stood on the sidewalk wondering if she was doing the right thing. Now she was here she was not so sure. It had all been too easy. No-one seemed to be looking for her, and here was this clinic where there was a good chance she would get a job, in fact they seemed keen to have her.

The white circular building gleamed in the morning sunlight. It was surrounded by an immaculate lawn on which sprinklers played lazily. The whole property was bordered by a tall hedge of some spiny plant. The only way in was through a solid metal gate with a small gatehouse behind it. As Matron approached the gate a uniformed guard emerged and asked if he could help her. She explained she had come for a job interview and gave her name. The guard consulted a clipboard and the gate slid open. She paused and studied the Tulsa Maternity Clinic. She sensed something odd about the building. It was only when she was inside it that she realised what it was. There were no windows on the outside. The place was a fortress.

The front door slid aside as she approached it and closed silently behind her. Once inside she found herself in air-conditioned luxury. Her feet nestled in a thick navy blue carpet. A copy of Van Gogh's Sunflowers in a gilt frame adorned one wall, she could hear soft background music, was it Vivaldi? A Louis Quatorze desk stood to one side with an enormous vase of gladioli beside it and an immaculate blonde lady seated behind it who greeted her by name. Matron thought it sounded like the same woman who had talked to her on the telephone. "So good of you to come and see us," she breathed, "I've advised Doctor Caine you are here, he's presently in a meeting but he'll be down to see you directly it's finished. He should only keep you a few minutes; would you care for a drink while you wait? Coffee, tea, coke, fruit juice?"

Matron opted for coffee. The receptionist spoke quietly into her phone and in a minute or two the coffee arrived, not the plastic cup of instant coffee Matron expected but a waitress with a tray bearing a cafetiére accompanied by cream, milk, sugar, sweeteners and a fine china cup and saucer.

Matron sipped the coffee gratefully and explained to the blonde receptionist that she was not just from Out of State but from far away England.

"I do so love that English accent, and so will the patients," she said encouragingly.

Dr Caine bustled in, a small well-scrubbed man, smile glued on, smelling strongly of aftershave, hand outstretched,. She followed him into a lift which appeared to be lined in black leather, and up to his office, which overlooked some snow-capped mountains; she assumed they were the Rockies.

"Wonderful, isn't it?" he exclaimed, seeing her looking at it.

Without thinking she said "I didn't see any mountains outside."

Dr Caine lowered himself into an enormous cocooning executive chair. "It's an illusion. Good isn't it. I had this great Italian artist take a photo and blow it up, then he put it behind this special glass so you think you're looking out of a window at the Rockies, snow, forests, rivers, the lot. Fools everyone. Including you."

She laughed. "For a moment I thought I'd come to the wrong town."

"City," he corrected her. "Tulsa is a city."

Her response sounded hollow. "I'm afraid I'm a stranger to American ways, Dr Caine. You'll have to excuse me - I've only been in the country a few days."

It didn't seem to matter. He swung round in his seat and gazed admiringly at the fake Rockies for a few moments. Then he swung back to face her and got down to business. "You got any qualifications?"

Without a word Matron reached into her handbag and handed over her certificates.

He studied them carefully. "These are Xeroxes."

Matron knew they were. They had to be, otherwise anyone would have seen the alterations. She was ready with her story. "There was a fire in my flat and the originals were burnt. I'm getting replacements, but it takes time. Luckily I had taken copies."

That was enough for Dr Caine. Nurses were like gold dust and he wasn't going to turn one away, even if her documentation was not quite right. That accent would impress the patients, too. He was not a man to beat about the bush. "When can you start?"

Matron seized the opportunity. "Right away, if you want me to."

Next morning she joined the staff of Dr Caine's discreetly expensive abortion clinic at a salary beyond her wildest dreams.

When Mrs Kinloch's sons had confirmed that the lady in the mortuary was indeed their mother, Stubble took them to Police HQ and broke the news that her death was not a natural one. Dr Ho's examination had confirmed his suspicions. The broken fingers and pressure marks on her chin and legs were evidence of some sort of struggle. Her lungs had been starved of air as well, but there were no signs of strangulation. There was nothing out of the ordinary under

Mrs Kinloch's broken nails. She had not managed to scratch her assailant.

Dr Ho's report made clear she had been done to death, and that she had put up a struggle. It was up to Stubble to find out who had she been fighting off when she had died.

Stubble favoured Mrs Sedge as prime suspect, with Matron in second place and Violet well back in third.

But first he had to deal with her sons. After checking that they had somewhere to stay and offering any help he could he asked if they knew whether their mother had made a will.

Alastair answered. "Sure to have. Mum was a very organised sort of person."

"Do you know what it said?" asked Stubble.

Cameron answered that one. "No idea. She didn't know where we were until I traced her. She wanted to leave us something, but we refused. We are both quite well off and don't need it."

"We didn't want to give mum the bother," added Alastair.

"Any idea who she left her money to?"

"None at all. We never asked."

Stubble probed deeper. "Were you paying for her care at The Poplars?"

"No, we suggested it, but she told us that was all taken care of." Alastair looked to Cameron as if to get confirmation.

Cameron knew a little more. "She told me that she had some sort of lifetime care plan. I believe these things are quite common; several insurance companies run them. It's a sort of inverse life assurance. I must say the care at The Poplars was very good, as far as I could make out when we spoke on the phone. Mummy was very happy there."

"No worries." concluded Alastair.

Stubble went into a reverie. Mummy certainly had no worries now. Funny how all old people were deliriously happy in their old people's homes. I must be getting old and cynical myself, but who wouldn't be in this business, listening to lies and half-truths day in and day out. Like these two lovelies. Mummy, he'd called her. Hadn't seen the old girl for fourteen years, didn't even know she was in an old age home until his brother hired a private eye to track her down.

While he was thinking these great thoughts the Kinloch brothers sat feeling vaguely guilty and slightly nervous. Police stations tend to have that effect on people.

Stubble came back down off his cloud. "I don't think I need to keep you any longer. We know where to get in touch with you if we need to, don't we?"

The brothers nodded as he went on. I'll get you a car to take you back to your hotel. Once again let me express condolences, personally and on behalf of my colleagues. Please let me know when the funeral is going to be, and if of course you need any help with the arrangements, do please let me know."

When they had gone he made notes of the conversation he had just had. As he wrote "Care taken care of" he paused. He should have got the brothers to tell him more about that.

The brothers were staying at the County Hotel. He was just about to phone them there when Alastair knocked on his door, wanting to know if he could recommend a good undertaker.

Stubble gave him Gladwyn's number and took the chance to ask if he knew anything about the care plan his mother had subscribed to. Did he have any figures? Any idea how much such a plan would cost? What company it was with?

Alastair didn't. He suggested Stubble ask Mrs Sedge. Possibly the policy would be found amongst his mother's papers.

Stubble's nose gave a sniff and his ears pricked up. "Could we go and look through them now?" he asked.

Alastair was not keen. "Can't it wait? We'd like a bit of time to ourselves. It's been quite a shock, Cameron isn't as well as he looks. He's got heart problems."

Stubble sympathised. It could not have been very nice to come and visit your old mother only to find she had been murdered, but time was dripping away.

"I'd like to look through her papers as soon as possible, before anyone gets hold of them and tampers with them."

Alastair changed his mind. He saw the logic in this. "I'll come with you," he said simply.

Cameron was waiting downstairs. Alastair suggested he go back to the hotel and phone the undertaker while he went along with Stubble to The Poplars to deal with matters there. Stubble admired the way he put that. This Alastair was obviously a tactful man

"What do you do for a living" Stubble asked him after they had dropped Cameron at the hotel..

"I'm a lawyer. Specialising in Aboriginal rights." Alastair told him.

"Used to walking on eggshells?"

Alastair laughed. "You could say that. Every morning when I come to work I ask myself whose back I am going to put up before I go home."

They drove along in companionable silence until they got to the Poplars. Stubble dismissed the policewoman who was sitting outside Mrs Kinloch's room, telling her to go and enjoy herself for a quarter of an hour. She took herself off wondering what she could get up to in fifteen minutes.

"Any idea where your mother kept her papers?" Stubble asked Alastair Kinloch.

"None at all."

"Well, it should not take long to go through one room. You don't mind being here? It must be rather painful for you."

"Not at all. I'm as keen to find out what happened to my mother as you are." Stubble began to warm to Alastair.

They started with the obvious places, like the chest of drawers and the wardrobe, without success. They had just taken down her suitcase from on top of the wardrobe and were looking through its contents which turned out to be of more interest to Alastair than Stubble, since there were several photograph albums and a box full of letters from his father to his mother. He was just showing Stubble his school reports when Mrs Sedge erupted into the room, demanding to know what was going on.

Stubble looked up from the suitcase, which he imagined would explain what was happening. It didn't. She almost shrieked "You can't come in here going through Mrs Kinloch's things without my permission. Where's your search warrant?"

Alastair Kinloch looked at Mrs Sedge as though she was turd on a tablecloth. "Are you telling me I can't look through my mother's effects?" he asked quietly? "Are you saying I need your permission?"

Mrs Sedge changed character instantly. "Oh, dearie me," she cried, "I didn't recognise you, Mr Kinloch! I thought it was the police searching the room."

"Mr Stubble here is doing that very thing, "Alastair told her. "with my permission and assistance. I don't think you need stay."

"I've got every right to stay, if I want to!" Mrs Sedge switched back to belligerency.

"I don't think so," said Alastair. "My mother has paid rent for the room, which implies you can only come in at her invitation."

"Aha!" cried Mrs Sedge in a voice that said 'Gotcha!' "The rent stopped the moment she died. I'm repossessing it!" unfortunately the last word came out as "resoppressing."

Alastair made to come round the bed with the evident intent of picking up Mrs Sedge and dumping her outside the door when Stubble intervened. "Let her stay. She may be drunk, but she won't have any grounds for saying we interfered with anything if she's present in the room. In fact she may be able to help us. Mrs Sedge, can you tell us where the insurance policy or document or whatever it is that enabled Mrs Kinloch to afford to stay here for as long as she lived can be found?"

Mrs Sedge settled herself on the end of the bed. She looked cunning, or so she thought. Actually her face exhibited a strange mixture of stupidity and rampant evil. "You'd better go to Wimpole Street," she cackled "Wimpole Street," she repeated before she lay back on the bed, closed her eyes and went to sleep.

"What an awful sight," said Alastair Kinloch. "To think my mother was in the care of that harpy, and what the fuck is all this about Wimpole Street?"

Stubble made to leave. "She means her solicitor has got it. His name is Augustus Wimpole. We'd better get down there before he 'loses' it.

Alastair stopped him. "Just a moment, a second or two won't make a difference. I just don't like the notion of that old bag fast asleep on my mother's bed. Grab her legs, will you?"

They dumped Mrs Sedge on the corridor floor, got the policewoman back to her post, ran to the car and drove off at speed.

When they got to Augustus Wimpole's office Alastair said "I'll go up alone, you wait down here ready to come up if I call you."

Before Stubble could protest Alastair was through the door and half way up the stairs. He burst into Wimpole's office leaving secretaries open mouthed, and demanded Mrs Kinloch's file.

"Who the hell are you?" Wimpole was indignation personified.

"Her son. And I want her file now! All of it!"

"Get out of my office" was what Wimpole was going to say but he only got to "of" when Alastair grabbed him by the hair and forced his face onto his desk.

"You're hurting me!" he howled.

"That's the idea. Now where's my mother's file?"

"I'll get it for you if you let me go."

"O.K." Alastair let go.

Wimpole immediately made a dash for the door. Before he got there he hit the floor as Alastair executed a perfect rugby tackle. His secretary appeared at the door. "Get the police!" he yelled.

Alastair ground his heel into Wimpole's back and gave the girl her instructions: "If you go downstairs you'll see a dark green car with a man leaning on the bonnet. His name is Detective Inspector Stubble. Please ask him to come up." He pressed harder into Wimpole's spine. "You fucking crook, you've got those documents and you're going to give them to me."

Wimpole was finding breathing difficult. "I'm not a crook!" he managed to croak.

"Yes you fucking well are. I'm a barrister at the Sydney bar. I know what a bent lawyer looks like, mate." He paused for thought and then added "I'm a scrum half in my spare time. Thought you'd like to know that."

The secretary returned with Stubble in tow. "Mr Stubble," said Alastair, "you know Mr Wimpole I presume."

"I do indeed," agreed Stubble

"So no need to introduce you. How can we persuade Mr Wimpole here to give us the agreement Mrs Sedge tells us is here?"

"I'll have you for assault! I've got a witness now." shouted Wimpole from the floor.

"So you have, so you have" Alastair turned to the secretary. "Am I hitting Mr Wimpole?" he asked.

Before she could answer he went on: "Mr Wimpole complained of a pain in his back, and I'm trying to help with some spinal manipulation. Isn't that the case?"

"He's hurting me!" whimpered Wimpole.

"If it's not hurting it's not working. You'll be on your feet in a moment, old chap, right as rain. I'm sure this young lady can show Mr Stubble the document we are looking for while I finish your treatment. It will be filed under K for Kinloch, I imagine,"

"Shall I do what the gentleman says?" the secretary asked Wimpole.

Alastair gently turned his heel, leaning forward at the same time. "You're breaking my fucking back!" Wimpole screamed.

"Foul language in front of young impressionable female staff, tut tut! I put it to you, Mr Wimpole, there is no need for profanity." Alastair was enjoying himself.

Wimpole capitulated. "It's filed under Kinloch in the Poplars drawer."

The secretary went to the drawer, opened it and started to look for the Kinloch file. "Most interesting" Stubble breathed over her shoulder. "I'm sure Mr Wimpole would not object to me looking through that drawer, would he?"

Alastair took his foot off Wimpole's spine, replaced it lower down and pressed harder. "Any objections, Mr Wimpole?" he asked. The answer was a low moan.

The secretary found Mrs Kinloch's file and made to hand it to Stubble. "Please give it to Mr Kinloch," he said, taking the opportunity as she did so to start going through the drawer. It was not difficult to find the documents he was looking for, since they were expensively bound to impress the clients. Stubble looked at the names on the front of the other folders. They meant nothing to him. Then he opened one casually and cried "Bingo!" The words 'the sum of £104,000' leapt from the page, the same sum that was deposited in Mrs Sedge's bank account.

Stubble closed the folder, took out another and saw the same sum. He put the folder down and radioed HQ. "I want two constables to the offices of Augustus Wimpole, solicitors, in The Close, immediately."

"Did your mother give Mrs Sedge £104,000 to keep her for the rest of her life?" Stubble asked Alastair Kinloch.

"That's what it says here," Alastair replied. "This agreement is only ten months old. When my mother signed this she signed her death warrant." There was an edge of bitterness to his words.

Stubble said "The same sum is on this agreement. £104,000. It looks like today is a lucky day," he looked at the folder again "for Mrs Oliver, assuming she is still with us."

The two policemen Stubble had called for appeared with commendable promptitude. He addressed Wimpole. "Augustus Wimpole, I am arresting you on suspicion of being an accessory to murder. You do not need to say....."

Before he could finish the caution, Wimpole was shouting "I never murdered anyone, you've got no evidence! I want this man charged with assault."

Stubble's only reply was to tell the policemen to handcuff him.

As he was led away, still protesting his innocence Stubble told Alastair he was going to arrest Mrs Sedge, "before she vanishes like that Juanita Standish. Want to come with, or do you want to go back to the hotel and see how your brother is getting on?"

"I'll come with you. I want to see that bitch get her comeuppance." declared Alastair.

When they got to The Poplars Mrs Sedge wasn't talking. She was slumped in her armchair in front of the television fast asleep. The bottle of brandy and the empty glass explained why. Alastair volunteered to stay with her until she woke up to allow Stubble to return to HQ to question Wimpole a bit further. Stubble told him not to bother. His nose told him she wasn't going to run, and if she did it would not be far before they caught up with her.

"If you'd just lie on your tummy for a moment," said Matron. "I'm afraid this is going to hurt, but after you've had the injection you won't feel a thing. Just a little prick..."

"If it wasn't for one of those I wouldn't be here" laughed Pollyanna Goldwater." I've never seen one so small. Thought one as tiny as that couldn't do any harm." She switched the gum from one side of her mouth to the other before turning over.

Matron wasn't listening. Her body might be in Tulsa, Oklahoma, but her mind was in Dununder.

How long would it take them to track her down? Wouldn't they pass the word to the FBI or the immigration service or something? Surely they had ways and means of tracing a single woman who flew to New York the day she fled The Poplars. It wasn't as if she had killed Mrs Bonnie, in fact she had kept her alive, well, on paper anyway. She'd given her a decent burial as well. They should be grateful, not hunt her down like a dog.

But it looked as if she had killed her. Why else should she bury her in the garden?

She'd be hard put to it to prove her innocence. But she didn't have to! They had to prove she was guilty!"

"You going to get rid of this fucking baby or not?" she heard Pollyanna saying.

Matron stopped day-dreaming and applied herself to the business of preparing her patient for Dr Caine.

Pollyanna was just a few days short of her fifteenth birthday.

It was the first time Stubble had had to deal with a bent lawyer. Augustus Wimpole wasn't talking. He simply declined to assist the police, over and over again. If they had evidence, then why did they not prefer a charge? Useless to tell him his silence would count against him in court - he knew that was a bluff. No good threatening him with wasting police time. What about the Lifetime Care Agreements and what had happened to various sums of £104,000? The agreements? They were between his client and others and perfectly legal, he had in fact advised his client against her taking them out. The money? He had no idea what Mrs Sedge had done with it. The premature deaths of the people who signed those agreements? He had no idea they had been premature. Stubble had no grounds for holding him and he had to insist he be released.

Stubble was forced to let him go.

When Wimpole got back to his office he was mortified to find Alastair Kinloch and his brother had convinced his secretary that they had the right to go through all the files that pertained to The Poplars. The girl, who had not been with him long, confessed that the Australian lawyer had taken some papers away.

He fired her on the spot and then stayed in his office nearly all night going through every file that that was left that anything to do with The Poplars. Nothing was missing except a few Lifetime Care Plans. As he read the various documents he convinced himself that there was nothing incriminating in them. He had merely carried out his client's instructions. If an elderly lady wanted to leave all her money to the care home where she had spent the last years of her life, it was his duty to advise her against such a course of action if he did not consider it to be in her best interest, but if she insisted, then he had to draw up the will as she asked. He had had his doubts about the financial aspects of Mrs Sedge's Lifetime Care Plan, and had indeed suggested that she would be better letting a well-established insurance company who had considerable experience of such arrangements, administer the plan, but again he had to accede to his client's wishes, and had drawn up an agreement which in his opinion protected the rights of both parties.

He went off to breakfast convinced he was in the clear. Untouchable. That Australian lawyer could do his worst. Wimpole was impregnable.

He reckoned without the Australian lawyer's brother. Cameron was a banker. He knew how the system worked, and more to the point, he knew how to trace his mother's money. It didn't take him long to find out that the cheque his mother had given Mrs Sedge had been paid into her account at the Cayman Islands Guarantee Bank. To find out more he needed only to talk to a slightly shady gentleman who had in the past found things out about nominally very confidential bank accounts all over the world. It didn't cost him very much to discover that a Mr Augustus Wimpole had an account at the same bank as Mrs Sedge, and the numbers of both accounts.

"What's the good of the account numbers?" asked Alastair. "We need to know the details, what went in, what went out, where from, where to, when?"

Stubble nodded his agreement. They were reviewing progress in his flat, eating a takeaway supplied by the Star of Bengal. Things were not going well. Wimpole was sticking to his story that he had merely carried out the instructions of his client, who had refused to accept his advice. His client, Mrs Sedge, was stoutly refusing to admit to having anything to do with the death of Mrs Kinloch. She tried to put the blame on Violet which had simply wasted some of Stubble's time. Scene of the crime officers have been over Mrs Kinloch's room with toothcombs and, as Stubble expected, found plenty of traces of Mrs Sedge, Violet, Matron and nearly every other member of the rest home's staff, none of which proved anything except that they had all given her every possible care.

There was no evidence that Violet had not killed the old lady, but there was nothing to say she had. He had questioned her at length and depth about her movements that night even though he knew he was on to a hiding for nothing. The poor woman could not account for every minute of her activities. She had listed which residents she had visited and what she had done, in one case helping an old lady to the toilet, which the resident corroborated, and in another escorting a gentleman, who was hopefully wandering the corridors minus his pyjama trousers, back to his room, again corroborated by the other carers who confirmed that Mr Dale went hunting for love almost every night, but she was not in the habit of looking at her watch, so none of what she told him helped Stubble.

Talking to Violet convinced Stubble she had nothing to do with the death. Violet was self-evidently one of those people who had not an unkind bone in her body. She spoke well of everyone. Mrs Sedge was such a good manager and such a kind lady too, all the residents were lovely people, even when they were being difficult, well, you had to make allowances, didn't you? She nearly managed to convince Stubble that no crime could have been committed in that earthly paradise they called The Poplars.

The mystery of the body in the garden was still open. Even though she had confessed, could he be sure that Matron had discovered her dead, buried her in the garden, and put Mrs Borland in her place? The Borlands must have realised something was not as it should have been when they handed over £500 in cash to Matron every week but they were so desperate to get the old woman out of their house they turned a blind eye. The question of that money was possibly fraud, possibly theft, but Stubble reckoned he could leave that to one side. It was a civil matter between Mrs Sedge and Miss Standish. The crime he was investigating was murder, and Mrs Sedge was the prime suspect, working with Matron? No reason why not.

Stubble wanted to get Sedge, wanted to nail Wimpole even more. Mrs Sedge was an ordinary malefactor, no doubt acting out of greed or envy or some sort of perversion. Wimpole was different. Wimpole was a solicitor, a fellow soldier in the forces of Law and Order, who had betrayed his sacred trust, deserted, committed treason. The various occasions Wimpole had got plainly guilty parties off was never a factor at all in Stubble's reckoning of the evil character of the man.

"So what's the good of the account numbers?" Alastair asked again.

"Leave it to me," said Cameron. "There are ways and means."

Stubble and Alastair understood him immediately.

"A touch illegal, are they?" Alastair winked.

"Breaking the Law" said Stubble bluntly.

"I don't recollect saying anything of the sort." replied Cameron. "I will have to go in person to Wronki."

"What, who or where," said Alastair slowly, "is Wronki?"

"It's in Poland." replied Cameron.

"And why do you need to go to Poland?"

"That's my business, but I guarantee I'll come back with every detail of those accounts." Cameron told him.

"Not good enough, Cam," said his brother. "We need to know what there is in Wronki that will give us this information."

Cameron considered for a moment, and then said "Between these four walls, and I shall deny everything if asked."

"Well?" said Stubble.

"It's a hacker. In fact the hacker. The greatest hacker in the universe. He lives there, in Wronki."

"His name?"

"Tadeusz, the surname you don't need to know. He broke into our bank's books, and our IT guys ran him to earth. Took them a year almost, but they did it. We turned him."

"Turned him?"

"In return for our people making sure he obliterated everything he'd got out of our system, and helping us make sure the friends who were using him got a bundle of false data packed with viruses we agreed not to pick him up by the scruff of the neck and feed him to the dogs."

Stubble grinned. "He works for you now."

Alastair suddenly regarded Stubble through new eyes. Cameron said nothing.

"OK by you?" Alastair asked Stubble.

"I'm not here and I've gone deaf."

Alastair turned to his brother. "O.K., Cameron. Let's do it. Do you think you can get the money back?"

"That I can't guarantee, but I'm pretty sure I can find out what happened to it. Even that isn't one hundred per cent certain though."

"Go ahead then. Do whatever is needed."

"Guess how old our hacker is." said Cameron.

"Ten years old?" suggested Alastair.

"How did you guess? Actually he's just turned eleven."

Stubble voiced a doubt. "Whatever you find out won't be any use. I can hardly present it as evidence, if you are going outside the law. Not only that, but could you get this kid into a witness box?"

"You've got a point there," said Alastair. "Even if you got him there he might not be any use. In my experience children are sometimes fantastic witnesses and sometimes hopeless."

Cameron had other ideas. "As far as I'm concerned the less courts and the legal system are involved the better. I reckon if we confront our birds with detailed records of their own off-the-record financial transactions they'll cave in."

"I'm not so sure," said Stubble, "but it's worth a try."

"Might break the logjam," agreed Alastair." We might be able to do a Capone on them."

"A Capone?" Stubble did not understand.

"Al Capone. They never got near him for murder, extortion or general gangsterism, but the Internal Revenue Service hunted him down and got him put away for tax fraud. We could do something similar." explained Cameron.

"When can you go to Poland?" Alastair asked his brother.

"I'll go first thing in the morning"

"How do you know you'll get a flight?"

"I'm going by rail. Much more pleasant, just as quick and no name on the ticket. I've checked the train times and I can be in Poznan by tomorrow night. Wronki is a few stops from there on the Szczecin line. I'll be waiting for him when he comes home from school."

"Does he speak English?"

"Of a sort. Geek English. Enough for me to tell him what I want him to do, and take him to a computer shop in Poznan and buy him any kit he desires by way of keeping him sweet."

Alastair declared the meeting closed and they repaired to the Green Man, where the brothers had discovered a cache of genuine Australian Castlemaine.

Somehow Alastair and Stubble managed to get up in time to march Cameron the few yards from the County Hotel to Dunuder Castle Station and to tumble him into the 05.15 to Paddington.

Pollyanna Goldwater was eating her dinner when she felt ill. She got up to go to the bathroom but threw up before she got out of the room. In spite of her protests that it must have been the burger she had eaten on the way home, her mother put her to bed and called the doctor.

By the time he arrived Pollyanna was ready to admit she was in agony. It did not take the doctor long to guess what the trouble might be. He gave her a sedative and went downstairs to talk to her parents.

"I'd like to run some tests. In fact," he nerved himself; what he was going to say – it might just produce an explosive reaction from her parents, "in fact, I'd like her to be checked over by a gynecologist."

"A gynecologist?" Mrs Goldwater said, "something down there not developing properly?"

Thankful for the out she had given him, he told her "Could be. It's not my specialism, but I'd like it to be seen to as soon as possible. Be OK if I call an ambulance? We'll get her to the Community Hospital and they'll take care of it."

Her father said "Whatever it takes".

It didn't take long for the gynecologist to find out what was wrong with Pollyanna. It took longer to get her to tell him where she had had the abortion, but he was a very persuasive physician.

Next morning there was a squad car outside the Tulsa Maternity Clinic. Dr Caine was very quick to refer the officers to his new English nurse. Her protestations that she had only administered the anesthetic before Dr Caine did the actual operation were brushed aside and she was taken into custody.

Pollyanna's story found its way into the local paper. Public feeling was aroused against the clinic and the foreign woman who was messing around with 'our fine American womanhood' and in no time at all the clinic was being picketed by a curious mixture of antiabortion activists, local rednecks, women's groups, concerned citizens and assorted religious fanatics.

That evening, as Dr Caine was driving out of the clinic's underground car park, his Lincoln was halted by a mob of screaming protesters, one of whom had a Mauser. The bullet went straight through the windscreen, entered and exited Dr Caine's brain and ignited the petrol tank which slightly singed some of the crowd.

It didn't take long for the police to establish that Juanita was in the United States on a tourist visa and had no right to work. They contacted the FBI who referred the matter to Scotland Yard, who in a matter of days found out that she was wanted by the Undershire Police in connection with the death of Mrs Kinloch.

Juanita still had the return half of her airline ticket which saved the American taxpayer the cost of sending her back to the UK.

CHAPTER FIVE
Cameron Goes East

Cameron was well received in Wronki. It was half term at Tadeusz's school, and his parents welcomed the arrival of an Australian child minder out of the blue with open arms. They spoke only Polish, so Tadeusz had to translate what they said.

"What did they say just then?" asked Cameron as they got into their car..

"No spend all day on that computer."

Banker and hacker looked at each other quizzically for all of ten seconds. Cameron broke the silence. "Come on then, switch the machine on and boot up!" Five minutes later Tadeusz was methodically searching the net for the Sedge bank accounts. It took him less than an hour to find Mrs Sedge's bank and another twenty minutes to hack into her Dununder current account. Getting last two years' transactions from the Cayman Islands bank was more of a challenge – their security was much tougher, but by lunch time Cameron had all the data he needed. Tadeusz also located a smaller holding at the Schweitzer Krediet Bank in Zurich. Evidently Mrs Sedge was getting nervous about the Cayman Islands.

When Tadeusz's parents returned they were delighted to find this mysterious angel from the other side of the planet playing football with their son in the garden. If they had been less trusting they might have asked why Tadeusz's friend's eyes never left his briefcase. They might also have asked what Tadeusz had done for the visitor that made him take the boy into Poznan and buy him enough mysterious packages to fill a taxi.

Tadeusz spent all day after Cameron left setting up his new computer and installing programs onto it. Cameron for his part spent only about half an hour on the train reading the printouts he had taken. He had considered e-mailing the information he had got hold of directly to his brother but that might have been breaking the law, and his brother was an attorney after all. Another obstacle was his having forgotten Alastair's e-mail address. Sitting opposite him in the compartment was a man in uniform who he guessed was a Polish police officer. The sight of the uniform made him feel guilty. Was hacking into bank accounts illegal in Poland? How many years could he get? He told himself he was being paranoid, but still found himself trying not to look at the man.

The following afternoon he arrived back in Dununder unaware that on the same train was a prison officer escorting Mrs Juanita Standish from Heathrow to Dununder Police HQ.

Stubble hated interview rooms. No amount of money spent on decor could dispel their cold formality. Whoever thought them up seemed to have designed them deliberately to make sure the interviewee said as little as possible. The presence of the tape recorder and a chaperone made it remarkable that anyone ever uttered a useful word in them. He preferred to talk to witnesses and suspects in familiar surroundings, spending time putting them at their ease waiting like a spider watching a fly for the vital word to drop unbidden from their lips. Nine times out of ten it worked.

He mused about what would be officialdom's reaction if he suggested taking Juanita Standish over to the Hanged Highwayman, and chatting to her over a drink and a packet of crisps. The Chief would go ape! Stubble was lumbered with the interview room.

How to open the batting? Look straight into her eyes and say "did you murder Mrs Kinloch?" or maybe "why did you murder Mrs Kinloch?" He had known coppers who got immediate confessions that way, but it was not his style. It would be hard to reopen the conversation after she had said "No" or "I didn't".

Better to ask why she had chosen to creep away to America. Be the sympathetic cop, trying to get on her side, trying earnestly to understand what had caused her to leave The Poplars without handing in her notice.

He drank up his coffee and decided on his opening sentence. He got up, opened the window and tried it out on the miserable horse. "How was your flight?" he asked it. The horse glanced up at him with a look of utter contempt.

He shut the window and went downstairs to Interview Room B. Juanita Standish was already sitting there, full of beans after her night's sleep on the plane, beans she was preparing to spill in all directions.

"Bang to rights" Cameron Kinloch told his brother, passing the printouts Tadeusz's computer had produced across the hotel breakfast table.

Alastair peered at the rows of letters and figures uncomprehendingly. "Explain." he said, passing the papers back and applying himself to buttering a slice of toast.

"The long and short of it is that Mrs Sedge has been..."

"More coffee?" asked a waitress, "or maybe a little more toast?"

"No thanks" said Alastair testily.

"You could go round the buffet again," said the waitress helpfully.

"Thank you," said Cameron, holding out his cup. "Quickest way to get rid of her," he told his brother as she departed. "Now, translated from computer-speak to banker's language, and then into plain English, Mrs Sedge has been taking £104,000 from any new resident she thinks is going to be a likely prospect."

"What makes them a likely prospect?" asked Alastair.

"That's more your expertise than mine. This coffee is cold and vile."

Alastair could not resist remarking "not such a cheap a way of getting rid of that stupid waitress, was it?"

Cameron chose to ignore him. "All I have here, after, I'm sure you will tell me, a trip to deepest Poland and back, is a list of eleven transfers of £104,000 into the madam's account in the Cayman Islands plus two for the same sum into an account at SKB in Zurich, matched in each case by a payment to a Mr A. Wimpole of £26,000."

"Twenty-five per cent commission to Wimpole," said Alastair. You don't pass someone a cut that big without there being a quid pro quo."

"Perhaps she was sleeping with him?" ventured Alastair.

Casmeron laughed. "Have you seen them?"

"Joke, brother, joke."

"Sorry, Al, I never know when to take you seriously."

"Seriously, then, what was she getting off Wimpole for his twenty-five per cent?"

"Fuck knows. Maybe he shunted the money round, maybe hc camc up with the idea in the first place, perhaps he has a twenty-five per cent share in The Poplars and so is entitled to a quarter of the profits, could check that easily at Companies House, could be anything. Could be just to keep his mouth shut. In any case, why he got it doesn't concern us. What does concern us is that he was getting it, which makes him a party to whatever was going on."

Cameron finished his coffee with a grimace, saying "I still think it was payment for sexual favours,"

As he said it he became aware of a coffee pot hovering over his right shoulder.

"Drop more?" asked the waitress.

Stubble had got as far as "Good morning, Mrs Standish, I trust you slept well," when his mobile rang insistently.

He held up his hand to indicate the interview was suspended while he listened to Alastair's news. When he had heard it he said "Thank you. The pieces are beginning to fall into place. I'll be in touch." Then he turned back to Juanita. "Well, Mrs Standish, how was your flight?"

She misunderstood. "I'm sorry I've given you all this trouble by running away. I realise now I should have come and told you when it happened, instead of waiting all this time, but I needed the money, and I thought to myself, I'll never have a chance like this again."

Somewhat at a loss, Stubble contented himself by saying "Go on."

She went on. "It was the Borlands, you see. They were getting desperate having to look after the old lady. Anyone could see that, and with Mrs Sedge away I saw a chance to help them and start a new life for myself at the same time. It seemed the obvious thing to do."

Stubble began to understand. "How did Mrs Bonnie die?"

"I don't know. I went in to see how she was just after Violet had helped her to her room after lunch."

"Was she awake?"

"Oh, yes. She said something like "What a lovely day, I'll just lie down and rest a little while." She had the window open. ""I'll be able to see the clouds, listen to the birds and smell the flowers, before I go to sleep."

"And then?"

"I went in to shut her window a bit later because it had got a bit windy, and there she was lying there."

"Stubble had to have her say the word. "Lying there what?"

"Dead. She looked so peaceful. She had a lovely smile on her face as if she had just seen an angel."

"What did you do then?"

"I checked her vital signs, of course, but she'd gone. It was then I had my idea."

"To keep quiet about her being dead and to put Mrs Borland in her place. Wouldn't Mrs Sedge have noticed?"

Juanita gave a short laugh, sounded more like a bark. "Not Mrs Sedge. She was much too busy being busy to get to know the residents, Guests, as she called them. "All the real work was left to me."

"Including giving them their medication." Stubble knew immediately he had made a mistake. She stopped saying what she was going to say and burst into tears.

"Not that again" she sniffled when she had partly regained her composure." I made one mistake and I'm going to be an outcast for the rest of my life. That's why I had to get away. She kept reminding me about it."

"A sort of blackmail," said Stubble hoping it would calm her. "She had you where she wanted you."

It worked. "Yes. She knew she had a hold over me. She kept telling me I was lucky to have a job at The Poplars. If I said anything she was going to report me for working as a nurse when I was barred."

"But she'd be just as much to blame for employing you, wouldn't she?" Stubble pointed out. "After all she knew you had been struck off."

Juanita looked up, startled. There was silence for a moment. Then she said "You know, that never occurred to me."

Stubble nodded. "So you didn't think you were doing anything wrong when you didn't tell her Mrs Bonnie was dead, and you put Mrs Borland in her room?"

"Not really," sniffled Juanita.

"She had asked for it. Mrs Sedge, I mean? Would you agree?"

"Yes," Juanita replied simply.

Stubble guessed the time had come for Juanita to have a rest. "Shall we break for elevenses?" he asked. He saw the young constable who was chaperoning Juanita look puzzled. "Elevenses – a cup of something to break up the morning at eleven o'clock," he explained..

Juanita relaxed visibly at the mention of a break, of a hot cup of something.

"Interview suspended at 10.51 hours." said the WPC decisively, as she switched off the tape recorder. 'Thanks a bunch' thought Stubble as he saw Juanita stiffen.

Stubble took advantage of the break to contact the Kinloch brothers. Cameron answered the phone. "So you've got evidence they've been salting away large amounts abroad?" he asked the banker.

"Yes. In Cayman and Switzerland. Thirteen tranches of £104,000 in all."

Stubble did a quick calculation. "That's getting on for one and a half million."

Cameron corrected Stubble. He was a banker. The word "about" was not in his vocabulary. "One million, three hundred and fifty two thousand, but the interesting thing is that every time a tranche was transferred..." he paused for effect. Stubble wondered if "tranche" was the same thing as "slice", "twenty-six thousand was passed to Mr A. Wimpole's account in a Luxembourg bank. He didn't even use an alias."

"So Wimpole got a quarter." said Stubble not to be outdone mathematically by the banker.

"That's right," confirmed Cameron. "So it means we can charge them with fraud."

"We can indeed, as long as we can prove they did not intend to use the money for the purpose for which it was intended."

Cameron understood what Stubble meant. He knew from experience that clients who indulged in fraudulent theft often wriggled off the hook by convincing gullible juries that they were hiding the loot in a safe place to protect the clients' interests, meant to give it back, were the victims of circumstances or were innocents who had had the wool pulled over their eyes.

Stubble was not quite sure how much he should tell Cameron. He finally decided to be vague. He said "This case is like an onion, you sort out one layer and then you have to get through the next, but don't worry, I think we are getting near the middle here."

Cameron wondered for a moment what onions had to do with the matter, but didn't ask. Stubble concluded "Tell you what; I'm in the middle of a pretty important interview just now. How about you come here tomorrow morning, say nine o'clock, with your evidence. I think I may have some good news by then."

Csmeron countered "Why don't you come to the County Hotel this evening. We can discuss things over a drink. More pleasant. Come and eat with us, if you're free."

"O.K. I'll phone you later if I can make it." replied Stubble.

As he went back to the interview room his nose told him talking to Juanita Standish was not going to get him anywhere. He should be sniffing round Mrs Sedge and her lawyer friend. Still, Juanita was here and in an interview room, so he might as well get as much as he could out of her while she was on the premises.

"Where were we?" he asked, almost to himself, by way of picking up the thread. "Oh, yes...... Mrs Bonnie? What did you do with her after you realised she was dead?"

"I put her in the wardrobe."

"You put her in the wardrobe?" He wondered if he had heard right.

"I had to get her out of the way before I showed the room to Mr and Mrs Borland." Stubble wondered at the things that went on in rest homes. Was this typical?

"Mrs Sedge didn't notice anything?"

"She was away."

"I see. And then what?"

"I took her out that night when everyone was asleep and buried her in the garden."

"On your own? Nobody helped you?"

She nodded.

"You are prepared to make a statement to that effect?"

She nodded again.

"Please say Yes or No."

"Yes," she replied in a low voice.

"Just let me be sure I've got it straight. You found Mrs Bonnie dead while Mrs Sedge was away, saw your chance to make some money by giving her room to Mrs Borland without Mrs Sedge knowing it, and put the money her family paid for her care into your own pocket. You buried Mrs Bonnie in the garden. That right?"

Again that small voice. "Yes, that's right. I'm very sorry. Shall I write the statement now?"

"Not yet. You may be able to help us with the death of Mrs Kinloch."

"Mrs Kinloch. Is she dead?" She seemed genuinely shocked.

"You didn't know?"

"No."

"She was killed, I'm afraid."

She put her hand to her mouth. "Killed? You mean .....murdered?"

"I'm afraid it looks that way."

"That's awful. Do you know who did it?"

"Not yet."

"You think I did it?"

"Let's just say we have to eliminate you from our enquiries, shall we?"

A tear formed in the corner of her eye and began to trickle down her cheek. The WPC passed her a tissue. She said "I didn't do it."

"My mind is open." He leaned forward and stared straight into her eyes. "Suppose you tell me exactly what happened that night, the night you left The Poplars."

Juanita went over the story of her departure from The Poplars in so much detail that Stubble was confirmed in his guess that he was wasting his time talking to her. He turned over the business of getting a written statement about the death and burial of Mrs Bonnie to the WPC and left to take himself over to The Poplars where Mrs Sedge made a show of being too busy to talk to him which forced him to use nasty words like arrest and charge. She had the choice of going to Police HQ for a formal interview or making him a nice cup of coffee and going somewhere private for a friendly chat to help him sort his ideas out. She chose the latter.

"It must be a great responsibility running a place like this." he opened after they had had the coffee and biscuits and exchanged a few observations about the weather.

"You've no idea," she agreed. "Old people can be very trying, you know."

"You must be missing Miss Standish."

"I certainly am. I suppose you'll be charging her."

"We're working on it. Can we go over the night Mrs Kinloch died again? I know it's a bore but I have to get certain details clear in my mind. So many people tell you different stories.... it's very hard to tell whether they're lying or just recollecting mistakenly. Miss Standish says she went round the residents with Violet between one and two o'clock to check they were all right. According to Violet you found Mrs Kinloch dead at," he made a pretence of consulting his notes, "at about ten past four."

"She's lying!" Mrs Sedge said viciously.

"Who is?" asked Stubble innocently.

"Matron. Miss Standish. I wish I'd never employed her."

"Why? You said she was not involved with the patients, I mean Guests, medically."

"She ran away. Wouldn't have done that if she hadn't done it!"

"Maybe she had other reasons for running. After all she had buried Mrs Bonnie in the garden."

"So it was her?"

"Oh, yes. She's confessed."

"You'll be charging her with that murder, then."

"Hardly. Mrs Bonnie died of heart failure, as far as we can make out. We may be charging Miss Standish with theft, but we have to be pretty sure of a conviction and we aren't there yet. We could certainly get her for illegal disposal of a body, there's quite a heavy tariff for that, but I imagine she'd get a suspended sentence. Now, about Mrs Kinloch...."

Mrs Sedge was a good poker player. She didn't even blink.

"About Mrs Kinloch. I believe she paid you £104,000 in advance on the understanding that in return you would keep her at The Poplars and look after her for the rest of her life."

Did Mrs Sedge blush? She asked "How do you know that?"

"Her sons found it out from her solicitor, a Mr Wimpole."

Mrs Sedge recovered her poise. "It's our Lifetime Care Plan. Guests pay a lump sum, and we keep them for the rest of their life, as you say. It's like an insurance policy; the average life expectancy of our guests is four years. If they live longer they win, if not so long we do. It gives them peace of mind and we know where we are financially."

"I see," said Stubble. "It seems like rather a good idea. How long has it been running?"

"Oh, I'm not sure, three, four years, maybe."

"So nobody has lived long enough, so far, to enjoy what amounts to free residence at The Poplars?"

"I'm not sure."

Stubble pounced. "I do, Mrs Sedge. Not one of the ladies who signed up for your Lifetime Care Plan lived longer than twelve months after doing so."

She was a cool customer. She just shrugged her shoulders and said "We've been lucky, I suppose."

"Very lucky. I imagine The Poplars must have a pretty hefty bank balance as a result."

Not a twitch from the lady. "It's invested. The interest is our profit."

"Good. No doubt it will show up in your accounts. After all you don't want anyone accusing you of making off with the Guests' money, do you?" He laughed. He saw her face begin to flush again. Her eyes, which had been meeting his were now staring fixedly at his shoes.

"Sindirt Ltd," he went on. "trading as The Poplars Care Home. One of those companies you buy off the shelf. They do give them funny names, don't they?" I see you haven't sent a return to Companies House for two years. That's breaking the law, you know. Do you have an accountant?"

Andrews and Zelig in the city. They look after our accounts. Mr Wimpole told me he sees to the legal side. I suppose that includes filing the accounts. He doesn't seem to have done it."

Stubble smiled. "Tut-tut. A solicitor breaking the law. I would not have thought it of him. Is he your partner by any chance?"

It wasn't a trap, but she fell into it. "She said "I thought he was but he did the dirty on me."

At first Stubble didn't realise what she meant. He was about to agree that it was unwise for a solicitor to have a financial interest in a client's business, but got the message just in time. He asked "You were lovers?"

Too quick. She had recovered herself and managed to sound suitably scandalised. "Of course not. He was my solicitor but as soon as this business came up he said he could not act for me."

"Why would he do that?"

"No idea. He said he didn't do criminal law, but there must have been more to it than that."

"He could have farmed the job out, I suppose, or recommended someone else. Didn't he do that?"

"No. Just told me he couldn't act for me any longer."

Stubble knew there was more to the Sedge and Wimpole relationship than solicitor/client. There was the twenty-five per cent taken out the so called Lifetime Care Plan for a start and no doubt other scams, large and small. Even if they hadn't gone to bed together carnally they certainly had done financially. If anything Wimpole stank even more than Sedge. Stubble's nose told him Wimpole was the driving force, had some sort of hold over her.

Which was not his business at that moment. Wimpole could wait. Mrs Sedge was here, now, and his job was to get her to admit to murder. He didn't seem to be getting very far

He kept on trying. "That's rather strange, Wimpole ditching you like that. In my experience solicitors hang on to their clients come hell and high water. It hurts their pride to lose one, and they've always got an eye for the income. What you've just told me leads me to think we'd better have a close look at his accounts, and of course we shall have to have a look at your, or rather Sindirt's, books."

That hit home. Why had he not thought of it from the start. She stammered. "I told you I left all that to Wimpole. I just signed whatever he gave me to sign. I trusted him."

"That's all right. We'll talk to him about that. You must have some records here at the home, though, and I'm sure you won't have any objection to our looking at your bank account and the company's account."

She realised that her refusal would almost be an admission of guilt. She said "That's all right."

"I'll need a letter from you authorising it – or better still, we could go to the bank together so if I've got any queries you can clear them up right away on the spot. Tell you what, why don't we get it over with, go down there right away. It'll only take half an hour or so."

Playing for time she protested "I'm very busy just now."

"Getting ready to get rid of another resident?" he asked without thinking.

She wasn't thinking either. "Not for the moment." she replied and then realised what she had said.

Stubble suddenly dropped the informality. "Maureen Sedge" he said "I am arresting you on suspicion of the murder of Mrs Eileen Kinloch. You do not have to say anything…."

It was a bluff. She could have said it was a slip of the tongue, or she hadn't heard him right, or that he hadn't understood her or even flatly denied saying it, but she didn't. She broke down, burst into tears, said it was all Wimpole's idea, she wished she'd never met him, nobody understood the pressure she was under, and finally, that she was glad it was over. Stubble listened patiently and impassively until she had finished and was drying her tears.

Then he said, not unkindly, "I think we'd better go down to Police H.Q. Come along now Maureen."

"I'll just get my hat, and it's Mrs Sedge if you don't mind, Inspector." was her only response.

In the aseptic environment of an interview room at Police HQ, faced with Stubble, a young lady constable and a tape recorder Mrs Sedge hastened to got it all off her not unimpressive chest. She sang like a canary and her song consisted of one word only. Wimpole. She had been quietly running an ordinary old people's home, aiming at the highest standards of care, until Wimpole the worm whispered his evil thoughts in her ear.

Wimpole had been her solicitor for years, their relationship entirely professional, until, she imagined, his wife died. He had changed after that. He had several times made improper suggestions which she had stubbornly rejected.

Stubble interrupted the concert to ask just what she meant by improper. She looked at him scornfully. "Do I have to spell it out, Inspector. Suggestions of a sexual nature."

"For instance?"

"He invited me to have dinner with him. I refused of course, but he kept on, well, you know what I mean."

"When did he suggest you got rid of residents and charged more to the new ones?"

"It was that Mr Warren. He offered me twice our usual rate to take his father as a Guest. I tell a lie. He didn't offer it, he gave it, I mean I didn't even ask for it, gave me a cheque for a year in advance at twice our normal rate.

"Hard to resist."

"I didn't realise what he'd done really. He literally dumped his father on our doorstep and thrust an envelope into my hand. It was only then I came to pay the cheque in that I realised he had not just added a little extra as he had said he would, but doubled the amount I had asked for."

Stubble did not believe this for a moment but he held his peace. Let the woman talk.

And she did. "I phoned him,"

"Who? Wimpole?"

"Yes. Wimpole, and asked what I should do. Was it all right? I meant legal? Should I tell Mr Warren? Maybe he had made a mistake?"

Stubble was very tempted to interject, but kept his mouth shut.

"And he told me to pay it in before Mr Warren changed his mind. Then he started talking about how he charged different fees to different clients according to what they could afford, and why didn't I do the same?"

"So you did?"

"Yes. Later he suggested some of the guests would be better off dead."

Stubble was puzzled. Surely no lawyer would be so indiscreet. "He used those very words?"

"He said," she paused to make sure she remembered correctly. "He said they should be encouraged to move over. To make way for people who could pay better."

"And you took him at his word."

"Oh no. It just happened that we had several deaths, one after the other, so we had the vacancies for guests who could afford that little extra."

Guests. That little extra. Move over. The woman spoke and most likely thought in euphemisms.

"You didn't have a hand in easing them out of this world?"

"Oh no, Mr Stubble. Not at all!"

He suddenly got up, scraping his chair as he did so. "It doesn't matter. You've confessed to killing Mrs Kinloch, so we can leave the others for the moment. What about the money though? £104,000 at a time. All sent offshore. Shunted round the world so we wouldn't be able to trace it.

She said nothing. Her face said 'how the hell does he know about that?'

"Oh yes," he went on. We know all about Your Long Term Care Plan. We've got the contracts, the glossy brochures and best of all, copies of your offshore bank accounts, so I don't have to bother you about that. I suppose you are going to say it was all Mr Wimpole's idea. That you left all the money side of things to him."

"Why don't you ask him?" she said sullenly.

"We have, and he blames it all on you. Says he knows nothing about it. Just drew up the contracts as requested. He came expensive, though, didn't he? I don't know what a top London solicitor charges, but £26,000 for drawing up a two page contract seems over the top to me."

That was all she needed. It was obvious Stubble knew everything. "It was Wimpole!" she shouted. "I was a fool. I thought he loved me."

She could not go on. Tears streamed down her face and she hid her head in her hands. Stubble gave her time to recover and when she had blown her nose and wiped her eyes and had a glass of water he asked gently "You were lovers?"

"He used me. God, what a fool I was! He must have thought I was a common tart. No!" She gave a laugh which came out as a sort of snort. "No! I wasn't a tart. Tarts get paid. I was paying him." She stared out of the window at a truck which was delivering to the canteen. "I was running a nice quiet little business until he came along with his big ideas!"

"Don't worry," Stubble told her, "We've got all we need to see Mr Wimpole gets what he deserves. He'll try to wriggle his way out of it, but all those sums of £26,000 going into his Swiss bank account – he's going to have trouble explaining them away."

"So dear Mr Wimpole's going to get what's coming to him?"

"I hope so. He's on his way here now in a police car. I just have to go through the business of formally charging you and then I'll be having a little chat with Mr Wimpole."

"Will I be able to go when you've done that?"

"Not my decision." he said, thankful he did not have to explain that with over a million pounds luring her to Grand Cayman, bail would be unlikely.

Case closed. A result. Now for Wimpole. Wimpole would be a much tougher nut to crack. Interesting that Mrs Sedge had refused a solicitor, most likely Wimpole was the only one she knew.

Wimpole came into the interview room with, 'how can I help sort out the mess that silly woman has got herself into?' written all over his face. His story was almost the exact opposite of hers. He had merely drawn up the contracts, advising her against what she was doing, but he had no power to stop her. He had his suspicions, but only suspicions.

Stubble asked "Why did you not come to us with those suspicions?"

"Client confidentiality, and anyway you would have laughed me out of court."

Stubble forbore to mention that Wimpole was not yet in court. He merely murmured "We might have been able to stop a couple of unfortunate ladies being killed."

"If I could be sure of that I'd feel guilty."

Once again Stubble resisted the temptation to tell him he should be feeling exactly that. He said quietly "Mrs Sedge has just told me you put the idea of getting rid of her residents into her head."

Wimpole jumped onto his high horse and rode away. "That is a preposterous suggestion, Inspector," he blustered, "I demand you withdraw it!" His voice was rising and his face getting redder.

"She says you seduced her."

"The woman's not just evil. She's mad! Deluded! How can she suggest such things! How can you take them seriously? This is a farce! I demand to see the Chief Constable!"

"I'm sure he'll be delighted to see you, since I understand you are personal friends, or should I say were. I don't know what the Rotary's attitude is to one of their members being an accessory to murder." said Stubble placidly.

"Murder!" shouted Wimpole. He held up his hands. "Are you saying these hands have killed someone?"

"You didn't use your hands. You used your tongue. Anyway I won't beat about the bush. I haven't got anything solid to go on when it comes to what you said to Mrs Sedge and what she said and did as a result. What I do have is this. He slid a copy of Wimpole's bank accounts across the table. How do you explain these?"

Wimpole went white. There was a long silence, and then he said icily "These figures are confidential. Where did you get them?"

"Not for me to say," said Stubble. "Do you deny the truth of those figures?"

Wimpole did not reply. Stubble went on; "thirteen deposits of £26,000. You don't win that sort of money on a horse. I suppose you're going to say they are dividends on an investment, or interest on a loan, something like that. Any idea how much they were before tax?"

Wimpole studied the table for a moment and then said "I refuse to say any more without my solicitor being present. I consider your line of questioning hostile."

Stubble ignored him. I'm sure our friends in the Inland Revenue will be able to do the tax calculation. Meanwhile, Augustus Edmond Wimpole, I have to charge you that at various dates you did conspire to with Maureen Elizabeth Sedge to murder Eileen Kinloch and others….."

Wimpole blustered "The charge is baseless. I'll sue for wrongful arrest!"

"Your privilege. You'd better say no more until your solicitor arrives. I think I ought to warn you the Revenue will oppose bail."

"What! I'll have you know...."

Stubble broke into what promised to be an entertaining diatribe by making sure Wimpole knew his rights before terminating the interview and asking the young lady constable to escort the lawyer to the custody suite.

AFTERMATH

Mrs Sedge got seven years. She was a model prisoner and got parole on her first hearing. Not sure what to do next she dropped into the nearest pub to sit down quietly and consider her options. As she sat there a furious row broke out behind the bar. It seemed one of the bar staff had been caught with her fingers in the till. Mrs Sedge offered her services as a replacement and was taken on immediately, no questions asked. It turned out the pub was one of a chain, and she has now worked her way up to being a popular area manager. The company maintains their new accounting systems are knaveproof. Time alone will tell.

Mr Wimpole was struck off and got five years, every day of which he served due to his habit of arguing with the prison staff. He was popular with the other prisoners by dint of giving them legal advice, paid for in cigarettes, drugs and sexual favours, among other currencies. On his release he obtained employment as a consultant with a finance company who specialise in lending money to people whose creditworthiness is so low that other moneylenders won't touch them with a bargepole. His knowledge of the law has enabled his employers to virtually ignore it.

Matron got a year's suspended sentence for illegal disposal of a body. She came to the conclusion that nursing was not for her. She still felt her forte was working with people and retrained as a nursery nurse, unaware that she was, with a criminal record, almost unemployable in that field in the UK. She answered a rather vaguely worded advertisement in The Lady and is now helping with the education of a Gulf State prince's children. She is engaged to an expatriate Texan in the oil industry, unaware that he has a wife back in Dallas.

The Kinloch Brothers buried their mother, went back to Australia, and carried on with their antipodean lives.

Sam managed to get mixed up with some of the cargo when it was being unloaded from the Largesse. Being white he commanded a premium and was bought for a crippling sum by a

Zanzibarean spice dealer. His master, a devotee of Wodehouse, is under the impression that he has got himself an English butler and has taken to calling Sam Jeeves. Sam doesn't mind; in fact he rather likes his new role in life.

Janine is at University studying for a Social Services qualification. She has ambitions to own her own old people's home some day.

Violet is now in charge of The Poplars, which was sold to a company who run about ninety similar homes. They describe her as the Head of Home, but the residents like to call her Matron. It makes them feel they are in safe hands.

Taddeusz was snapped up by the Apple Corporation. Vary possibly some of his brainpower is in your computer.

Stubble is still following his nose.

85924

17867116R00136

Printed in Great Britain
by Amazon